FOIL

A NOVEL

EVAN KLONSKY

Copyright © 2026 by Evan Klonsky

All rights reserved. No part of this publication may be reproduced, stored or transmitted in any form or by any means, electronic, mechanical, photocopying, recording, scanning, or otherwise without written permission from the publisher. It is illegal to copy this book, post it to a website, or distribute it by any other means without permission.

This novel is entirely a work of fiction. The names, characters and incidents portrayed in it are the work of the author's imagination. Any resemblance to actual persons, living or dead, events or localities is entirely coincidental.

Designations used by companies to distinguish their products are often claimed as trademarks. All brand names and product names used in this book and on its cover are trade names, service marks, trademarks and registered trademarks of their respective owners. The publishers and the book are not associated with any product or vendor mentioned in this book. None of the companies referenced within the book have endorsed the book.

First edition

Published by Red Oak Books
New York, New York

Cover art by Jake Friedman

Identifiers:
Print: 979-8-9927833-1-5
eBook: 979-8-9927833-2-2

ADVISORY NOTE

Foil addresses themes of self-harm and emotional distress in a manner that some readers may find triggering. The novel explores these issues with sensitivity and realism, striving to shed light on the complexities surrounding mental health and personal struggle.

If you or someone you know is struggling with self-harm or suicidal thoughts, please know that help is available from the following free resources:

- **Crisis Text Line:** Text HOME to 741741 for free, confidential support from a trained crisis counselor, available 24/7.
- **National Suicide Prevention Lifeline (U.S.):** Dial 988 for immediate support.
- **SAMHSA Helpline (Substance Abuse & Mental Health Services Administration, U.S.):** Call 1-800-662-HELP (4357) for free, confidential treatment referrals.
- **National Alliance on Mental Illness (NAMI):** Text "NAMI" to 741741 for crisis support or visit nami.org for resources.

For Sydney

"I'm the father; I'm the archaic medium of male violence that literature is supposed to overcome by replacing physicality with language."

BEN LERNER, *THE TOPEKA SCHOOL*

"We are going to eat ice cream and we are going to eat shit. The trick is to use different spoons."

SAM LIPSYTE, *THE ASK*

PART 1

1

HOLLY

I picked up something strange about Xander that morning. His shiftiness, the intensity of his distracted, faraway stare. But what could I have done? There was no reason to think our field trip to the Met would be anything out of the ordinary.

Xander showed up at the Bayside station a few minutes late, looking flustered after getting dropped off by his mom. He wore the same tan-colored overcoat he'd been wearing to school lately, zipped all the way up even in the warmer weather.

"Look who decided to show up," Hal said to Xander, standing on the platform a few paces away from the rest of our twenty-person class and Mrs. Duprey.

"What's up, man?" I said, trying to glimpse his eyes behind his transition glasses, though the lenses were too dark.

Xander didn't answer, just smiled weakly at us, as if the simple act of speaking to his friends pained him. Did that seem particularly strange to me? Xander always looked pained, flustered, weighed down by the curse of his own existence. Even back in middle school, when we went to our support-group meetings for kids from broken homes, Xander was difficult, unreachable with his eyes obscured by the changing shade of his lenses. He always looked like he'd seen more than he should have, like the rest of us were only faking it. He'd shrug off the suspensions for acting out in class, hiding firecrackers in his bookbag. Small potatoes next to the belt lashings in store for him at home.

"Hey," I said, nudging him. I noticed how pale he looked, how hard he stared down at the tracks in anticipation of the coming train, running several minutes late. "You okay?"

"What?" He looked at me for the first time, his eyes wide as if startled by the question. "Yeah. No. Everything's good."

Behind him, Hal had his nose in his phone, biting his nails while playing a video game or texting. But I was already obsessing over how Xander made me feel any time he sounded so distant, mechanical, his body as stiff as an action figure's. Did I notice the extra bulk underneath his coat? How little he actually moved his arms? Maybe only when I thought back on it later. All I felt at the time was the hardening rock of anxiety that lived inside of me, lodging up in my throat before spreading to my stomach, wrists, hands. I feared he might go off on another classmate or teacher, maybe a stranger who bumped into him. And even knowing how powerless I was to stop it, I still wanted to shake him loose, somehow, to tug on the knot of his coat, expose his naked anger and tell him it was okay for everyone to see.

"Guess what," I said.

He looked at me for the slightest trace of a second before moving his gaze back to the tracks. It shocked me to notice how hard I fought for his attention sometimes, how hard I wanted him to like me.

"I think I'm finished with The Gross Girl," I said, referring to an abstract sketch I'd been working on. It was inspired by a recent chat we had about what it means to live inside of a body, to fuss and ache and feel everything much too deeply. The chronic migraines and crazy-high fevers I experienced every few months, trembling and paralyzed from the waist down. "I want you to see it. You know, whenever you have the time."

"Sounds good," he said absently.

Inside, I cringed. *Whenever you have the time?* Xander was a high school senior with a part-time job and no extra-curricular activities other than helping out with set decoration for the school plays. All he had was time.

"I just texted you guys a link to this new online trivia game," Hal broke in. "Me and Remy are obsessed. Wanna play a quick game on the train?"

Xander stared at Hal like he had fourteen heads.

"Maybe later," I said. I can't lie, I wasn't really in the mood myself. Maybe because of how sensitive I was to Xander's moods.

"Really?" Hal stepped towards me to show me his screen, all flashy with color. Hal was frail and timid and probably Xander's closest friend. The two of them spent long nights holed up in Hal's attic, worshipping David Lynch or surfing the darkest corners of 8chan.

"Look, you can play in our group," he went on, "Or they have these leagues—"

"We're good!" Xander said. Hal flinched, looked down. Sweat rose on the back of my neck. I couldn't deny that everything about Xander seemed off, strange, as if we were invading his thoughts.

"It does look cool," I told Hal. Out of the corner of my eye, I saw Xander staring off toward the Manhattan skyline. "I'll check it out later, maybe on the way home."

Another awkward silence. I looked at my phone, scrolled Instagram to pass the seconds.

A moment later, finally, came the low hiss of the arriving train. It grew to a whistle, followed by a deep roar. Warm air brushed our faces as the train thundered in.

I didn't have any other close friends on the trip, so I stood next to Xander and Hal for the duration of the 12-minute ride into Manhattan. I thumbed around on my phone, my ears getting stuffed up from the pressure inside the tunnel.

Once we arrived at Penn Station, it felt like cattle being herded into the swarm of late-morning commuters. Some of the normie kids from our class like Annie Felton and Conner Day giggled or shrieked as we walked, always drawing too much attention to themselves. But Hal, Xander, and I walked with our heads down, stayed quiet.

I felt a tugging at my sleeve. It was Xander, a tiny smile on his lips, a pink cardboard box in his hand. He handed me the box, which I recognized as cupcakes from the place we liked in Manhattan. My heart sizzled in my chest. My earlier fears seemed to quiet. I grabbed his hand and squeezed it tight, smiling sneakily at him as if this was some big important secret. Sure, the gesture was unlike him, but it was also somewhat like him to share his feelings with actions over words. I swung my bookbag around to the front of my body, the bright pink of the box attracting a funny look from Hal—curiosity, but also embarrassment. I couldn't deal with anyone else noticing, so I unzipped my bag and buried the cupcakes inside.

Mrs. Duprey rounded us up for a headcount outside one of the coffee shops, then asked if anyone needed to use the bathroom. When no one did, she led us to the 1 train at the east end of the station.

The normal mix of serious and weird-looking people elbowed past us on our walk through the corridor. A woman wearing a furry tunic stared at me through wild, gray eyes. I looked away, took my MetroCard out from my pocket, then swiped through the scanner and climbed the stairs with the rest of our class, feeling little more than the anxiety I tended to feel in crowds. These masses of faces sweeping out of the subway cars and onto the platform, off to their jobs or schools or meetings. We moved past them in a jumbled dance, each of us happy to make it safely aboard for our twenty-minute subway ride uptown. The train car was far too warm and packed in, and it smelled like feet. But this wasn't anything I wasn't used to as a New Yorker with a moderate case of OCD. I found a spot at the front of the car next to Ross O'Neil and Drew Stanton, separate from Hal and Xander, who lingered towards the back. I grabbed the handrail, warm and slick from some previous passenger's greasy palms. A shiver of nausea ran up into my throat. I pulled my hand back, spread my legs wide as the train rocked forward. Subway surfing, my friends called it. Riding the twists and turns without needing to grab on.

The swerves and rattles of the subway brought me back to that summer. Xander and I would take the train to hang out in Washington Square Park, alive with the sounds of street musicians and vendors, skateboarders hammering the pavement. Afterward we'd travel to parts of town like Harlem that we had no reason to visit otherwise. One day I took him to the MoMA, where we stayed for hours, sharing which piece we'd pick if we could only take home one—a game my grandpa and I would play when he'd take me to museums around the city as a girl. Xander chose an oil painting of an old, abandoned SUV in a field. I chose a bright, two-headed bust of the Pink Panther and Little Mermaid, hugging. Maybe it was silly, but I looked forward to playing the game again today, to see what pieces might catch our eye. I even thought I'd be open to dating again if that was something he wanted. Did the cupcakes signal he was ready? I remembered how lonely I'd been feeling lately without him. How we came together to drown out whatever it was we inherited from our fucked-up parents. What was stopping us from giving it another try?

I must have been lost daydreaming about the possibility, because the next thing I knew, Hal was tapping me on the shoulder. He'd made his way to the front of the car with several stops still to go.

"Have you seen Xander?" he asked, not looking or sounding too concerned, just genuinely curious.

I kept my voice low so none of the other kids would hear. "No, I thought he was with you?"

"I thought he was with you?" he repeated, the words coming out sharper now.

We wheeled our heads around to scan the train car. There were pockets of our other classmates, chatting or looking intently at their phones. In between them were strangers, reading books or listening to music or nodding off. Just then the train braked in a sudden, jerking fashion, throwing all my weight straight into Drew Stanton. He stumbled backward into Conner.

"Holly, you serious?" Drew said. "What, you never take the subway before?"

"Shut up, Drew." My heartbeat flapped in my throat. Conner smiled at us. The two of them weren't on the trip because they cared about art history. They cared about Mrs. Duprey being hot. Getting bossed around by her, licking their lips behind her back, like savages.

"Wow," Conner said. "You got her to speak to you!"

I grabbed onto a handrail, ignored them. Tried to ignore the sweat from my hands seeping onto the gross, warm metal. As the train slowed for the next stop, the rattle that had brought me such comforting memories, moments earlier, now clamped down on all the unstable parts of me. An urge came over me to bolt out onto the platform right when the car doors opened. I could search the cars in front of us and behind us for him, even take the train back in the opposite direction, to Penn Station. But I knew this made no sense, since our entire class was in this car. I turned to Hal.

"What do we do? Do we have to tell Mrs. Duprey?"

"I'm not sure." He sounded just as frozen with confusion as I felt. We looked over at her with her nose buried in a pamphlet of the exhibition we were going to see. "Maybe he just wanted to hitch a ride into Manhattan to go god knows where? Let me text him."

My lungs pushed out a dark laugh. "You think he's gonna answer his texts?"

He shook his head. "Well if he doesn't, I'm sure he's fine either way, Holly." He sounded extra defensive. "He's 17. He can handle himself."

The familiar, two-note chime played over the loudspeaker. "Stand clear of the closing doors please," the robotic voice said.

Panic gripped me in this huge, unexpected way. Helpless to stop the closing doors behind us, I couldn't believe I ever thought today would be the start of something new or exciting between me and Xander. That the cupcakes represented anything the least bit romantic. Did he intend something else all along? Were the cupcakes an apology to me for what he had in store? I pictured him boarding the train downtown, getting off at Washington Square Park, approaching shady-looking characters to ask about the pills they had. With open arms he'd welcome the third-strike suspension he'd receive from school in response to simply drifting off, regardless of whatever else he was up to. Another week or more of missed class would follow, making it that much harder for him to graduate on time. Not that I thought he cared. In fact, I knew he didn't.

We sped uptown in uneven bursts, trapped inside the car moving further and further away from where I wanted to be. Already the innermost parts of me seemed to know we were approaching the point where nothing would be the same, ever again, and with each passing subway stop, the lump in my stomach hardened. It was only a matter of time before the rock that lived inside of me would take over my wrists and hands and feet. Then grow bigger and bigger and bigger. And sooner or later, it would become me.

2

SAM

Entering Penn Station that morning, a Tuesday at the height of rush hour, I didn't feel on the verge of doing anything noble, much less heroic. See the golf clubs clanging heavily over one of my shoulders. The frenzy I joined in with the other commuters, our ears budded and faces planted in cell phones, barely dodging each other. *Look at this place*, I thought. Ever since Penn Station moved from across the street, where the old stone façade still stands like a mausoleum, it was a dump. I'd accepted this, by then. My girlfriend Audrey and I agreed on it.

Audrey grew up north of the city in Westchester, coming down like an angel from Grand Central Terminal. Early on, I loved her for the status that coming from Grand Central seemed to represent. The Hellenic, white stone pillars, the zodiac symbols painted onto the turquoise ceiling. I loved the way she'd turn her nose up at Penn's grime whenever we had to travel through here to visit my family on Long Island, always calling it *gross*. But maybe this was a mistake, too, a kind of overcorrection. As I walked through Penn Station with my golf clubs and unearned disillusionment, I tried to stop pretending I was better than the place.

From one end of the station came the sound of minimalist funk music, a guitarist wearing a ski mask, a bassist standing next to him. I dropped a dollar into the Tupperware container in front of them—something of a karmic ritual I maintained, a tribute to my past and those still trying to make it. The bassist nodded and I rearranged the clubs on my shoulder, swaying like a mistimed dance step. Backtracking, my golf bag swiped the knee of a tan, broad-shouldered executive type. He snarled and I mouthed *sorry*. He shook his head at me, returned to his cell phone. Onward we all went. Upstream.

I found a ticket line, dragging the clubs along with me during my wait. This was actually the first and only time I'd skipped work like this. My friend Gelb was off on a two-week sabbatical required by his finance job, and he'd called asking me to join him at his soon-to-be-father-in-law's country club. While Gelb could be persuasive when he put his mind to it, it'd be wrong to blame him for my bad decisions. I didn't put up a fight. Gelb knew how to lap up all the excesses provided by his soon-to-be-in-laws, and I didn't mind taking part in the ceremonies, particularly with the weather so mild for late October.

The show of security was everywhere: muscular buzz-cuts in camouflaged sandstorm, leashed to German shepherds, bearing M16 rifles.

Ten spots ahead of me in line, a pair of women ran their slow, hesitant fingers over the touchscreen. People sighed, folded their arms together, jounced from leg to leg, but I remained patient. My cap brim angled low over my eyes, I scanned faces and imagined they were coworkers at the magazine where I worked: A snowy shock of hair might've been Ron, our creative director who commuted on the New Jersey Transit. A passing woman's deep-set hazel eyes summoned Karen, front-of-book editor, also of New Jersey. But as the commuters came into focus, each image proved deceptive. I told myself I wouldn't mind being seen—that's how I felt towards my job. I wouldn't mind being fired. Then I remembered I still had to put in for my sick day.

I brought out my cell phone, sent Claire the pre-drafted note from my outbox: *I've come down with a stomach bug and can't make it in and here's where I've stored the PowerPoint.* In the meantime, my inbox showed a new unread message:

Dear Mr. Reid,

Thank you for your interest in a job with RazorEdge Media. While we enjoyed meeting with you, there were many applicants of exceptional quality and we will be moving forward with another candidate at this time. We will keep your information on file and be in touch if there's an opening we think you may be suited for.

Thanks very much for taking the time to meet with us.

Crack through the chest, hot rippling across the face and hands, aftershocks spreading out. Rejection was an earthquake, a reminder of all the ways life dunked on you, and kept dunking. I looked up towards the Amtrak departures board. Using fewer than fifty steps, I could board the next train to the South, the Midwest, anywhere. Switch off my cell phone. Disappear. Buy an acoustic guitar and then dump my credit card, ride the trains like Kerouac.

A three-word response from my boss Claire hit my inbox: *thx feel better.* That's all it took to snap me back to reality. That Amtrak sign in the distance wasn't real life. That wasn't the kind of fucking-up I did. I'd stay and pound more job boards and write more smarmy cover letters. I'd pay for my train ticket on the Long Island Rail Road, sweep the golf bag back up over my shoulder, ride eastward, and meet Gelb out in the idyllic fall countryside. We'd drink too many beers on his soon-to-be-father-in-law's dime, because that's the kind of fucking-up I did, and did well: one day of playing hooky. Not a full-on runaway.

The women in line were getting an assist from the couple behind them. I clicked around my phone some more, revisiting group texts from the day earlier. Gelb and my other former bandmates were romanticizing bygone days: the time Abe punched that bar manager in the mouth. The time Gelb puked on the bus ride back from Rochester. The time Nick contracted gonorrhea, again. Then, as always, how we should get together to play again. Even though it would never happen. For them, it was just talk. Not for me. I yearned for this past, the rich history that came before the ordinary, cubicle-bound present—marketing and job-searching—which had become something like my identity.

When I reached the front of the line, I moved my fingers rapidly across the screen, sureness bred from a lifetime of shuttling back-and-forth to the Island. Twenty minutes remained before my train's scheduled departure, so I corkscrewed over to the Hot & Krusty at the other end of the station.

A short, damp-shirted fellow eyed me from behind the glass display. There were several appealing options—cream cheese varieties and mayo-thickened salads, stabbed with placards. I ordered an egg and cheese sandwich, hash brown, and a yellow Vitamin Water.

I paid him. He asked my name, and I watched him write on the white paper bag in fat, uppercase Sharpie strokes—soon to be etched into my memory like a scene from a film—SAM.

I watched the blinking red digits on the schedule board, leaning against a cold metal pillar. Fifteen more minutes to go. I held my food bag, grease already blotting through the sides, and set down my golf bag, relieved of the weight on my shoulder.

SAM

I drew small sips of Vitamin Water, forestalling hunger, grinding the ridged cap between my fingertips. Then my pocket vibrated. A call from my dad.

I nearly laughed out loud. We still hadn't spoken in months. Not since the night the long-simmering resentment between us finally bubbled over into the threat of physical violence, actual property damage. In that time he'd systematically exercised his righteous indignation over me. But now, today, he'd had enough? Enough of the standoff? Enough of my mom forcing us to attend family gatherings together, where we quickly discovered how to avoid eye contact.

A second ring shook my phone, followed by a third. With the job rejection swelling through me, the Performance Improvement Plan, a thought crossed my mind: maybe I *should* answer. Get it over with. I remembered the roar of his voice that night, the echo of shattered glass. His voice always jangled me up like dental work, including through the phone, but now I could use it as fuel, tell him all the things I never could. How I no longer needed to listen to him. How I no longer needed to accept his credit card or tax return help as the price for listening to him.

I was getting ready to do it—hovering my thumb over the answer button, steeling myself with a breath—when a sound caught my attention: a nearby, high-pitched wheezing sound. It came out sharp as a balloon squeak over the rise and fall of voices and footsteps. Two steps to my right was a kid, no older than high school age, wearing a pained-looking expression behind his dark eyeglasses. He had on a spring-mud-colored overcoat that covered his whole lanky body, a white baseball cap on his head, and watching him—his fidgety hands commanding more and more of my focus—I let the call from my dad lapse unanswered. You might say I was happy to have the excuse, but something seemed uniquely wrong about this kid. The stiff, determined stare behind the wide, wet eyes. The wiry frame underneath the too-big overcoat. Inhale, exhale, wheeze. That stare.

I felt my feet clench in my sneakers, wondering if anyone else saw what I did. Or maybe I was only imagining it? When I was ten years old, my family and I were returning from a vacation late on New Year's Eve, a couple years after 9/11, taking the connecting flight from Philly to La Guardia. A few seats away from us sat a turban-clad gentleman, reading a book and eating the packaged nuts they handed out. He posed no harm to me or anyone else, but I hawk-eyed him throughout our entire descent into New York. I whispered to my mother I was scared he'd be taking the plane down, straight into Times Square, and, to her credit, my mother tossed her head back and laughed out loud, her certainty as reassuring as it was embarrassing. But then she took my hand and held it, low, so no one could see. She wanted to comfort me.

I was alone now, I remembered, an adult who'd seen one too many movies. I knew better. A certain comfort came from knowing it was all in my head, knowing I could watch this kid out of the corner of my eye, unbothered.

He didn't seem to notice me watching him. Head tilted at a 45-degree angle, he scowled at a single block of the tile like he was mad at it. Or perhaps he did notice me and was intentionally avoiding my gaze? He removed a hand from his pocket. Very calmly, he unknotted his overcoat, revealing dark electrical wiring, duct tape, and Velcro wrapped roughshod around his torso. My breath quickened. I still seemed to be the only one with a clear view. To my left, a woman was typing into her phone, nose two inches away from the screen; on the other side was a man in a black, flat-brimmed Yankees hat, eating green grapes from a Ziploc bag. Farther away, the uniforms: soldiers chatting up the officers by the NYPD welcome desk.

So this is how it ends? I thought.

SAM

Unless I could stop it—the responsibility of which angered me. Why was this on me? Not the cops and guardsmen with their unconcerned, clueless laughter. Why couldn't they see what I did? Didn't they know I did *nothing* in situations like this? I was the one who froze with doubt, second-guessed myself, and let others step in to handle it.

But then, there was no more mistaking it. Something inside me transformed when I saw the yellow Bic lighter emerge from his pants pocket. Way down in my gut, I knew the time for second-guessing or relying on others had ended. He glanced at the lighter before burying it back in the palm of his hand. He ran his shaky thumb over the metal wheel, testing it out. I dropped my greasy food bag and reached for the nearest weapon I could find. A golf club.

I drove the face of my 9-iron straight down on top of his head, the impact softer than I expected. He covered his head with his hands and then fell, the lighter skidding out across the tar-colored tile, his coat thrown open. Someone shrieked. "Oh my god!" came a woman's voice, more incredulous-sounding than alarmed. "A bomb?" And everyone around us scattered. Everyone but me.

Because I was only getting started. I lifted the club up and brought it back down on his head. Over and over again. The crack of shattered bone shot up thrillingly to my fingertips. What was I thinking? I can't remember thinking anything good—not of safety or integrity or saving lives, or my family or Audrey, of safeguarding our future. I only remember thinking of myself. Rather, of the absence of myself. I was altering destiny, cheating death. I wasn't supposed to *win*. I wasn't even supposed to *survive*. I was so close to him, I'd have been the first to go up in the flames.

I ground my jaw so hard I bit my own lip, tasted my own blood. But I couldn't stop. The kid lay in the fetal position, surrendering. He heaved and seized beneath me.

My hat came off. Someone grabbed my wrist and wrestled

me groundward. I gave no resistance. I could feel how far I'd gone already. Much too far. The soldier's hair was red. He smelled of citrus-flavored dipping tobacco, and he made quick work of me and my golf club. He pinned me down with one hand, fastened handcuffs to my wrists with the other. Screaming bystanders ran in all directions, down every corridor. The PA blared repeatedly, its rhythm comforting somehow:

Please move safely and calmly towards your nearest exit.

Pockets of rubberneckers remained. From the ground, I made out approving nods from all kinds of people, all colors and ages. I closed my eyes as the soldier gripped the back of my neck, digging the cuffs harder and harder into my wrists. The force made me feel oddly better—just what I deserved.

Muffled requests for backup went out over the walkie-talkies. Then there were more officers, leaning over me, questioning: *What's your name? Where are you from? Are you hurt? Do you know this man on the ground next to you?*

I nodded to the white paper bag where the counter guy had written out my name: SAM. I couldn't speak, my throat gone dry, one ear pressed hard against the tile floor. I tasted blood. And though I was crying, the pain from inside my lip wasn't the reason why.

Because something strange had started happening. I saw flickers of it, even then—in the nearly peaceful-looking eyes of the young man next to me; in the seams of red spreading through the white of his cap; in the faces of the officers turning from puzzlement to slow recognition. It shot out clear from the haze: I'd been wrong about my destiny. It wasn't to die, or to want to. My destiny was to stay and fight. To walk out of there, free.

3

HOLLY

When we reached the subway stop for the Met, Hal and I hung back on the platform for an extra couple of seconds to look for Xander, to see if by some miracle he was in the car behind us. We stood watching more businesspeople traveling to work, a pair of nuns shuttling off the train, a set of middle schoolers with skateboards in their arms. Then I saw Hal walking furiously in the opposite direction. My heart swelled, thinking he'd picked Xander's face out of the crowd? I followed him, until I saw him stop abruptly and spin back toward me.

"Did you see him?" I asked.

His face fell. I had to look away. "I thought I did, but it wasn't him."

"Fuck! Fuck, dude."

The rest of our group had already reached the front of the platform, beginning to climb the stairs. Annie Felton bounced on her toes, ponytail swinging merrily behind her head, completely oblivious. We scampered up to join them, my breath quick and heavy in my chest once we reached the top. I eyed the rest of the kids in our class to see if they held any clues about Xander. But no one else seemed to notice a thing.

Aboveground, Drew Stanton and Conner Day were shadow-boxing in the shade of a small tree. I fished out the travel-sized bottle of hand sanitizer I kept in my backpack and applied it to my hands, just like I did every time I rode the subway. But the ritual felt more necessary now, like if I could kill the germs, I could ward off the rising waves of anxiety in my chest, too. I saw Mrs. Duprey using two fingers to mark the pairs of heads in our small group. The image of a countdown clock, like one next to a proctor during a test, entered my mind. I punched Hal in the arm as hard as I could.

"What the fuck? What was that for?" he said.

We watched the recognition settle on her face in degrees of confusion, giving way to all-out frustration. I knew Mrs. Duprey had only wanted a nice, drama-free morning at the museum. When she finished counting, and double-checking her work, she walked straight up to us with purpose to her steps.

"It looks like you two already know why I'm here," she said, reading the worry in our downcast eyes.

"I swear, he was with us back at Penn Station," I blurted out. "I have no idea where he wandered off to."

A breeze swept in, and I watched Mrs. Duprey's dark, docile eyes look out over the expanse of trees in Central Park on the other side of the street. "You know I have no choice but to call the school now," she said. "Unless one of you can reach him?"

"We've both texted him," Hal said.

"And?"

"Nothing."

A shot of irritation spiked through Mrs. Duprey's brow, resigned to the fact that she was the latest victim of Xander's behavior. Teachers pranked by him, detention sentences served by him, all-out absences for days on end. Maybe because of my closeness with her, Mrs. Duprey had been spared—until now.

HOLLY

"Do you know how screwed I'm about to be?" she asked us, without waiting for us to respond. "Teachers who let students out of their sights—nothing good ever comes of that. I have young kids to care for at home. How selfish of him."

"I'm sorry," I said, even though I knew it wasn't my fault. She'd already turned her back on me, though, making me fear our relationship might never be the same. No more after-school instruction, no more guidance on how to prepare my portfolio for college applications. She was in full micro-managing, student-escort mode now. She instructed the class to cross the street and wait and not to do anything stupid.

"Your classmate Xander has wandered off somewhere," she announced, trying to sound casual, but the defeat in her voice was obvious. "I need to call the school to inform them and see what they want us to do."

A few eye rolls passed over our classmates' faces, but no one really seemed to make much of it. Obviously, Hal and I were the only ones who cared. As she stood off to the side and dialed and put her phone to her ear, I wondered if I looked as pale and stricken as Hal did. Probably, I looked worse. We didn't have to say anything to each other to know we should have mentioned something to Ms. Duprey sooner. With the guilt building up inside of me like a volcano, I kept looking at my phone, then Mrs. Duprey, back and forth over and over, unable to make out any of the words she spoke. At one point my phone lit up with a notification at the same time as Hal's, making my heart just about stop beating. Had Xander texted our group chat? No, I quickly saw. It was just Remy, sending us a Snapchat video from gym class back at school. Most of the other kids had their phones out, too, for what we all expected to be a short time.

But when Mrs. Duprey hung up the phone, she had a cold, pissed-off look on her face. She led us under a tree in the park across the street from the Met, its stone columns towering in the distance.

"I suppose you can all thank your friend Xander for ruining the trip for us," she said.

"What?" Lucinda Green asked. "You mean we're not going inside anymore?"

"Nope," Mrs. Duprey answered. I heard myself groaning in chorus with some of the other students. "School policy. A student goes missing on a trip, we're required to return everyone back to school safely. A bus is on its way already."

Murmurs coursed through the group. "That *freak*," Annie Felton said. "Wasn't he almost suspended two weeks ago? Why was he even allowed on the trip?"

"Everyone deserves a second chance, Annie," Mrs. Duprey said.

"Where is he?" Conner asked me and Hal at once. "You must know."

"We don't!" I shot back. "Asshole."

He snickered, too gratified to have provoked the reaction in me. "Bullshit."

"Settle down, guys," Mrs. Duprey said. "No need to make accusations we can't back up." She waved for us to follow her to a set of green park benches. "Everyone, grab a seat. It'll be a little while before the bus gets here, but if we end up locating him before then, we still might be able to take an abbreviated tour through the museum. At least it's a nice day out."

Hal and a couple others slumped down on the benches, readying their phones with video games or social media scrolls. Only then did I notice how my chest seemed lighter. Mrs. Duprey seemed to recognize that I hadn't been the one to let her down. The anticipation of something bad happening was always worse than the reality of it, no matter how confused and frustrated I felt still. The little argument with Conner had broken up the balled-up rock of anxiety, to the point where I could power my legs to drift over with the rest of the class. Still, I preferred not to sit. Too worked up from Conner, too consumed by my fear of Xander's whereabouts. I didn't have the heart to take out my phone or talk with anyone or think about anything besides how dumb it was for me to be wasting my breath on someone like Conner. I knew he still held it out for Xander. Every Halloween, Conner used to throw eggs at Xander when he rode by on his bike. One time, he filled his locker with shaving cream, ruining his notebooks. Xander retaliated by slashing the tires of Conner's bike, which of course ended with them both being suspended. Boys, with their never-ending grudges, were the *dumbest*.

We waited another twenty minutes until the next bit of news arrived.

"Guys, something just went down at Penn Station," Drew Stanton announced. "It's all over Twitter."

"What? Let me see," Conner said, snatching the phone from him. Even Mrs. Duprey looked up in curiosity.

"A bombing, they're saying!" Conner called out, waving the phone in the air. The corners of his mouth seemed to curl into a smirk, whether out of shock or pride in being the one to break the news, I didn't know. Or maybe he got some sick thrill out of being a teenage boy so close to something so serious, so real, for once.

"Oh my god," Reggie Tate wailed. "Don't tell me—"

"Everyone calm down," Mrs. Duprey said, even as we were the complete opposite of calm, a muttering racket. All at once, every single one of our classmates seemed to have their phones out, tapping the screens like pigeons pecking at breadcrumbs. "It's probably nothing."

"I'm seeing there was a stampede!" Reggie called out.

"Are people hurt?" Lucinda Green asked. "Dead?"

"Let's not jump to any conclusions," Mrs. Duprey said. "Instead of checking social media—which might be getting it wrong as we speak—I'd encourage everyone to get in touch with their families, to let them know you're safe. That would be the most productive use of your time right now."

Some of the other kids listened, but I stood frozen in

place, like moving a single muscle required monumental effort. The cement brick had returned to my stomach, my neck itched all over. Time seemed to stand still. No branches or leaves swayed in the trees.

"Hey, Holly," Conner said from the other side of the semi-circle. He had a huge, menacing smile on his face, and right then I could tell he was thinking the same thing as me. "If Xander turns out to be involved, I'm gonna lose it. Legit, the funniest thing ever."

He and Drew fell apart, laughing. Annie smacked him.

"It's not funny!" she said, tears welling up in her eyes. I fiddled with the zipper on my windbreaker. Up and down, up and down. When I looked over at Hal, his mouth hung open in the shape of a small o.

"It's not him," he whispered. "There's just absolutely no way."

"I need you all to know that you're all completely safe here," Mrs. Duprey said, failing to stop the onslaught of collective hysteria whatsoever. "The bus will be here soon."

Hal and I stood off to one side of the huddle of kids crowded around Mrs. Duprey, watching as questions rained down on her. She tried to comfort them by placing a hand on their backs, nodding through gritted teeth. But there was nothing for any of us to do anymore but wait.

4

SAM

A muddled stretch of seconds: cuffed and pinned down, a hand gripping the base of my skull. My pants were rifled through, my cell phone and wallet lifted. The voice of my captor barked out instructions, received them. "Cover five. Over two. Third flank from the east. Set?" Beyond this, the repeated PA announcement became an earworm in my head, soft pleasantries heightening my terror. Figures hazed in the periphery of my vision, some tending to the unconscious attacker on the tile floor near me. Had I killed him? I couldn't imagine myself the kind of person who had killed and yet it seemed he was dead; the way they inspected and hovered over his limp body, its purple swellings more awful than any I had seen in any movie, worse—realer—than I had imagined a dead body would actually look. Blood leaked slowly from one of his ears. I wanted to vomit. I was a killer. I had killed.

"You good to walk?" someone asked me. Before I could respond, I was on my feet, lifted and then on the move. My head pushed down to duck under the yellow tape. I kept my head down, the metal of the cuffs digging deeper into my wrists. We turned against the tides streaming toward the exits.

Between the voices rushing past me, the repetition of the PA voice, and the clusters of armed personnel in shades of blue and camo-green, SWAT-embroidered chest protectors, I couldn't make out much, but thought I heard someone use the word *timer*. The man with me kept my head down, as if to avoid eye contact with anyone, except that was unavoidable. Eyes hardened when they met mine—glares that judged me for being handcuffed and bloody, as though I were the perpetrator of whatever had happened here, whatever derailed their commutes. I recalled reading that when 9/11 hit, an extra 1,600 people died in car accidents because they switched their travel plans from flying to driving. What kinds of unforeseen consequences would arise today? How many other deaths or lost jobs or ruined marriages? And how many people would come away with the wrong idea about me?

What was the wrong idea?

We kept moving, deeper into the bowels of the station, and soon arrived at an unmarked metal door. There was a man there, waiting for us with a set of keys.

"Sam," he said. "Sam, that's you, right?"

His voice sounded familiar, though I couldn't place his face. He wore a man bun and had soft green eyes that settled on me as though I were telling an interesting story. We entered the room, humid with dull porcelain-tiled walls, a moldy sheen built up along the floor and wall edges.

"It's all over, Sam. Look at me. Everyone's safe here."

I couldn't decide if I should trust him. The room had rough concrete floors and rows of drab gray lockers on either end, the air warm and thick like someone else's breath. I wanted to run straight back to my apartment, where I could plunge my face into a pillow, alone. But the circumstances wouldn't accommodate these wants. Blood had stiffened as it dried on my chin, brownish splotches stained my yellow polo shirt. The plainclothes police officer nodded to the presence behind me and carved a circle with his forefinger, signaling for me to be un-cuffed.

"What is this place?" I asked.

"Wait." He turned to the man who'd brought me there, the redhead with ruddy cheeks and lots of freckles. "Rust, keep watch, okay? Sam, you're safe in here, trust me. I'm coming back. Five minutes tops."

Rust handed him my cell phone and wallet. The officer handed Rust a first-aid kit.

"Are you sure we're safe in here?" I asked Rust as the door shut. I was certain there was still some ongoing danger out there. I had the pounding heart to prove it.

"We're good," Rust said, and I didn't argue. He popped open the kit, withdrew some gauze and a tube of antiseptic cream. "Lift your chin," he said. I saw the creases around his eyes soften as he daubed the small wound. Rust assured me we were far enough away from any blast radius, he'd heard over his receiver that bomb techs had already moved in. I pictured burly men in riot gear, huge beige suits like from the movie *The Hurt Locker*. Another thought occurred to me as he spoke, starting out as a question: Did he admire me? Were we *bonding*? People like him never admired me. People who wore camouflage and spent years in war zones overseas never thought much of those of us whose biggest complaint in life was the monotony of a desk job. He went on to tell me he wished he could have gotten a few punches in himself, to be honest, he knew from the second he spotted us what was going on. But he did what his line of work required him to do.

"Sorry if I got a little carried away with that form tackle," he said. As Rust carried on, I realized he must've thought that was the reason I bit into my lip, and I saw no reason to correct him. Instead, I pictured the world outside this stuffy room— the crush, the commotion—and even further out, the people in my life who would find out about me, in short order, without me. I saw my mother—not her reaction, but hassling me over whether I'd gone to the dentist lately. I heard the rare cooing sound of my dad's voice, that friendly tone he used when playing with our dog, Jenkins. Rust's words somehow gave me license to imagine the warmth of Audrey's fingertips, smile, belly.

Picturing my return to the world came on like hunger. Chips and guac. Hand-cut fries. I heard music playing, old Motown music, and saw dancing. Hot and sweaty, I thought of shouting out lyrics at a concert, playing my guitar, ripping my pick across the strings without even playing any chords, just to feel something simple and natural and good.

Rust finished up and paced the small space, occasionally spitting onto the floor. I figured it was a nervous tic, until I remembered the smell of his dipping tobacco. From one of the lockers came a noise that made my heart jump through my chest. "That's a phone," Rust said, reassuring me. The locker was vibrating with a silenced ringer, rattling the tinny walls. In the back corner of the room, I saw a crumpled-up navy blue shirt with the MTA logo printed on the breast pocket. Some poor MTA worker must have left her phone in here for her shift. Now her family couldn't get ahold of her.

"Is your name really Rust?" I asked him.

He chuckled. "What the hell else would my name be?"

"I don't know. I thought maybe it was a nickname."

There was a rap at the door, three quick knocks followed by a pause and one more. Rust seemed to know that this meant to open the door.

"Check it out," the guy with the man bun said as he entered, smiling and shoving a cell phone into my face.

@BethHull8
DEVELOPING: Several reports of an attempted suicide bombing at #PennStation. Eyewitnesses say attacker was halted by another commuter before he could detonate the device. Stay tuned.
9:33 AM - Oct 23, 2018

Reading the words lent a higher order of truth to what I'd done. A rush of something began flowing through me. Maybe I puffed my chest out or did something equally stupid. I know I must have smiled, because I saw him smile back. It wasn't the type of smile you enjoy, though, it was the type of smile that leaks out of you, like after you score in youth-league basketball and jog back on defense with extra sets of eyes on you. Pride at having scored, but shame in being seen. Not wanting to gloat.

Man Bun placed a hand on my left shoulder and told me he'd be there with me, the whole time. I'd get my belongings back soon, my golf clubs, my forever-changed life. They were scanning my cell phone for any connection to the suspect, any text messages or emails or links between us, which he insisted would be unlikely.

"What happened to him?" I asked. I had to ask. The image kept crossing back and forth in my mind—the pooling blood, the nausea.

"He's fine. Just a little banged and bruised. You did what you needed to do."

I shook my head, seeing him appraise the spatter of blood on my shirt. They'd get me back to normal soon, he said. "But there's a protocol we have to follow. You're just gonna need to wait here a little while longer."

They brought in a metal folding chair for me. Man Bun identified himself as Officer Marsden, a member of the MTA Police, which was apparently a real thing. He didn't have the proper authority to question me. They needed to wait for the arrival of the Joint Terrorism Task Force—another real thing—made up of federal, state, and local officials. He described the hierarchy meticulously and, in a self-deprecating way, placed himself low down on the totem pole.

"Our friend Rust here is in what's known as State Active Duty Deployment. That's why he gets to carry that M16 around in public."

"Yes sir," Rust said.

"What about those dogs?" I asked. "Why didn't they react? I thought they're trained to sniff out bombs from like a mile away?"

"It depends on the type of explosive," Officer Marsden said. His voice was deep and matter-of-fact, trustworthy, as if trained to make people believe he would take care of them. "Say it was a peroxide-based device, which has become more common, then yes, the dogs would sniff it out. But it sounds like this guy might've gone old school—dynamite or C4—and those devices are harder to detect, particularly during a rush hour period."

Part of me found the inside information fascinating, I'll admit it. But as they kept going on, detailing the ranks of a domestic terrorism response—the NYPD, the FBI, a Title 10 deployment versus a Title 32 deployment—I wanted them to stop, to leave me alone with my thoughts. As distraction, I tried thinking about Audrey—how late into the school day she'd find out, how alarmed she'd be—and then about Gelb. He'd already texted me, it turned out, the first in a long series of them:

Where are you bro

I pictured Gelb's bleary-eyed confusion, wondering if I'd overslept or just plain stood him up. He came to me in perfect clarity. He was never hard to pin down, sitting in horror inside Amy's family's vacant and brightly lit kitchen—the mahogany table, baby blue pads on the chairs, a glass centerpiece filled with hollow wicker balls. With Amy working, and her dad working, and her mom at yoga class, Gelb had the house to himself. He had free rein to use the blender and Lexus and golf course, a real accomplishment if you thought about it.

But now, my sudden disappearance threatened to ruin all that. When he took out his phone to check Twitter—something we each did no less than fifteen times an hour, every time we ate, finished sending an email, got off a call, every time we took a shit, we checked Twitter—he scrolled over to the trending topics. And that's when he saw it, the tweet that made his heart sink down through his intestines:

@KyleStanhope
#PennStation in an evacuation right now, alarms
going off, cops storming, everyone rushing toward the
exits. Just saw an old woman getting trampled.
Complete chaos here.
9:46 AM - Oct 23, 2018

Looking at the metal door, half-listening to Rust and Officer Marsden, I somehow managed to feel bad for Gelb. Even in my imagination, I worried about his reaction to seeing all the confusion and worry already circulating, the facts unraveling to disrupt the order he worked so hard to maintain. Look at the comforts that he surrounded himself with—the organic, omega-3-enriched eggs he ate on mornings like these, the hobbies as impractical as golf. He dealt so poorly with disorder that at any moment I half-expected to see all 230 pounds of him blast through the door like a battering ram, grab hold of me and drive us straight to the first tee.

In reality, he could only work his thumbs over the bits of hysteria and misinformation that popped off his screen with the reckless force of a tornado. Even if I couldn't investigate for myself, behind that closed door, stuck inside those moldy walls, I identified with the gathering frustration Gelb and everyone else must have felt, any time my mind flashed with the yellow lighter and wiring. Or my fingertips trilled with the echo of shattered bone. Stuck in a looping replay of what I'd done, not thirty minutes earlier. I kept seeing the disfigured hairline and torn-open flesh of the attacker, sagged from his face like leather straps.

And who was he? What drove him? Where was his family? Why was he so…young?

"You know, I always wondered something," Rust said to Officer Marsden, brow knit in curiosity. "Who signs your checks? State or local?"

"Cuomo," Marsden replied. "We're in 14 counties across New York and Connecticut."

They looked at me and I nodded and smiled but didn't speak—I couldn't—not to these officers I'd only first met. I tried to relate what I felt to anything recognizable—getting up in front of the board to deliver a presentation, lungs gasping for air under the heat of their withering stares. But what I wouldn't give for the return of that panic—over nothing at all, it seemed to me now—as opposed to this one. My lip still burned and pulsed, the only reminder of my physical existence in the world. I never wanted or asked for this near-death experience, but now that I had it, there was no going back, I saw, no denying the momentous irony: I may never have done what I did that morning had I not been as fed up as I was. And for what? Because I couldn't handle some job rejections? Some stagnation in my relationship? Some arguing with my family?

How ordinary were the things that made me feel so terrible inside?

Lip throbbing, panic-stricken on my metal folding chair, I mulled these questions continuously with no clear answers.

SAM

But one thing became clear: I had it much better than I knew. I wanted to tell someone, Audrey, if only I could get out—a possibility that seemed less and less certain with the more time that passed—I'd commit everything to her. I'd drown fewer nights in the self-pitying wash of red wine and prescription meds. I'd thank my parents for offering me a safe upbringing, a way forward, as long as I could escape.

I stared at the door and longed to break out with a restless energy I never would have expected. Meanwhile, Officer Marsden and Rust continued to walk me through the finer points of emergency response protocol, disrupted only by the sound of a cell phone vibrating from inside a locker.

5

HOLLY

I watched Mrs. Duprey walk up to a hot dog stand, take a bottle of water out of the cooler, and slide two singles across the counter to the vendor. Strangers bought pretzels for their kids, sped by us on bicycles, filed into the museum entrance across the street. My mind couldn't process how everyone around us kept going on about their business as if nothing had happened.

Some minutes later, Annie Felton let out a shriek. "Guys! The bomb never went off," she called out. We all turned to look. A couple of students clustered around her as she read the tweet out loud: "Witnesses say a bystander disarmed the suspect before he could discharge the device. Both the bystander and suspect are now being held in police custody."

"Thank god," Mrs. Duprey said. I turned my neck around, making out more than a spray of colors—smudged browns and greens of the trees bleeding into the blue-gray stone, the faces of the people passing by completely blurred.

"Wait, there's more," she said. "I think they released their names."

My heart flapped up in my throat like I was being zippered, suffocated, from the inside out.

"Oh my god. It's him. It's Xander."

My knees buckled. I staggered and fell purposefully to the ground, not worried about my pants getting dirty from the city street. Not worried about anything besides the feeling of being grounded, as close to the earth as possible. All around me, words were being spoken, people were congregating, but I couldn't make out any of them.

There was a hand on my shoulder, a light touch.

"Holly, I'm here," Mrs. Duprey said to me. She knelt next to me, and I met her wet eyes for half a second before bursting into tears myself. She wrapped her arms around me. "I know how close you guys are. We're going to get to the bottom of this."

I drew back from her embrace. "He didn't do it. He'd never do something like this, I swear."

"I believe you."

She hugged me again, allowing me to fill the shoulder pads of her blouse with my hot, eyeliner-ridden tears.

Drew read out loud from his phone, "One witness characterized the head injury to the suspect as *blood pooling out of his head*."

More gasps. Tears. My friends and classmates covering their mouths with their hands. I noticed Hal staring over at us, his typically easy and gentle features marked by utter shock. Then, behind him, I saw Conner. All the color had drained from his face.

Could Conner have been the target of Xander's plans today? His pale disbelief seemed to indicate he was considering the possibility. And I even wondered whether this was revenge for the bullying he put Xander through back in middle school. To think, this minor pre-teen drama of ours might soon play out in news reports, on Twitter. I watched as Conner's shock quickly turned to anger. His nostrils flared. He and Drew Stanton pointed fingers into their phones to confirm the news. *This is not real*, my mind kept saying, over and over.

"C'mon, let's get you up to the bench," Mrs. Duprey said. She and Hal lifted me up from the ground and dropped me onto the bench like a rag doll, attracting attention from everyone around us. But I didn't care anymore.

"He's not dead, is he?" I heard myself ask.

It was such a stupid question, she didn't know how to respond. She shook her head, half shrugged.

"Please don't tell me," I said

"I don't know, I really don't. But they're going to figure it out soon, I promise."

I didn't believe her, didn't believe anything anymore. I couldn't speak. I rocked on the bench, my face pressed into her shoulder, drool spilling out from the corner of my mouth.

"Whenever you're ready, we're going to call your dad," Mrs. Duprey was saying. "I don't know what he does or doesn't know at this point. But I want him to hear your voice. He needs to hear from you. Just as soon as you're ready."

6

SAM

I never thought I'd be so thankful to hear cops knocking on a door. The knocks came in a group of three, followed by more chatter over the walkie-talkie. When Officer Marsden opened the door, a woman and a man appeared in the doorway, both wearing navy blue parkas. She had a ponytail and a striking black-eyed gaze, and he had flecks of gray in his hair. Nods were exchanged, they already knew the protocol, what would happen next. Officer Mardsen told me he'd be stepping outside to confer with them.

"Hold on a couple more minutes, okay bud?"

He acted like I had a choice, but nothing about my circumstances felt that way. Marsden closed the door behind them.

"So, what do you do for work?" asked Rust, who'd been standing so quietly in the corner, I'd nearly forgotten about him. I studied him a moment—red cheeks, wide blank eyes. It was the first time I realized I was caught skipping work. Or about to be. Claire, my boss, would find out I'd been lying.

"I work for a magazine," I told Rust.

"Oh yeah? Which one?"

"It's called *Ether*." Rust looked stumped. "Small magazine. We cover music and tech mostly."

"You write for them?"

"No, I work in marketing."

"Oh. Marketing. You must get cool perks, like concerts and stuff?"

"Not really. But the other week I got to meet Dave Coulier, you know, from *Full House*?"

"No shit? Hell yeah, man, I love *Full House*."

The door creaked back open, and they returned—Marsden, the guy with the nice salt-and-pepper hair, and the woman with the eyes like bullets. She spoke first.

"Sam, my name is Agent Laura Ramirez. This is my colleague, Lewis Bender. We're with the FBI."

I nodded, trying to be friendly. I was so tired, suddenly, that moving my head hurt. "How much longer do I have to stay here?" I asked. "Can't I at least get my phone back?"

"We're keeping everyone informed," she said. "We've spoken with your parents. We've put in a call to Audrey's school. All your loved ones know you're okay."

The mention of Audrey's name shook me awake, more so than the thought of my parents. For all she knew, I'd gone to work. Agent Ramirez continued, "I know you've been through a helluva lot this morning already. But we feel this is the best approach—for you to give your statement now—when things are freshest in your head. The more time passes, the more things can start getting, let's say, hairy."

"Hairy?"

"Listen. Here's the honest-to-god truth. I have a suspect who's still unconscious. It's possible he might not even be able to speak after this. You did quite a number on him."

Rust let out a little snicker. I felt my stomach dropping. She gave him a look before continuing. "How do we know you two didn't have some disagreement related to what happened here this morning?"

"Are you kidding me?" The temperature inside the room went up several degrees. My tongue rubbed up against the hardened, toxic-tasting mound where I'd bitten my lip. "You searched through my phone. I mean, look at me: I'm wearing a golf polo, for Christ sake."

"We're doing our jobs, Mr. Reid."

"I'm just saying. I was going out to Long Island to play golf. You found my golf clubs back there, yes?"

"We've seen some elaborate props used before."

I shook my head. "Would you like me to lie and say I knew this man?"

"We'd like the facts, Mr. Reid. That's all. I'd like to know how out of the thousands of people here this morning, including dozens of armed security personnel, the miracle happened that you of all people spotted him first. And not just that you spotted him first, but that you decided to beat him halfway to death."

I had no words anymore. "I don't know," I muttered. "I don't know." I looked around at the tight, muggy space. The lockers, the table. The awful lightless light.

Agent Bender spoke next. "What Agent Ramirez is trying to say is that we feel this is our best shot at getting the facts right, when it's the freshest in your memory. We have no presumption of innocence or guilt. We just want the facts as clearly as possible."

"Are you doing a good-cop-bad-cop thing on me?" I asked, feeling suddenly frantic. "Because good-cop-bad-cop sounds like the type of thing you do to someone you think is guilty. I haven't done anything wrong. I saved people." I could hear the anger rising in my voice, I knew they could hear it too. I couldn't hold back anymore.

"Let's start over," Agent Ramirez said, calmly now. "Let's start from the beginning. So you're going out to play golf this morning, out to Long Island, right? You're standing there waiting for your train to be announced and what, you see this guy acting strangely? Is that right?"

"I heard him first, actually."

"And what did you hear? Or think you heard?"

This puzzled me, the hypothetical line of inquiry. What did I think I heard?

"I heard him breathing," I said. "Very heavily, like he was wheezing."

"And this got your attention."

"Is that a question?"

She frowned. "We're not your enemy here, Sam. We're only trying to understand what happened this morning. What did you see next?"

"I saw him with his eyes closed, like he was breathing or meditating or something. Then when he opened them, I saw a look I didn't—I don't know—I guess I didn't trust."

"You can speak freely," she said. "You can be honest."

"He looked fucking *terrified*," I said.

"And then what?"

"And then I'm looking around to see if anyone sees what I'm seeing, if anyone even *cares*, and when my eyes return to him, he's taking out this lighter. A yellow lighter."

She turned to her partner and said, "Did we find any lighter? A yellow lighter?"

He started flipping through his notepad and while he did, I thought back to a very specific movie scene. *The Truman Show*, when Truman sails out to the edge of his artificial world, when he hits the wall. I must have been around nine when I saw it but never forgot the premise: What if I was I nothing more than a pawn in someone's experiment? What if people were only constructions? This guy here, today, wasn't a real attacker, was he? He was an actor in a social experiment, there to measure my growth. A whole sweeping arc of misguided anger, drawn out and plotted over twenty-six years.

"We can check the tapes, but our notes indicate he had a detonator in his hand, a red button on it."

I felt my heart beating very fast now. "You can't be serious," I said.

All the symptoms hit me, all at once—weakness in my hands, lightheadedness, dry mouth and drier throat. I motioned to my tongue.

"What's happening."

I looked up. The ceiling seemed to cave in by the second. "I don't. I don't. I don't think I can breathe in here?"

A few hundred feet above me, inside Madison Square Garden, giant men received large sums of money to run and leap at each other, to dunk and smash each other into plexiglass. Elephants shat on the floor when the circus came to town. Now there I was, down beneath the place where all that happened, buried under the weight of their performances. My armpits were soaked through, and the tiny room seemed to have less and less air, and somehow this was the way the universe worked now.

"I need air," I said. I would've given up one of my own feet for fresh air. "Water. Anything."

They were asking me what was going on, but I couldn't understand. She placed both of her hands on my shoulders. A gleam of discernment spilled out of her black eyes.

"Sam," she said. "Sam, take a few deep breaths. We're going to get you out of here, alright?"

She led me out through the door and into the empty corridor. Walking had a fuzzy, dreamlike quality. When I used to take the train in from my parents' and stepped out into the rushing river of activity, brightly lit beneath the gray, arched ceiling, that walk down the corridor was how I knew I'd arrived in the city. Now the faces were blank and empty, suspended in the air like ghosts, the bodies that should support them replaced by dust and little else. Storefront lights blended together into the flat, swirling whiteness around me—a mist of unrecognizable, anti-color. I felt the hand at the top of my elbow, steering me left or right, then up a set of stairs. We emerged into the morning, the sun high overhead with a brush of wind in the air.

What was I expecting? Police barricades? Fire engines? Half of the New York press corps? There was none of that. There was just Manhattan, busy and self-assured, like ancient Rome. Traffic on Eighth Avenue lurched and stalled. Crowds gathered in every direction. A small police presence hovered on the outskirts, little more than you'd see on an average day.

"Welcome to the big show," a gravelly voice called out, matched to a crazed stare.

My head was pushed down into the back of a midnight blue town car. Once I settled back against the rough leather seating, I couldn't take my eyes off them—the columns from across the street, the old Penn Station. They possessed their own deep history, were there to remind me, a thought that lingered even after we rode north and they faded from view.

7

HOLLY

The bus ride back to Queens took forever. Traffic clogged the crowded city streets and more of it built up as we made our way over the bridge. Below us, the diesel engine rumbled in the synthetic green seat coverings. The driver lurched forward to speed up or switch lanes. Meanwhile, the pink box inside my backpack was burning up a hole in my brain. All I wanted to do was return home, away from everyone else, where I could look inside and figure out what to do about it. But there was no opening where I felt safe enough.

My heart kept jumping up and down, reacting to the bus's every sway. Next to me, Mrs. Duprey took several calls from Principal Sands and some of the other faculty members. I didn't have the strength to ask her about the latest developments. The longer I stayed in the dark, the longer I could pretend none of this was real. But I knew it was, I'd spoken the words to my dad over the phone, once we got ahold of him at his job site in Long Island: "Some bombing attempt they're saying...Penn Station...I can't believe it either. I can't. I keep praying that we learn it was just a mix-up, but there's no actual info yet. The only thing we know is that he was stopped, apparently. Someone got to him before he could do any harm."

A sudden, shrieking giggle rang out from a few rows behind me. It felt like nails dragging across my skull, my whole body going cold, and when I turned to see Annie Felton's smiling face, I shot her my meanest glare. She blushed and looked away—I knew Annie, we were lab partners in Chemistry class—but her remorseful expression showed that the other kids wouldn't keep their distance from me forever. Sooner or later, I'd have to face the actions Xander may or may not have taken. At the very least, I'd have to find some explanation.

And how much did I know already? What could I have prevented? What did I owe my classmates, my friends, my family?

It wasn't like I couldn't have seen some version of today coming. Maybe not exactly how it happened. But I knew he was contemplating suicide all the time, threatening his mom with it. There were even times when I felt the same way as him. The subject became the basis for some of my drawings, his writing. We didn't have the same interests as our other friends, didn't find the same jokes funny. We related to each other in our desperation to escape. Hence *The Gross Girl*, my attempt to make an abstraction of the physical discomfort I felt all the time—featuring stooped shoulders, fat rolls, bug eyes, lots of period blood. But lately I'd begun to sense that his obsession with suicide was getting more and more serious, dangerous even. And when I begged him to get real help, it backfired. I explained how seeing a therapist had helped me, gave me a framework for separating the thoughts from the feelings I tried to express in my art. He only mocked the idea, though. So I told him I refused to see him anymore if he didn't get help.

Is that what pushed him over the edge? It was impossible to say, but equally impossible to not start feeling the return of all my guilt. A guilt that I'd worked hard with my therapist to overcome.

When we arrived back at school, the twins were waiting for me in the parking lot, sticking around to give me a ride home. I watched the other students from our field trip file into buses or cars. Conner, with the same troubled look on his face, climbed into his mom's SUV.

"This weekend was so normal, wasn't it?" Piper asked once I made it inside their car.

"I actually thought he seemed fine at Hal's," Remy responded. "Chipper, even. And chipper isn't a word I'd ever use to describe Xander."

Their necks were turned to look at me, faces hovering over the center console like Muppet heads anticipating a response. I suppose you could call the twins my closest friends. Mostly by default. They each had many other close friends, and I didn't, so we stayed close because we were family friends more than anything. I knew their mom pressured them to invite me to hang out at their house any time they had people over. And I knew they pitied me for my parents' divorce, even if they'd never admit that was the reason they included me so much. I often wondered if we would've remained close had the divorce never happened. Maybe I might've branched out more, not played everything so safe. Maybe I wouldn't have sought out someone like Xander.

"He seemed okay," I told them. A silence lingered before they recognized I didn't want to get into it, turned back around, and Piper hit the gas pedal. My mind traveled back to Hal's backyard, the first night Xander hung out with us as a group following his return to school. His mom had pulled him out to stabilize his antidepressants. And I'd told him I couldn't hang out anymore if he didn't get help. So him joining us at Hal's should've been a sign of progress. But Xander largely stood off to the side that night, not engaging with anyone. A brown hat shaded his eyes. At one point, he and Hal gathered

FOIL

in the backyard to work on a new flag they'd designed together, though Xander didn't seem to get much joy out of it.

"Snacks are ready!" Remy called out, setting down a tray of nachos made up of microwaved, store-bought tortilla chips. Piper followed her with a plate of Funfetti cupcakes. Hal approached the deck where the rest of us sat. But Xander hung back and busied his hands with the nylon, stencils, and cans of spray paint.

"You sure you're not hungry, Xander?" I called out to him, watching as the boys began devouring the snacks. "Come before it's all gone!"

"Yeah," Teddy said with a mouthful of food, "come join the rest of the human race, bro."

Xander kept his head down, refusing to give the insult oxygen. Piper flicked Teddy once in the ear. He shuddered, shot her a look. Teddy could dominate the group dynamics, but Piper held him in check. Such was the power of sex, dating in high school. A few minutes later, Teddy went inside and returned with his backpack, bringing out a cheap, plastic bottle of vodka.

"Maybe this will cheer everyone up?"

We crowded the bottle. Even Xander shuffled back over. He took a swig when it was his turn, wincing from the afterburn. And the more we drank, the more animated we all became, Xander included. He mentioned how his grandparents would be away soon. We could drive up to their house in Connecticut if we wanted, have it to ourselves. Maybe take out the boat. I didn't think that sounded like such a great idea, and when he went inside to get ice, I followed him, touching his elbow with my hand. But he jerked away from me.

"What's up?" he asked, not looking me in the eye.

"Do you want to talk some more?" I asked him.

"What's there to talk about?"

"I don't know. You know. It's just me."

He flashed me a big disarming grin. His face looked

gaunt, cheek bones in shadow. "You don't want to hang out anymore. You've made up your mind."

"It's not that I don't want to hang out." I tried to organize my thoughts. "I like seeing you. I just can't support you not doing anything to get better, given everything you've told me. That's all."

He paused for a second, spilling orange juice into his cup. "This is cute," he said, jiggling the ice in his glass and brushing past me. "You did me a huge favor, you know that? The breakup was exactly what I needed. I'm journaling about it. I haven't felt this good in months."

Had he been trying to warn me? Protect me? Or maybe keeping his distance because he knew what would be coming.

"Garage or front?" Remy asked me, snapping me out of my trance to realize we were around the corner from my house.

"What? Oh, garage is fine."

"Are you sure you're okay?" Piper asked.

Things seemed to become apparent to me for the first time, urgent and new things: Remy had a blue line on her neck, just above where her gold necklace rested. Was it a vein? How had I never noticed before?

"No, yeah. I'm fine," I said.

"Do you want us to come keep you company until your dad gets home?"

My throat was still bone dry from crying, my eyelids crusted over. All I wanted was to wash my face with cold water, and take the hottest shower, and do those two things over and over until the world returned to the mildest form of normal. The twins keeping me company—gossiping, speculating—that was the last thing I wanted.

"He'll be home soon," I told them, lying, pulling open the car door and stepping outside. They looked down in disappointment. I thought I might feel the same as them if I thought Xander was acting normal recently. They must have always found him so elusive, so strange.

I walked straight up to the garage, punched in the code, and went inside. I took some deep breaths from the space I finally had. The time I needed to inspect the so-called gift Xander had passed me, buried in my backpack and lodged in the back of my mind.

Up in my room, I unzipped the backpack and removed the pink cardboard box. I placed it on the rug in front of me like some haunted charm from a teenage horror movie. I crossed my legs to steady myself against the faintness that arose any time I thought about opening it. Could the cupcakes be poisoned? Filled with tiny explosives? Tossed back and forth between my hands, the box tipped with the weight of the two cupcakes inside. In the silence, I feared our neighbors could hear them smacking against the paper walls, no matter how faint the sound. The lengths I'd taken to conceal the box would come out eventually, I thought, the way I felt any of the few times I hid water bottles of vodka under my bed. I ran my hands along the cardboard exterior, reinforced with scotch tape. My fingers hesitated with fear, like waiting to hit the call button on a phone call you were putting off but knew you needed to make.

Fucking Xander.

It was my anger toward him—the whole situation—that broke through my reluctance. I tore open the scotch tape, flipped the lid, and took my first look at the two cupcakes. One chocolate frosting with yellow cake, the other vanilla frosting with vanilla cake. The careful swirls of frosting had collapsed from knocking around in my backpack, smudges built up along the lid and sides. A strange urge came over me to run my finger through the frosting to take a taste, the way I might on any normal day. But even if I hadn't eaten for days, I don't think I could have worked up an appetite today.

I looked underneath the cupcakes and inside the side flaps

for anything else the box might have contained. The interior lid of the box held a card with the bake shop's logo and a 15% discount offer towards a future purchase. But there was nothing else, not in any of the sides or hidden anywhere under the wax paper. It came as a deep relief to know Xander hadn't passed me some secret sign of his motive. Instantly, I felt less guilty about keeping it hidden inside my backpack all morning.

Had he merely wanted to end things on some type of optimistic note? Give me some strange parting gift to remember him by? There was too much confusion. Too much to wrap my head around. I needed a break.

I shoved the box into a small, standalone drawer on my desk, where it barely fit inside. I went to the bathroom and turned the shower on, convincing myself a hot shower would bring me clarity and comfort. Already, though, I must have known there was no such thing. Xander was dying in the hospital, head bashed in with a golf club. The next in line to desert me. Same as my mom, when she picked up and moved across the country for a job.

Curls of steam ricocheted off the ceiling. Heat tingled over my skin. Inside the shower, for the briefest of moments, I almost fell for the lie that I was something other than all alone.

8

SAM

Was it the lighting inside the hospital that made everyone seem so happy? Good-looking, too. A tall, tan doctor with a huge smile leaned over a desk, chatting with a nurse who sat behind a computer screen. Two blonde women in light blue scrubs strode through the hallway, tossing their heads back with laughter. I sat on a hard synthetic bench, inside a small white room, and waited for my call to connect. My skin itched from the hospital gown they'd forced me to change into, admitting me for *physical and psychiatric evaluation following exposure to acute trauma.*

"Standard procedure," said the nurse who took down my height and weight and blood pressure. She'd given me pale green hospital socks to wear, little chevron balls on the bottoms that gripped the linoleum. "You come into the ER, you get a gown. That's how it goes."

I breathed in the gluey hospital air and stared at the wall opposite me, which had a pattern of indents in the plaster as though someone had taken a pair of brass knuckles to it. They had me fill out a ton of forms when I arrived, most of them designed to determine my levels of anxiety and depression. *Put a checkmark in the box that best describes how you have felt in the*

SAM

last six months: *I have trouble concentrating, I have little interest in doing things, I have thoughts of harming myself or others.* They recommended I answer as honestly as possible, which I did, although a new anxiety questioned whether this was the best idea.

I heard my mother come over the line—her coarse voice repeating my name as if from outer space.

"Sam is that you?" she said. "Sam please tell me what's going on."

"Mom," I said, breathing heavily on the cordless phone they'd given me. "Mom, calm down."

"Calm down? You almost had yourself blown up and you're asking me to calm down?"

I pictured her behind the wheel of her Mercedes, writing sticky notes on the steering wheel as she drove, the bangs of her blonde hair falling just above her eyes, the scent of her perfume infusing the air in a frenzied way. "Are you going to act like this when you get here? Because I can't deal with that right now. I need you to be calm. Normal."

"What's happening? Start from the beginning."

I filled her in on as much as I could, sticking to the contours I told the cops: how I'd been going out to play golf with Gelb; how I made a split-second decision to act; how I'd maybe gone too far.

"I'm concerned about *your* safety, Sam. Why are you in the hospital?"

A robotic and vaguely female voice said, *In half a mile, merge onto I-278 East, Robert F. Kennedy Bridge.*

"They felt they needed to evaluate me. I'm not entirely sure why. I think they want to make sure I'm lucid, that I'm okay. Also, I hurt my lip while it was happening. It looks bad but it isn't. It's all just pretty distressing."

Heavy traffic reported ahead. Re-routing.

A car horn sounded in the background. "Fuck."

"Pay attention to the road, mom."

"Can you put me on with the doctor?" she said. "I'd like to ask him a few questions."

In middle school, my mom brought me to get tested for attention deficit disorder. I remember the doctor with his hair like marble rye bread, his home office out of a converted garage. The good doctor couldn't draw any conclusive findings from the cognitive tests. I had normal working memory and reasoning skills—paired with an ability to concentrate on things for too long, where I had trouble transitioning between tasks. Not abnormal for a middle schooler. But something was wrong with me, my mom knew that much. All my dithering. I continued to act out in class, to grow angry and sometimes violent, to struggle to maintain close friends. Even if my particular disability didn't have a name, my mom would make it her job to fix this thing, to shake me from my stupors and set me on the path with everyone else.

"You can talk to them when you get here," I said. From the corner of my eye, I saw Agent Ramirez poke her head in. "They'll explain the rest then. Pay attention to the road."

"Fine."

"Agent Bender got ahold of Audrey's principal at school," Agent Ramirez said when we hung up, stepping inside along with one of the doctors. He was bald and fat and friendly-faced, *Dr. Speer* written in black cursive on his coat. "We told him to reassure her you're totally fine. They're scrambling to find a sub for her to finish out the day. Then she'll be on her way home."

"Right."

The light from overhead cut across the crags in Agent Ramirez's skin. Somehow this made her look less intimidating than she'd seemed inside the locker room.

"Can I show you something?" she asked. "Something you might actually like to see."

She sat at my side and removed a cell phone from her jacket pocket. She scrolled, showing me a screenshot of a local

SAM

TV news program, my Facebook photo taking up one half of the screen. *Local Kid Does Good*, the chyron read. The first thing I felt was embarrassment, stinging my cheeks as I studied the photo of me with my arm around Audrey. Our features reversed, a glossy glow on our skin from the pixelation.

"You're a celebrity," Agent Ramirez said, smiling, and I reflexively covered my mouth with my hand. I couldn't believe how fast it had spread, that my name and face were out there already. I only had the still-mysterious circumstances that Agent Ramirez brought me here under—partly related to my sanity, I knew, and that I was no longer a person of interest. Then there were the practical and physical: my stomach growled from not eating all morning; my swollen inner lip throbbed; my chest pumped with a general, low-level apprehension. I imagined the notifications lighting up my social media feeds—tiny red flags of inquiry. But before I could process these images—before they were anything other than fleeting and surreal—I needed answers.

"Why haven't I gotten my cell phone back?" I said to Agent Ramirez, looking her straight in the eye. "And what's the deal with the lighter? Have you found it yet? When can I go home?"

A tiny ripple of a smile played at the sides of her mouth. "That's exactly why we brought you here."

She dug her hands into her pockets as I scowled. "You might not believe it, but we're here for your protection. Your safety. What can you tell me about Gelb?"

Gelb? What did he have to do with this? Gelb was nosy, bloated but harmless.

"How many times has he called and texted?" I asked her.

"Quite a few," he said. "But that's not the reason I'm asking."

Out from her pants pocket, she drew a translucent orange pill bottle. My heart did a little backflip.

"We found these in your golf bag," she said, dangling the bottle so that the few pills inside clattered around.

"*This* is what you're asking me about?"

"We want to know why you have it," she said. "You're not in any trouble. We're worried about why you have it."

The agent's lips tightened. I felt the defensiveness swirling in my chest. I'd been using the pills to lighten my mood, to accompany a glass of wine, to improve my sex life. I didn't put them there because I needed more from Gelb, or to give them back to him, or for any other reason than that's where I kept them—my hiding place.

"Can you tell me why this is relevant?" I asked. If word of the pills got out, somehow, it wouldn't only jeopardize me. Gelb's drug habit had already spun out once, several years earlier, shortly after his dad died. He couldn't afford Amy finding out he'd been abusing his prescriptions again. "Do FBI agents really go sniffing around for people who borrow prescription pills from their friends?"

She nodded, very pensively now. "The lighter we can't find. The pills we found. I imagine you've been under quite a bit of stress lately, Mr. Reid, yes?"

"I've been job searching? Most people get stressed when they job search."

That's when she exchanged a look with the doctor, who'd been listening in with his hands clasped, a serene and knowing look on his face. "Have you ever read anything about stress and adrenaline?" he asked. "It can have strange effects on the brain."

A silence gathered. I put some pieces together, looked off to think. He spoke more.

"You were in a combat situation. Your senses change—they've done studies on this—your whole field of vision changes. You're not even forming proper memories, but flashbulb memories. Your mind functions only in terms of action and reaction. This applies even more so to people who aren't used to this sort of situation."

Bits of confusion and frustration and curiosity boiled up, but mostly shock. He continued speaking more quickly than I could follow.

"Speed is important too. You only know that you need to act faster than your opponent. And you did—you acted very fast."

I snorted. "Most people tell me I'm slow. That I talk slowly, act slowly."

He said, "That might confirm something I'm thinking— that you entered a combat state. Have you ever experienced past traumas that might've caused you to get angry and combative?"

It would be wrong to say I thought of my father for the first time then. He'd been there with me all day, unacknowledged in the back of my mind. He called me that morning and stayed with me through when I swung the club, when the cuffs dug into my wrists. Even now, when I sat helplessly in a dotted hospital gown, I thought of him. That didn't mean I wanted him there.

"Do I need to answer these questions? Now?"

"You don't have to do anything," Agent Ramirez said. "We can let you go if you'd like. But here's my fear. Our fear." She paused to study my face and chose her words carefully. "Let's say you go home, and everything is normal. You're happy to be home. But you're still in an agitated state, you just don't quite know it. Then let's say there's a confrontation— maybe between you and Audrey, or you and a family member. And you release your anger in a similar manner to what you did today. That wouldn't be very good for you. Or for them. Or anyone."

I thought about this. "What are you suggesting?"

Dr. Speer answered. "We keep you here, under supervision. We examine and evaluate you and figure out what's going on—if there's a medicine course we need to start you on, for example."

My mind saw contorted faces shambling through sterile hallways. Unruly spills of hair. Guttural shouts ringing out in the middle of the night.

"You're asking to institutionalize me, am I hearing this right?"

"It's an option we'd like you to consider—as a bridge to treatment. The forms you filled out earlier indicate that you've been feeling dangerous levels of anxiety and depression. And the actions you took this morning confirm that, too."

I thought back to the forms, my earlier fear borne out: I was wrong to be so honest. But didn't everyone have their days? Didn't everyone gloom? Suicide, as a subject matter, appeared in much of the comedy I liked. Then again, maybe they were right. I needed help—not just from the half measures of pills I took, but professional help. Maybe this was the start, the long-awaited answer. Look at what I'd done that morning. I'd unleashed my rage on an unwitting party—a threat, but also an excuse. I'd pummeled him past the point of recognition.

I was considering the option when a set of footsteps rang out from the doorway—black suede pumps clicking across the linoleum. Then her blonde hair, clear-framed glasses, tight frown.

My mom hugged me so hard my windpipe constricted against her collarbone. I felt the urgency and necessity of her hug. That's when I lost it. Full on. All the tightness bottled up in my chest, the contortions in my face, each conversation that morning—they were the coils of a spring pushing further and further back. They needed to release at some point, and that point was now.

"I'm not okay," I said, blubbering, snot running from my nose like an infant's. "I can't do this."

SAM

The doctor cleared out, followed by Agent Ramirez, giving us our privacy.

"Sam," she said. "Look at me."

I did. There were tears in her eyes, too, snaking down in muddy black mascara rivers. Years of worry suddenly visible in the creases by her mouth. Something I hadn't noticed before, something I maybe hoped to never notice: There was regret.

"You did absolutely nothing wrong today," she began. "I can promise you that."

I nodded, because I couldn't speak.

"I don't know what these people here have been telling you, but you did a *good job* this morning."

She hugged me again. She swept a hand through the back of my hair, pressed my head into the hollow of her neck. "You did so good."

I spent some more time like this. Reverted to the most elemental tendency, I stayed stuck against my mom for as long as permitted me. I had little strength left to answer questions, to face the world with its mixed-up opinions and disappointments. Out there, people got to tell me I was good or bad. They got to form huge messy thoughts, and I had no say. But clutched to my mother's bony collarbone, with her long fingernails splayed like tentacles over my scalp, I could think. Or I could not think. Or I could remember things I'd forgotten.

"What'd he say?" was what I asked her first. "What's he saying now?"

She pulled back, tightening back up in her gaze and mouth. "Not now. We need to get you home."

"No," I said. "Tell me what he said."

She looked down at her hands. "I don't know. Maybe he was surprised. Maybe not. He was the one who told me what happened."

"Excuse me?" I heard my gasp vibrating against my inner ears. How could my dad, who barely kept his cell phone on him throughout the day—my dad who barely used email—find out about this first?

"Carol was in the break room at Dad's office, saw your name pop up on the ticker. When he called, he said, 'Do you know what your son is up to right now?'"

I could hear him saying exactly this.

"And then he wanted to know whether it was you or Gelb who had the brilliant idea to skip out on work to play golf."

"What, he thought this was funny?"

"No, Sam."

I balled my hands under my thighs, up to where my underwear cut off beneath the gown. I saw a kind of undercurrent forming. She said, "You could lighten up a little, you know. You should be happy right now. You're on the news. The mayor will probably be calling any minute."

As bad as things were, there was also good to come, wasn't there? I'd seen the tweets earlier. A lot of good, maybe: curiosity about me. Credibility. Job opportunities. Facebook friends and Twitter followers. Still, within the smallness of our white hospital room—within the intense purity of that smallness—I had only one thing on my mind.

"This doesn't change anything," I said.

"He tried to call you. He wants to work it out."

"For the eight-thousandth time."

She threw her hands up. "Let's not do this now. I think we have bigger things to worry about right now, no?"

Our eyes flicked towards the door, which had a glass window at the center. Earlier, a nurse had pressed a button outside the door that made the window fog up. Next to the door was a black chair with reflective metal legs. I stood and pulled the chair out towards the middle of the room. It was so heavy, as if bolted down, that I needed to use both hands.

"Are you ready to call the doctors back in?" she asked.

"Why?"

"Oh, Sam. I'm not accusing you. You're startled and

nervous and upset, and rightfully so. But I know you. I know you're not crazy. You're brave. A great kid. You stopped someone who needed to be stopped."

I lugged the heavy chair further towards the opposite corner. The plastic seat had much more give than the composite bench. Sinking down, I felt tiny, undeserving. I shouldn't have told them how I felt. Aired my dirty laundry, involved doctors and cops in my petty saga, distracting them from others with pressing needs—*real* drug addicts, domestic abusers, the bipolar and manic and worse. The attacker from this morning deserved that kind of attention. What made me think I did?

"Let's get this over with," I said.

My mother sprang for the door, but before she got there, a loud chirping sound rang out from her purse. My heart stopped, drawing me back to the tinny walls inside the locker earlier, the ceaseless vibrating phone. My mom looked down at the caller's name, then at me, drawing her hand open as an offering.

"Audrey," she said.

"Please," I said, reaching for the phone, watching her slip out of the room. She shut the door behind her.

"Hi," I answered.

"What's happening? What I'm hearing...I just can't believe it."

Her urgent tone, the rushed sequence of questions, drove home an unprecedented fact: The experience that morning was, above all, a near-death one. The bomb, steps away, threatened to upend the very foundation we'd worked for years to build. Where would I turn when I needed someone? Where would she? Who else would listen to our every anxiety and bad joke?

"I still can't believe it either," I said. "But it's true. And I'm fine. Totally fine."

"Good! I'm so glad to hear your voice."

"Me too."

"Do you want to get into it?" she asked hesitantly, knowing my prickly aversion to having conversations I didn't want to have. "Or not?"

I pictured her brown eyes, marbled on the brink of tears, the same as when I told her about receiving another job rejection the week before. She'd applied for it on my behalf and afterward expressed a mutual frustration I couldn't have expected from anyone else. Just as I grasped the gravity of what I'd experienced that morning, I realized how badly I needed her. Not my mom or my fucked-up family. But Audrey, the totality of my world.

"No, sure," I said. "I just saw him there. I saw the fucking wires under his jacket, Audrey. It was so insane. Terrifying."

"I can't even imagine. Just talking about it is giving me anxiety."

"I did it, though. I stepped up and took him down, using my golf club of all things."

She let out a nervous laugh. "Yeah. About that."

My stomach dropped. "I'm sorry I didn't tell you I was going to play," I said, trying to infuse my voice with as much feeling as I could muster. "It's just, you know, between the job search and everything else, I knew you might not think it was the best idea."

"It's fine," she said quickly, unconvincingly. "Don't sweat it."

I filled the dead air by describing the cut on my lip and the locker room and people I'd met along the way, who were all taking good care of me. I assured her I'd be leaving the hospital soon—without saying why they were keeping me there—and after that my mom would drive me home. Brushing over these logistics, a swirl of guilt rose in my stomach—one I no longer wished to feel. Silently, I made myself a promise. I'd come clean to her, when the moment was right. I'd tell her about the Xanax. I'd refuse to lie to her ever again if it meant keeping her by my side.

"I should be home in a half hour," I told her. "I'm gonna give you the biggest hug."

"Ugh, I can't wait," she said. "They found someone to take over the rest of my afternoon at school. I'm thinking I'll take the subway back."

"The subway?"

"Is that not okay?"

I wanted to say no, it's not okay, if this isn't the time to spring for an Uber, here on the day I almost died, what would be? Her commute took an hour, more when the trains stalled out, as they often did. Did she not feel as urgent about this as I thought she did? Or did she not feel as urgent about *me*, given what we were going through?

"It's fine," I said, deciding not to press, not now. "I'll see you soon. I love you."

"I love you."

After hanging up, I took a deep breath, stood, and walked to the door. Knowing what I needed to do. I signaled to my mom, leaned up against a desk with her finger saving her place in a magazine, and gestured everyone inside. The four of us packed back into the room—my mother, me, Agent Ramirez, and Dr. Speer. Dr. Speer folded his arms behind his back before speaking first.

"So," he began slowly, "have we reached a decision?"

The doctor and Ramirez watched me with a kind of distant, friendly awe, as if I were a doe slipping through a forest clearing. My mother nodded to say, *Go ahead*.

"I'd like to go home," I said. I thought of Audrey, the silent promise I'd made. I'd phrased it as merely getting it over with to my mother earlier, but now I heard the certainty in my voice. My stomach grumbled with hunger, rejuvenation.

Dr. Speer didn't seem surprised. He refolded his arms, this time in front, pale skin crossing the bright white of his lab coat. "My assessment is that you seem like a normal, well-functioning member of society. What I would like you to do is make me one small promise."

"Yes?"

"If you think you're in trouble, or might pose harm to yourself or anyone else, you'll stop what you're doing, take a deep breath, and call 9-1-1. Or Agent Ramirez. Or your mother. Can you promise me you'll do that?"

"Yeah. Sure. Of course."

"Good. Now we're going to have you fill out some paperwork—clearance forms and all that."

"Wait a second," my mom said.

"Yes?"

"What about medication? If he's feeling a certain way and wants to take the edge off, isn't there something you can prescribe? I could give him some of my Xanax, but I don't think—"

"No, no," he said, his smile chilly and disapproving. Still, he didn't out me. He must've sensed she didn't know about the pills I'd been borrowing from Gelb, and he was diplomatic. "I can write a small prescription for Ativan, which is very similar to Xanax, and also has a sedative quality, so it can help with sleep."

"Question," I said.

"Yes?"

"Do you guys have any food?"

9

AUDREY

Commuting home from Brooklyn to Manhattan in the afternoons, I liked to take in the spaciousness of Stuyvesant Heights where I worked. The wine-colored brownstones, the historical Dutch architecture, the leaves changing in the small park that neighbored the above-ground subway station. In these moments, I could almost envision a life with Sam out here or another outer borough, less crowded than our Upper East Side neighborhood. We talked regularly about escaping the city at some point, decamping north for a town along the Hudson. All part of our big bright future, laid out together the summer we started dating after our senior year of college. Mid-twenties marriage, two kids, modest home north of the city. I saw this future being realized by some of our friends like Amy and Gelb, freshly engaged and soon to be married. But like them and everyone else we knew, we stayed in Manhattan for its convenience. Everything we could ever need within a short-to-medium-length subway trip.

Would we have been better off in Brooklyn or Queens? Simply for the space to breathe? People in Stuyvesant Heights always struck me as friendlier or, at the very least, calmer. I'm talking about the barista at the coffee shop, the clerk who made my sandwiches and salads at the bodega, greeting me every day with his big smile and, *How are you, sister?*

These comforts grounded me as I commuted back to Manhattan each afternoon. My lower back would ache from standing all day. I'd often be too tired to read or grade papers or even look at my phone. But on the day of the incident, in need of supreme comfort, I didn't head for the subway like I told Sam over the phone. After giving our vice principal the detailed instructions she needed to finish out the school day for me, I stopped at the cute new coffee shop on the corner. I ordered a coffee with extra creamer, a chocolate croissant for good measure, then slid into a nook by the window. Notifications had piled up on my phone, even on the five-minute walk. Tweets cascaded down my texts in droves: Sam, my boyfriend, a real-life hero. His name blasted all over the internet. I couldn't deny I was tantalized. Felt my lips smirking with something like pride.

I composed a message to my family group chat first, even though I'd already spoken to my parents on the phone back at school. *It's actually true,* I wrote. *Sam's still recovering at the hospital. They're doing some basic evaluation but saying he should be out soon. Thanks for checking in!!*

After hitting send, it occurred to me I could copy and paste the message to share with each of my friends and family members who had reached out. I chuckled a little while doing it; two somewhat dense friends of mine would use this approach to tell me and our other friends about the most mundane developments in their lives. Behind their backs, my other friends and I would share screenshots to show how we each received the same text about, say, a pasta dish from the night before. Not that I worried about any of my friends making fun of me today, as I fired off text after text. It was simply a matter of practicality.

Chasing my croissant with coffee, I didn't find that I was in any rush to get home. With Sam still in the hospital, I knew I had some time to sit and take in the news. I tried to process Sam's explanation for why he couldn't tell me he was going to play golf with Gelb that morning. Sure, I might've tossed off a snide comment about it not being the best idea, but I wouldn't have told him not to go. He was grown. Capable of making decisions with or without my input. The caginess, on the other hand, I minded. I pictured myself rushing home to question him, like I might have if he hadn't lied. Listen as he told the story and stroked his hair at the appropriate times. I just felt like I could use more time to access that part of myself.

Unlike Sam, who was addicted to Twitter, I rarely used my account. But modern life made it impossible to avoid whenever someone shared the latest news or meme or batshit celebrity meltdown. I quickly found the hashtag #PennStationBombing and scrolled through the feed—populated with eyewitness accounts of the stampede and descriptions of the suspect, a high school kid, of all things.

@MichaelDavenport
Here's everything we know so far about the #PennStationBombing suspect, Alexander Shine of Bayside, Queens 1/x
12:11 PM - Oct 23, 2018

The thread had already received more than two-thousand retweets. His age, all of 17 years, horrified me. You didn't hear of many high school kids engaging in the kinds of activity they were describing, carrying a bomb and a gun into a busy transit center to inflict maximum damage on innocent lives. People always liked to complain about the subways getting more dangerous, but this seemed like a bigger deal than someone getting stabbed or pushed onto the tracks. Penn Station served so many trains and subway lines, I got dizzy thinking about all the disruptions and delays. But with the threat neutralized so quickly, confined only to the LIRR section of the station, the MTA announced they would be resuming normally scheduled service within the hour.

When I came across the video footage, I couldn't resist clicking, watching the developments unfold in real time. Overhead helicopter shots of Penn Station. Concerned-looking police officers wrangling the crowds.

"We're fortunate that there are no fatalities to report at this time," the chief of police said from behind a podium in a live press conference.

I was watching him take questions from reporters when Amy's name popped up on the top of my screen. Amy, my best friend since college, and the fiancée of Sam's best friend, Gelb. Amy and Gelb started dating freshman year, Sam and me senior year. The four of us had been inseparable ever since.

The phone flashed and buzzed in my hand. A FaceTime call. Was I ready? Ready to acknowledge Sam's failure to tell me about his plans that morning? Maybe I didn't need to. Our little secret. Even though I hated the thought of that. Hiding our moment of weakness. Hiding secrets from our friends.

The screen persisted in its flickering. When I picked up, the two of them appeared to be in the back of an Uber, heading from Long Island back to the city.

"This is the most insane fucking thing I've ever seen in my life," Amy said. "I'm weak."

"I'm just disappointed he stood me up," Gelb said, cracking a sly smile as if he'd been waiting to use the line since the moment he'd found out. They were "On a day as nice as this? He owes me."

"I'm really still in shock," I said. "But we spoke, and he sounded fine."

"We're coming over later," Gelb said. "I need to shower that sick son of a bitch in champagne. Who knew he had something like this in him?"

A good question, one that I didn't have the slightest clue how to answer. It reminded me of how people have sometimes used major disasters and terrorist attacks as an escape latch, a chance to leave their miserable lives behind forever. Something didn't sit right. All the accolades lavished on him only intensified my suspicion that the story wasn't as simple as it was being made out. I knew Sam had anger issues, and he was going through a particularly tough time between his job search and hatred for his job at the magazine. But could Sam have initiated the altercation? It didn't align with the facts, sure. I just sensed something deeper beneath the surface. Then again, maybe I'd spent too much time on Twitter already. Maybe I was succumbing to the same conspiratorial thinking that ran rampant on the site.

"I'll talk to him again and see how he's feeling later," I told them, knowing he wouldn't want them to come over.

"Ok ok, go back to figuring it out," Amy said, perhaps picking up on my hesitation. "Where are you right now, by the way?"

"I just stopped at a coffee shop near my school to take a few calls," I said. "So many people texting and calling."

"Makes sense," she said. "Okay, talk later, ily."

"Ily, bye."

"Ily," Gelb sang.

More texts were waiting for me when I hung up—my younger brother Taylor checking in, punctuating his words with all the relevant emojis—but already Twitter had its hooks in me. I kept scrolling through descriptions of the scene that morning, new reporting about the suspect's cousin and supposed accomplice, Lance Tiernan, picked up for questioning in the aftermath of the failed attack. Lance had connections to a far-right extremist group armed with militia-style weaponry. It struck me how close Sam had been to the fast-growing phenomenon of domestic terrorism that continued to make national news. How close I was, now, by extension. I never thought I'd see the day when these groups would target a place as close to home as Penn Station. Even when 9/11 happened, all those years ago, I was still only in middle school, nestled safely in the Westchester suburbs. It always seemed like an isolated incident, a freak thing, never to recur. But as a New Yorker, I felt an intense connection to the city, its culture and diversity and convenience. Waves of panic were gripping the city already. All over Twitter, people were saying how unthinkable it was for domestic terrorists to be living and plotting in our own backyard.

The news had awakened a feeding frenzy in me, as delicious as the coffee and croissant I washed it down with, if not more so. I was scrolling through a thread on standard transit protocols in response to these events when I finally snuck a look at the clock. *Shit*, I thought, not quite urgently, but with enough sense to know I couldn't afford to linger. No matter how much I longed to remain forever inside the safe, warm, uncomplicated café. I knew I should get back. But at the same time I couldn't stop reading. Once I polished off my croissant, I looked up from my phone with a delirium usually reserved for Instagram binges. As squirrely as I still felt about the specter of returning home to Sam, at least I felt like we could now relate on one matter: Twitter was addicting as hell.

And yet Twitter was only the start. A few minutes later, a pink and purple banner swept down from the top of my screen: *You have 3 new followers on Instagram!*

A surge of panic raced through my heart. My jaw went limp. Three new randos were following me. Bots, possibly, or just plain freaks. Within minutes, I had another six followers. Then another nine after that.

They weren't all New Yorkers. People from all over the country wanted to know more about me, the girlfriend of the guy who stopped the #PennStationBombing suspect.

Except I wasn't anyone! My page featured an obnoxious amount of family photos. Some art we'd seen together. Boring scenic backdrops with Sam and me, same as every other couple out there. Sam never quite understood why I kept my account public. But only because he was a far more paranoid person.

As all these new followers swarmed—and I saw myself, from afar, like a lost soul surrounded by predators—the only thing I could think to do was switch my account to private. Maybe start removing or deleting followers. I wasn't even sure I knew how!

"Still planning to come by to pick up your workout bag?" my friend Jillian texted just then. I winced remembering I'd told her I'd get it after work today. "It's with the doorman but he keeps giving me shit that it's been sitting there for days."

Poor Jillian. She worked as a teacher, too, and probably had no clue about the news. But today seemed like the perfect day to make the pit stop now that I was out of school for the afternoon. Right? The initial high of the sugar and caffeine was wearing off, I noticed. I hadn't eaten a real meal all day. My gut was growling at me to move, to break free of the stagnation I'd assembled in the coffee shop, no matter which direction that took me. I packed up my stuff, plugged her address into Uber. I texted Sam's mom that I'd be back at the apartment a few minutes later than expected.

10

HOLLY

I knew it would still be another half hour before my dad returned home from work. So after showering and drying off, I shut the blinds, turned off my phone, and climbed into bed. With each breath, I imagined the parts of my body going numb. First my feet, then calves, then knees. The numbness crept up to my elbows and neck until I became nothing more than a head, as close to a dead body as possible. It was a trick I learned way back before my parents' separation. I've heard of kids who hide in their closets or cover their faces with pillows to drown out the sounds of their parents' fighting. But somehow, I only ever wanted to go inward, breathing and breathing until I could almost erase their voices from my head. Another OCD tic, I guess. My dad would be giving my mom a hard time over the credit card bill, buying me a new pair of sneakers or pajama set to match Piper and Remy. Meanwhile I'd be engaged in a secret competition with him, trying to drown him out.

But my dad's voice could travel. On my first day as a freshman in high school, our science teacher Mr. Karabatsos saw my name on the attendance sheet and said, "Ken Palmer's kid?" When I nodded, he told me how they used to work construction sites together. "Loud voice, Ken Palmer. Good guy. Passionate."

With each bark out of my dad's mouth, each hissing taunt, I'd lay as still as possible, as if moving a muscle would upset the magnetic forces to such a degree that he would know I was listening and take it out on me or worse, her. My mom could provoke him, though, she didn't back down like I did. I guess I admired her for this, but when I started therapy earlier this year, I learned that my anxiety and obsessiveness developed in direct response to their fighting, to form some order out of chaos.

Lying in bed, wet hair spread across my pillow, my brain pored over the evidence, not on Xander's side. He had a bomb strapped to his chest, right there in one of the busiest transit centers in the country. He'd be facing years of jailtime even if he didn't carry out the attack, even if he escaped with his life.

I paced my room and turned my phone back on. Too restless to stay in bed. As always, each of the apps grabbed my attention along color lines. I didn't even have to think of the names when I went to open one. I thought of colors: green for Spotify, yellow for Snapchat, pink for Instagram. My personal rainbow of digital connectivity. There were several voicemails and DMs, too many texts to process, but the one from my mom stood out from the pack:

I don't care if you're ignoring my calls. I'm on the first flight out tomorrow morning, we're going to figure this out as a family.

I was fifteen when she sat me down in the kitchen, took a deep breath, and told me she was moving to San Francisco, California.

"I have an opportunity to take a big step forward in my career," she said, as I sat across the table from her in an emotionless state of shock, pretending this wasn't happening. "I would be foolish to pass that up. It'll only be three years apart, then maybe you can come join me out there."

My shock soon gave way to an outburst of anger. How could she up and leave for a paycheck? Leave me behind with my dad's moodiness and weird distance. But she stood firm. And afterward sent me to talk to a therapist, a woman in her mid-30s named Lauren. She gave me a year to call my mom every name in the book. Lauren let me blame her for my crippling anxiety, my long hermit spells when I couldn't get out of bed. But then we focused on the so-called *controllables*—my grades and college applications, my art, my babysitting job. Even my hopes to reconcile with my mom, further down the line, when I felt ready. Then there were the things like breaking off communication with Xander that Lauren wouldn't allow me to blame myself for, no matter how hard I tried.

I couldn't think of what to say to my mom. I didn't have the energy. Sitting at my desk, I waded through two dozen more texts, half a dozen social media notifications.

Remy: *Still home? Just checking in <3*

Piper: *Holly, HELLO?*

Teddy: *Can you just send us a quick note to let us know you're okay? Piper is really upset you aren't picking up or texting back.*

Fucking Teddy. He'd throw himself in front of a bus for Piper, who was already looking to find any way she could to make this about her and her feelings, somehow, as if that was the most important thing.

I'm fine, I wrote back. *Catch up later.*

My dad's name dropped from the top of the screen: *I'll be home in 10-15.*

Remy: *Also you left your History binder in the back seat of the car earlier. Maybe I'll come drop it off later?*

I sighed, unable to remember taking the binder out of my backpack for any reason. I worried: How else had I been clumsy? What else would I struggle to remember? When I went to text Remy back, I saw she had shared a tweet I must have missed the first time around.

@KyleStanhope
Police have put out an APB for Lance Tiernan, a relative of this morning's bombing suspect. Recent posts by Tiernan online reflect far-right extremist sentiments, including connections to various anti-government militia groups. He hasn't been seen or heard from since the attempted bombing this morning.
12:33 PM - Oct. 23, 2018

That's when it hit me, the memory of going to his cousin Lance's house. Xander had taken me to see the collection of weapons. The guns. The suicide vest. How on earth had I forgotten? I felt so foolish, so ashamed of the limits of my own memory.

We met up there one night in early fall, once Xander finished his shift at the grill. Lance and his friends were away on a fishing trip, but by then we were used to hanging out there on our own. Some at school called Lance's a *crack house*, but I simply knew it as the place kids went to escape. They went during periods off to smoke hookah, after school to get high. Weekend nights to drink and blast each other with knock-off pepper spray.

That night, Xander told me he'd figured out the combination to the light chrome safe in Lance's storage shed. "I gotta show you," he said, a small smirk drawn across his lips as he brought us inside. The safe's contents blazed in my mind: a beige Safari-style vest with rectangular pockets up and down the front. Red and yellow wires hung down from the sides, patched together with duct tape. Next to the vest were two guns, unopened packages of bear spray, blue-tooth earpieces, and zip ties. A set of weapons that could have tempted minds far less vulnerable than Xander's.

"Imagine being born into Lance's privilege and still blaming minorities for your shit," Xander said, taking the seat next to me in the backyard.

"The privilege is beside the point, I think?" I said, picturing some of the construction workers my dad worked with, grown men who fell asleep to Tucker Carlson at night. "There are plenty of less privileged people who feel the same way he does."

I threw the back of my head against the netting of my chair. We said nothing for a while. The air felt warm for fall, and sitting in Lance's backyard, I kept expecting Xander to make his move. Because…Xander brought me here to have sex, right? I didn't care about this nonsense problem of Lance. He'd brought me here to go inside and have the most awkward sex inside this basically abandoned house. Instead, Xander just kept staring off in thought, or looking at the storage shed so intensely I thought he might explode.

"So, what do you think you're going to do?" I asked him.

His mouth moved around, fingers crisscrossed behind his head. "I'm less concerned with what to do. It's more a question of when."

I didn't know what to say to that, just waited for him to go on.

"Lance might be dumb, but he's not dumb enough to spell his plans out on the Internet. They use these encrypted messaging apps that I can't see. So, there isn't enough evidence probably."

"He has a homemade suicide vest in his backyard! How isn't that enough evidence?"

Xander smiled up at me and grabbed me by the hand. He bore this remarkable calmness, none of the mumbles or trembles that sometimes accompanied his words. His jaw stayed set in place like when he would be excited to share his latest fun fact, how Hungarian had 41 different phonemes, the most of any language. "I don't just want them to get him on illegal weapons charges. He goes away for a couple of years, then maybe he comes back even worse, more radicalized. No, I want to see him go away for good."

His words seemed to snap against the air, punctuating the insane thought of wanting to lock your own cousin up in prison for the rest of his life. Did it matter that his cousin was some hyper-online, neo-Nazi fascist? I couldn't imagine hating a family member so much I fantasized about putting them in jail. One important place where Xander and I differed.

I noticed how the initial shock of learning all these new facts, all at once, was starting to wear off. In its place, some new focus had taken hold of me. Some movie plot recollected, some book.

"What about if you, like, sabotaged him?" I heard myself say.

An eyebrow arched on Xander's face. My heart was bursting. "Excuse me?"

"Let's say you pretended to be on his side? Maybe even casually at first. You tell him you agree with some of what he says. It's not like he knows you disagree. As far as he's concerned, you're an open book. Maybe even an ally. You gain his confidence . . . and then you rat him out."

Xander eased back in his chair, flashed a devilish grin. "That's crazy, you know that?"

I smiled back. "Yes. Obviously."

We chuckled some more and glanced at each other from across the fire pit, but didn't talk any more about Lance that night. Kids like us—kids who wore goth clothes, pierced our noses, and took ourselves so seriously we couldn't imagine a future that didn't involve making art—had little thought to spare for domestic terrorism that may or may not be happening in our backyards.

The next time I checked my phone, I noticed it had gotten late. My dad would be expecting me home any minute. We packed up our backpacks and found our bicycles in the driveway, then rode toward the park separating our houses. Once we pulled up to the pond in Golden Park, we came together in a tight, drawn-out embrace. Moonlight leaked through the trees and reflected off the pond, a striking romantic vision that made me yearn for more. But I knew Xander didn't. While we could be intimate sometimes, mostly it felt like we were just close friends. He claimed he'd been on so many anxiety meds over the years that his sex drive had been driven out of him. Either that or we were both too awkward still, too uncomfortable inside our weird bodies.

I mashed my face into Xander's bony chest, and he kissed me once softly on the cheek. Then we said goodbye.

At my desk at home, I took a moment to sift through the layers of meaning behind Xander's actions that morning. *Foil* was the word many articles and tweets used to describe Sam Reid's role in stopping Xander. A word I couldn't recall ever hearing before, at least not outside of the kitchen. But that word only seemed to tell half the story. Xander wasn't only foiled in his attempt to set off the suicide bomb. He was foiled in his attempt to foil his cousin, Lance.

Xander never intended to harm anyone. That much I saw clearly. The less clear part? Getting anyone in the universe to believe me.

11

SAM

A hospital administrator named Mary cautioned me that word of my location had gotten out. There'd be media waiting outside, did I want help negotiating them? I considered it, but not for more than a moment. Compared to what else I'd been through already, members of the media seemed easy to negotiate.

I stepped out of the hospital's rotunda, my mother at my side, into a small huddle of reporters, video cameramen, and photographers. It's not like you imagine, with a police escort and bulbs flashing, a firing squad of questions. There were maybe eight people in total. I sensed my photo being snapped without hearing the clicks. The video cameramen switched on the white lamps above their cameras and with practiced stares and calmness in their voices, reporters asked me questions. As if by predetermined rule, a plain-looking blonde woman went first.

"Sam, Caitlin Gustafson with Channel Five. How are you holding up?"

"I'm okay," I said, looking her square in the eye. "A little shaken up, and tired, but I didn't sustain any real injuries. Just this cut on my lip from when I hit the ground."

"Have you had the chance to learn more about the attacker and the device? It seems like this thing had the potential for some real damage."

"The police briefed me," I said. "But mostly in relation to my role. What are they saying?"

"They're saying it could've caused dozens of fatalities, maybe as many as a hundred."

"Wow," I said, because I had nothing else to say. Sweat crested on my hairline. A thumping in my chest. This was a bigger deal than I could ever have imagined.

"How does that make you feel?" another woman asked—bright red curls, pointed stare, irresistible.

"Strange," I said. "Really strange. I can't comprehend it. Wasn't there a stampede? I feel bad for anyone who got caught up in that."

"They brought a few bystanders to Montefiore," said another reporter, male and raspy-voiced, with a scraggly beard and black tape recorder. "But they only sustained some bumps and bruises like you."

"Oh. Good."

"There's no reason to be humble, man. You saved lives this morning. You're a hero. How does it feel?"

I turned to glance at my beaming mother. Embarrassed, I looked away from her, concentrated on what I had to say.

"I'm not a hero," I said. "I'm not so sure this came out of anything other than self-interest, to be honest. Occam's Razor. I saw someone standing in my way. I felt I needed to take out the person who was standing in my way."

I saw their eyes and smiles growing, digesting my words like a steak dinner, exploding all the taste buds. As good as it might've felt to bask, an unsteady bubbling sensation began happening, too, creeping up from way down in my stomach. I knew what this bubbling meant: I couldn't stand to go any further, not then.

"It's been a long morning," I said, veering back from the

light. "I'd appreciate a bit of privacy, so I can collect myself and head home. Thanks, guys."

They all extended me the courtesy except for the male, who as I walked off, handed me his business card. I grabbed it out of some primal reflex, equal parts politeness and avoidance.

Michael Davenport, Senior Reporter, the New York Post.

"If you're ever in the mood to talk more," Michael shouted after me, "give me a ring any time." I followed my mom towards her car, parked in a garage a block away. After placing the card in my back pocket, I got the cynical sense that he knew exactly what he was doing. He sought to capitalize on this basic human reflex, that people take things that you hand them, particularly disoriented people. As we waited for the parking attendant to retrieve the car, I fussed with the plastic bracelet on my wrist. It felt alien, light, a little itchy. I didn't wear jewelry or even a wristwatch. I looked forward to the satisfaction of severing it with a pair of scissors. Each time my mom and I caught each other's eyes, something knowing passed in the unspoken space between us.

"Do you want to go pick up your prescription now?" she asked me once we were sealed inside the car, smelling clean and vaguely of the mints she kept in the center console.

"No," I said, more petulantly than I intended. "Can't you run out and get it later?"

"Okay," she said. "And what do you want to order? Something from the diner, maybe?" "What was it that Audrey texted again?" I asked. "She'd be on her way soon?"

"What time is it, 12:55? She said she'd be back around 2, I think."

"Let me see."

I reached for the cup holder where the phone sat, woke the screen to find a browser window open—the *New York Post* article my mom was reading in the waiting room. It described the event that morning, featured a big blurry photo of travelers scrambling, a lady in a head scarf who had fallen in the crush.

An eyewitness confirms another traveler, Samuel Reid, 26, of Manhattan, halted the alleged attacker before he could detonate the device strapped to him.

Inside the cool, sterile car, I became aware of a soft buzzing in my head, a swelling that seemed to lift me off the ground. I could only liken the feeling to texting with Audrey during the summer we started dating. I'd re-read her texts before I fell asleep at night, fastening myself to the certainty they would be there again the next morning. Not just that they'd be there, but there would be more of them to come.

Driven to intoxicated distraction, I forgot all about the reason I grabbed the phone to begin with, to check in with Audrey. I headed straight for Twitter. I ran a search for my username, @SamuelJReid, and uncovered over 160 mentions. I took my time scrolling through them.

> @alanfulbright: without a gun, saving lives. Thank you, sir.
> @taralippmann: Many of us can use good victories over bad right now
> @dexter18: Your parents must have done quite a job raising you! A true model citizen, right before our eyes

Some pop song played on the radio, Katy Perry or Ariana Grande, and even though I couldn't name the song, it seemed like I could hear the entire history of pop music happening— Elvis to the Beatles, Bruce Springsteen to Blink 182 to Britney Spears. Variations of the same sugary chord progressions, spread out across a fifty-year exercise in store-bought bliss. I became aware of an acute and dangerous current running through me, pushing me higher and higher, riding as though strapped to the roof of the car instead of in the passenger seat. It reminded me less of being on drugs than the anticipation of being on drugs—the thirty minutes of jangly suspense that it took for the pills to kick in. It scared me, to be honest, made me feel edgy and unpredictable. My focus went wild, a million miles a minute, with every new bit I read.

@NumberOneStokely: Yes, @SamuelJReid deserves our admiration today. But does anyone doubt that if he were a black man, he would've been gunned down right there where he stood? Beating someone half to death? He's just as lucky to have escaped with his life as anyone he saved.

I hadn't considered this interpretation, but I could sympathize. Or I thought I could. In a certain mood, I might have retweeted this comment, along with the 200-odd people who already had. But I didn't need to go seeking further attention.

I looked out the window as we arrived at our block. My mom pulled the car up to the curb and let me out, then drove off to park nearby, telling me she'd be up soon. A brisk and familiar wind whipped in from the East River, intensified by our proximity to the 59th Street Bridge. The good-natured doorman, Ali, held the door open for me with a bright and oblivious smile. The glossy blue and yellow tiles of the wall inside the lobby were a comfort, their irregular shapes and sizes like a bathroom inside an art museum. Did I take special notice of the wall? Or was it only that after being bunkered down in the locker room earlier, returning here seemed like a remote and unimaginable possibility? With some sadness I remembered the everyday strangeness of returning home. The comedown from my sugar high. I remained a foreigner in our ritzy building, despite my attempts to acclimate. I never forgave myself for caving to Audrey's requirement that we live in a "doorman building," allowing her parents to cover the cost. No matter how drastically certain things could change—the unthinkable events of that very morning, for instance—others would remain the same forever.

12

HOLLY

The rumble of the garage door opening downstairs. I looked out the window to see my dad's truck pulling into the driveway. When we locked eyes in the kitchen, I saw the tiniest flicker of fear cross his eyes. Maybe for the first time ever. He was so strong, so strong-willed, that I never considered what it might have meant to lose me. His only daughter, his only child.

I collapsed into my dad's broad shoulders, making me as small as I needed to feel. Tears falling down my cheeks. Breath too labored.

"I'm so happy you're safe."

I cried into his plaid shirt, smelling of sweat and cigarettes and fried food eaten behind the wheel of a car. We weren't especially close. He cooked the same three meals every week, drove me to tutoring or school, gave me far more space than many of my other friends received from their parents. I appreciated the independence but knew there was a forlornness about him, some trauma that still haunted him. No matter how much time we spent breathing in the same air, it often felt like I barely even knew my dad.

"I spoke to Joan," he said, referring to Piper and Remy's

mom. He pulled back to look at me, gestured for me to join him at the table. Just like that, his eyes were back to the business at hand. "I knew this Xander kid was part of your friend group. But he was your…boyfriend?"

"No," I said, sniffling. "I don't know."

I took the chair across from him at the table, scattered with old receipts, a paper towel roll, sticky notes, car magazines. How could I tell him? Not just about how close we were, but about Xander's dark side. The side that led us to today. I never opened up to my dad about all my insecurities, ample as they were. One time I told him it was hard growing up with the constant drumbeat of social media and group texts and cyberbullying. His only response was to say at least I didn't have to engage in hand-to-hand combat during recess, like he did.

"So, let me get this straight," he said, hands flat on the table. "You're on the trip this morning and he has this device, or whatever, on him. And no one notices?"

"It was under his jacket. His dad's old raincoat. It was big on him. He'd been wearing it a lot lately."

"And then he just disappears from the group?"

I nodded, dabbing my eyes with a paper towel, grabbing another to blow my nose. I hated how little ability I had to stop myself from crying. I only ever confided in my mom about things like this. And even that was minimal. I'd hardly spoken to her since she moved to San Francisco in the wake of their divorce.

"What were you thinking when he disappeared?"

Again, how was I supposed to tell him? That at first, I thought it was nothing, a kind of prank. But then that gathered into a sinking sense that he'd escaped to do something extreme.

"Everyone was just annoyed at first. He has a reputation for pulling pranks, getting into trouble at school."

"And this is what attracts you?"

"Dad!" I rose to my feet. "This is why I don't tell you things like this."

"Fine," he said. "Sorry." He stood, walked to the stove, and twisted the knobs to boil water in the kettle. He took a tea bag out from the cupboard and dropped it into a mug. I stood back, scrolling through my phone, where I saw the latest development making the rounds on Twitter.

@MichaelDavenport
"Police have conducted a raid on the Bayside home of this morning's bombing suspect, Xander Shine, as well as the home of his cousin, Lance Tiernan. There they found ghost guns, bomb-making materials, drugs, and riot gear, among other materials.
12:01 PM - Oct 23, 2018

"I just need to know the basic facts of what happened today," my dad was saying. "So that I can protect you."

"What does that mean?"

"Here," he said, pulling a magenta sticky note out from the back pocket of his work pants. He dropped the note in front of me on the table. There was a phone number scribbled in black ink, alongside the name *Agent Laura Ramirez.*

"Seems like they're questioning everyone already," my dad said. "She left me a voicemail on the drive home. So, again: Did Xander ever tell you he had plans to do something like this?"

"Dad," I said again, coming out as more of a groan this time. "No. Obviously not!"

"Fine. Good."

I took out my phone again, snapped a quick photo of the sticky note on the table. I wasn't exactly lying to him. Our meet-up at Lance's hardly counted as Xander telling me his plans. Anyway, I was so motivated to find out what happened,

I'd talk to anyone who could help pull on the tiniest thread. My dad didn't notice me taking the photo. He was scrolling on his phone, too, the red-and-white CNN logo pinned to one corner. Such a Boomer. Xander's face appeared at the top, right next to the other guy's, Sam Reid. The whistle of the boiling kettle arrived a moment later. I watched him pour the steaming water into his mug and take a seat at the table. He grimaced while reading more of the article, eyes popping with interest over all the facts we were still processing.

"I'm sure everyone's grateful that nothing worse happened. A few people injured in the stampede, it looks like, but sounds like he could have done far worse. They found a gun on him? Jesus Christ."

"It doesn't make sense."

He looked up at me. I heard the bottled-up defensiveness in my voice, the eagerness to defend Xander against Conner and the rest of the kids, who didn't know what he was really like inside. I thought of Xander's hands, too soft for fighting. His painful shyness. He barely ever made a move on me, barely even touched me without asking if it was okay. Because of his Sensory Processing Disorder, he always assumed everyone felt everything as sharply as he did, no matter how much I told him otherwise.

"Xander is really mild-mannered to be honest. Though also withdrawn a lot of the time. But he loves animals. His cats."

My voice caught in my throat. He extended a hand to mine. His other hand wrapped around his mug, still sending up thin plumes of steam.

"I can't imagine what you must be going through. It sounds like you guys are awfully close."

I nodded, directing my eyes to the window, where I saw how late it was getting, how quickly the day had passed. Clouds moved in to blot out the radiant morning. The sky gone from blue to granite. Long shadows threaded through the houses across the street like spider legs. With the sunset came sudden, cruel memories of earlier. The itchy rash that broke out along my neck when we found out. The knot down in the very bottom of my stomach. If Xander couldn't defend himself, if he was on his deathbed like the news suggested, would I have to be the one to do it for him? Despite the issues we'd had, despite the supposed weapons, I still couldn't square the day's events with the Xander I'd gotten to know over the past two years.

"I've filled your mother in on the basics. But I really think you should give her a quick call. Just to let her know you're safe."

"Okay, fine. I will."

He took a few more sips of tea, reading the article on his phone. A minute or two later, he said, "Can you believe they're calling this other guy a hero already?"

I tossed my head back, not knowing how to answer. I couldn't process how complicated it all was. A part of me felt Xander did, in fact, deserve what came to him. But I would've given anything to hear his voice again, just to listen to him describe what the hell he was thinking. Why he gave me that box of cupcakes, if the vest and the gun had come from Lance's.

"It sounds like he delivered a hell of a beating," my dad went on. "Golf clubs can do some serious damage."

"Maybe he deserved it, honestly," I said. Rose to my feet. "Maybe it's better that he just goes away forever and leaves us all alone."

I stalked out of the room, back up the stairs to my room, threw myself back into bed with the lights off. Unlike earlier, when I was powerless against the racing thoughts, a radical exhaustion had unraveled inside of me. The anticipatory anxiety and the real anxiety drained me from the inside out.

FOIL

Sniveling under the covers, I felt myself slipping, too quickly, into the heaviest, worst form of sleep. The one that existed to drown out my parents' voices. To escape when left with no other choice.

13

SAM

"I think I'm gonna quit my job," I said, sitting across from my mother at the kitchen table in my apartment.

"What?" she asked. She was dangling the salt shaker in front of her eyes, squinting to measure out the precise amount to apply to her egg-white omelet. She sprinkled some onto her palm, then dropped it over the top.

"I'm quitting," I said. Forks in hands, we watched one another, unmoving.

"You better not."

"Why?"

"Now's not the time to be making rash decisions."

"Who says it's rash? Audrey and I have been discussing it for a while, actually."

"Is that right?"

"Maybe I'll go back to freelancing."

"When was the last time you had anything published? Two years ago?"

"Two and a half years ago."

"Good, Sam."

"It's never too late to start over."

"Smart."
"Maybe I'll start a charity."
"A charity?"
"I'm blowing up!"

    I went over to my cell phone, charging inside the small kitchen. Even in the short period I'd been without it, the mentions and follows had piled up—dozens more each. This latest round came in response to the release of the video they'd taken outside the hospital.

@ABC7EyewitnessNews: EXCLUSIVE: Sam Reid speaks for the first time. "I'm not a hero," says the 26-year-old New Yorker. WATCH.
4:11 PM - Oct 23, 2018

Replies:

@LiveOrLetLilah: There goes my Hero…
@RiRiGoggins: Not only is he humble, but CUTE?!
@EllieSayers: I can be your Hero baby…
@MasonDee: Wtf is Okum's razor?

    My mother and I sat and watched the clip together. It hadn't occurred to me that anyone other than my friends would post video of me online, for any other reason to shame me, much less an account with 650,000 followers. I noticed the glassy screwball look in my eyes, the clumsy pronunciations, tongue flicking over my wounded lip. I wished I could have done another take. My mother's face snuck into the background frame at one point, the lenses of her transition glasses darkened like a lingering Dr. Strangelove. Watching the clip over my shoulder, she wore the same smirk of self-satisfaction, as if my success belonged to her.

@Heather2412: We can be Heroes…just for one day…

@KarenTibult: Is he gay? I think he might be gay.

"Well, you do look handsome," she said, as she scrolled through the replies. "They're not wrong about that."

I returned to my side of the table, where my eggs and hash browns sat, hearty and greasy and just what I needed. I shoveled the food into my mouth like a death-row inmate.

"And what's work saying?" she asked.

"Oh," I chuckled uneasily, not wanting to explain what was weird about this. "Claire wants to come and wish me congratulations in person."

"That's nice of her."

"No," I said. "It's just like her."

"What?"

"She can't stand not being the center of attention. I had to tell her that today didn't sound like the best day."

She gave me a fishy eye. "Don't be so cynical."

She spoke some truth. Social media wasn't the only category of attention I'd begun receiving. There were voicemails from friends and cousins, family friends I hadn't heard from in ages, each of them eager to commend me on my bravery. Not that I viewed them coming out of the woodwork in a cynical light. I didn't think they wanted or needed anything from me. I only saw how they sought to mark their proximity to the rare beam of Good News that shone out from me. *That's my nephew*, I could hear my aunt Pearl saying, speaking to the cashier at the grocery store tomorrow morning, indicating a copy of *Newsday* on the newsstand. I guessed the attention wouldn't have been anywhere near as full-throated if the reverse outcome had played out. Who would outwardly brag about our relationship if the bomber had gotten me, instead of the other way around?

Other forms of attention were less personal, though equally surreal and insane, like when Mayor DeBlasio called. He told me a story about a police officer in Queens who'd been shot in the head several months earlier, attempting to apprehend a suspect.

"You acted with no less distinction than that officer," he said, speaking so fast and loud I could hardly get a word in. "It takes a certain uncommon trait to run towards the source of danger rather than away from it—a heroic instinct that I can't claim to understand. You should feel assured that we're all in your debt today, Mr. Reid."

Afterward his handlers told me they'd be sending a member of the NYPD over to deliver a personal show of thanks. And to return my golf bag.

The final form of attention was more ambiguous, and maybe the most personal in a way that sometimes accompanies ambiguity—all due to a wave from Gelb's clumsy hand. Without my knowledge or say-so, he'd sent the link to our SoundCloud page to a music blogger he kept in touch with. I couldn't help but think he'd been sitting on the connection all these years for just this reason, just this day. The blog post went up early afternoon.

The Penn Station Hero Played in a College Band, and They Were Actually Pretty Good

The post summarized our history—how Abe and I scored early production credits and opened for a now much-more-famous rapper-producer. Reading through it made me feel sick—falsified and incongruent. I knew Abe would feel the same way, in whatever Austin-area art collective he called home. In college we handed out flyers to get the word out, we posted to our modest social media bases, but we never prostrated ourselves on the altar of self-promotion. We were idealists maybe. But by then I'd come around to the idea that music existed only within the pure, untroubled waters of history. I

SAM

couldn't bear the thought of getting back up on stage, sweating and doing vocal exercises, herding the same fourteen friends to a sticky bar in Brooklyn. That's what I told myself anyway.

Gelb's gesture wasn't only hasty and poorly thought out. It clarified all the ways we differed—the diverging paths we'd taken in recent years and in our more fundamental identities. He kept calling and texting. That was in Gelb's blood. I pictured him fidgeting on the edge of his seat, his boredom more profound from losing out on the day's activity. Call it spite, if you like, but I suddenly found myself in no great hurry to return his calls. The thought of him forced me to confront the fact that I had another one of his Xanax prescriptions on me, tucked away in a plastic storage container under our bed. In between the calls and texts, I snuck a look to ensure the bottle remained where I'd left it, under a pair of old hats. I closed the container drawer, not knowing when or how I'd deal with this, just knowing that I should. Especially if I was going to be the focus of so much attention. If cops were keeping tabs on me.

Eager for distraction, I stayed glued to the spigot of news that kept coming out, like a little kid placing my mouth under the soda fountain at Burger King. I read and read about him, the attacker, my supposed adversary, Alexander Shine.

The first thing is that he went by Xander. Reporters had already begun to question members of the Bayside community where he lived. They explained how Xander had received an Asperger's syndrome diagnosis at age seven. By his teens he began closely guarding his privacy, filling his computer with encryptions to surf websites like 8chan. He'd lined duct tape over the egress windows in the basement, where he'd moved his bedroom, shutting out the watchful-seeming light. His throwing off the bomb-sniffing dogs was nothing short of a miracle, it came out, given the patchwork of homemade chemical propellants he used, lifting the recipe from a dark web forum.

Then there were the photos. There he was being hauled out of Penn Station on a gurney, his head gashed red, his neck in a chunky, taupe-colored brace. The cameras captured the haunting glimmer in his eye but also a youthfulness I failed to notice the first time, when I merely saw him as a threat. He had a short fuzz of hair and smooth skin, still visible over the livid red. At 17, he was nearly a decade younger than me, the person who'd issued these gruesome injuries. And what, exactly, was I capable of?

More than I knew. When I saw photos of him from before the incident, I sensed I could pick him straight out of my high-school graduating class—the guy who wore dark clothes exclusively, so proud to tell you how stupid he knew everything was. Now I felt like the bully going after the oddball on the playground, even though I'd never done that kind of thing growing up. I feared being exposed for my vengefulness—the monster that had burst out of me. Of course it turned out to be tainted in this way. My achievements were never as meaningful to me as my failures. I succeeded at the aspects of my job that were required of me—those and nothing more. Now here it was again, an achievement tainted by the disillusionment I worked very hard to hide. Like a bull rider at the rodeo, I held onto the forces inside of me that threatened to buck me off track—the angry and self-pitying outburst towards my dad and others. Then I managed the fallout the best I could. Even as I knew that this wasn't any real way to live.

My mother wouldn't have understood. I was thankful she kept me company, but as the afternoon wore on, and she took calls from everyone in her phone book, repeating the story each time with different parts accented in the telling, I grew weary. Ready for her to leave.

SAM

When Audrey called, I was scrolling through Twitter, sinking deeper and deeper into the pits.

"Where are you?" I asked her, over the frenzy of sirens and street noise, voices calling out.

"I'm making a quick pit stop downtown, I need to pick something up from Jillian's."

Bitterness spiked through me. The same as earlier. Why was she being so cavalier? Did she still think this was an average day?

"You needed to do this today?" I said, adding some deliberate frustration to my tone. My mother looked up from the other end of the table. "Of all days?"

"Sorry! It's my gym bag that's been sitting there for like a week. It'll take ten extra minutes, I promise. Then I'll be right home."

During the summer that Audrey and I started dating, I once asked her if she ever felt any remorse for the way she ended her relationship with Craig, her college boyfriend. She cheated on him with me, and no matter how much I suggested cutting ties earlier in the school year, certain as she was that they didn't belong together, she didn't seem to mind the drama. "I don't spend very much time caring what other people think of me," she told me, nearly laughed as we sat by the pool at her parents' house. Her eyes remained obscured by sunglasses and a big straw hat. "I must get that from my mom. She was always teaching me to move forward, save face, rather than backtrack. The more you dwell on what others think, the more trouble you're going to bring."

She wasn't wrong. I spent too much time thinking about what others thought of me. But this was also one of the few things I sometimes liked about myself in comparison to Audrey, who discarded people like Craig so easily, he must have questioned whether he ever meant anything to her at all.

"I'll see you soon," I told Audrey on the phone now.

"Great. Love you."

FOIL

"Love you," I said, and despite the uncertainty over when she'd return home, I did look forward to seeing her, to settling back into our small, commonplace routine, and even to hashing out our problems—like this one—that seemed bigger because they were ours.

14

HOLLY

I woke to the sound of car doors closing in front of our house. An all-too-familiar set of voices. Even in the dark, peering out through the window in my room, I made out Piper, Remy, and their mom Joan climbing out of their SUV. Remy held a big aluminum foil tray in her hands. Joan carried a plate covered in cellophane. One of her famous cakes.

I smiled faintly. The knot in my chest shook loose, if just for a moment. As our closest family friends, the twins wouldn't surrender to my earlier plea to be left alone. Our families took vacations together, shared season tickets to the New York Rangers together. Each of us had keys to each other's houses for times of emergency, and it wouldn't be too much of a stretch to say today qualified as one.

I needed to use the bathroom before going downstairs to join them. I heard my dad greet them in a muted tone, not knowing if I was still sleeping. I looked in the mirror and splashed water over my face, brushing and re-arranging my hair, mussed and frizzy from sleep.

When I arrived in the kitchen, Piper ran straight over to me, wrapping me in a forceful hug. Remy shot me the most pitiful smile from the other side of the kitchen. She opened the aluminum tray with its layers and layers of ribboned pasta, cheese, meat sauce.

"Lasagna, Joan?" my dad said. "What have I told you about my cholesterol?"

Ignoring him, she looked at me and said, "You poor thing."

She stopped mixing the salad bowl in front of her on the counter. Remy opened the oven, lifted the tray, and set it down inside.

"You didn't have to do all this, guys," I said.

"Sweetheart," Joan said. "It is our absolute pleasure." She wiped her hands with a rag before gesturing to me and saying, "Get over here."

She hugged me and I felt more secure than I had all day. Secure in the physical sense of a human being I knew and knew well, squeezing me tight. But I also felt secure in the deeper sense of being part of a community of friends and family. Those who wouldn't blink to come to my side in a time of need. There to fill the glaring hole left behind by my mom's decision to move away.

"That boy. What I'm hearing." Joan shook her head and swept a hand across her forehead. "I can't believe the kinds of trouble kids are getting into these days. I don't think I've ever heard of anything so…depraved."

"Mom," the twins said in unison.

"What?" she cried. I noticed the twins moving unsteadily around each other, giving each other extra space. "We can't acknowledge the elephant in the room? Not at all? That boy was sitting in my living room three weeks ago. Who knew all this was going on in his head?"

My dad sucked air through his teeth. Remy and I exchanged a brief glance before she said, "Wait." I watched her take my History binder out of her bag. "Here, remember? You left it in the car earlier."

I grabbed it from her. "Oh, right. Thanks." My cheeks

burned with embarrassment. I frowned. "Let me bring it to my room." I slipped out of the kitchen as the rest of them busied themselves with the food and made small talk. Inside my room, I shut the door behind me and sighed, pushing out all the air built up in my chest. I remembered hearing once that extroverts feed off the energy of others in social situations, while introverts only find everyone exhausting, and I never needed to guess which category I belonged to. The energy of socializing, even with people as close as them, was draining me already.

Back in the kitchen, our conversations stuck to less serious matters than what Xander may have done that morning. Remy told a story about Charlotte Brandywine getting hit in the nose with a Nerf ball in gym class. Piper asked if we knew the term *acid reflux*? She always thought it was *reflex*. We all laughed at Piper's willingness to be the butt of the joke, as long as she took center stage.

Sometime later, Piper and Remy's dad Roy joined. He owned a hardware store a few neighborhoods over and his naturally calm manner, compared to my dad's grouchiness, sometimes made me envy the twins. Not that I didn't think they had issues as a family. Joan could be extremely overbearing, for one. Piper and Remy were always competing for grades and after-school clubs and who would get which part in the play. But I couldn't ever picture them having issues as serious or upsetting as ours. As we sat at the dinner table, passing the salad bowl around, I was overcome with the same warmth and depth of feeling that made me feel like crying earlier, surrounded by people who rushed to keep me and my dad company in our time of need. They weren't the only ones, either. Friends from my extended social media circle checked in at various times throughout the day. I was taking a moment to respond to an Instagram DM, in fact, when we heard a knock at the front door.

"At this hour?" my dad said, sounding annoyed. From the

kitchen, I watched him stand from his chair at the dining room table, drop his napkin on his plate, and storm off to the front of the house. Roy followed a few paces behind. Joan watched with a mix of curiosity and concern. The four of us tried to eavesdrop, exchanging wide looks of confusion between each other in the quiet.

"I'm a reporter with the *New York Post*," we heard a man's voice say.

"Oh my god," Remy said.

"No," Piper said. "I'm actually freaking out."

"Shhh!" Joan said, waving her arms frantically at them.

"I've had sources share that your daughter knew the suspect, Xander Shine, quite well. Would you or her care to comment?"

The twins looked at me with their eyes bulging out of their heads. A charged silence followed, and even though we couldn't see my dad or Roy, I pictured them scrambling with the same shock we all felt, unable to come up with a single thing to say.

"Are you serious?" my dad said finally, his voice rising.

"Yes? It's not that uncommon—"

"No, I would not like to comment," he said gruffly. "And please don't ever come back here again."

The door snapped shut. They rounded the corner back to the dining room, a look of utter revulsion on my dad's face.

"It's not enough what you're going through?" he said, pacing, agitated, unable to sit down. "Now they come out here and *stalk* us?"

"Unreal," Roy said.

"Please tell me this is not how this is gonna go from here on out," my dad said. "I might end up dropping one of these sons of bitches before all is said and done."

"Dad," I said. "It's not that big of a deal. That's just his job."

"I don't care," he said. "It's not right, cookie."

HOLLY

I hated him then. How he used my childhood nickname to demean, to muzzle me. He didn't even bother to look at me, as if I was unworthy of the chance to respond.

"How could they even have found out so quickly?" Remy asked, perhaps to ward off the tension rising between us.

"Someone must've talked," Roy said. "She was snooping around town and someone, another student maybe, said you guys were close. *Why don't you go ask Holly? She's the one who knew him best.*"

"Unbelievable," Joan chimed in, shaking her head. "The nerve of these people."

"Scum," Roy said, one of his nostrils flaring, breaking through his bearing of calm.

Joan stood. "I guess that means it's time for pasta," she said. "Girls, you can each pour yourselves a little wine. But only half a glass each."

Piper and Remy smirked at each other before stepping to the bar in the corner, drawing three wine glasses out from the rack. Roy and my dad found new ways to express their disgust. Joan retreated to the kitchen, and the twins poured the white wine into our glasses. Joan returned a few seconds later with the dish and spatula, filling everyone's plate with a hearty serving of Costco lasagna.

We couldn't help but talk about Xander for the rest of the meal, as if that reporter had not only punctured the protective layer of courtesy we maintained, but broke it wide open. Everyone asked one unanswerable question after another: How could Xander have done it? Why wasn't he caught sooner? What role did his cousin Lance play? And how crazy was it that he disappeared? Lots of speculation flowed, serving only to intensify my feelings of confusion and hurt and anger. But it was something Roy said, toward the end of dinner, that settled me down slightly. That and the wine, I guess.

"I know you guys are going through a lot right now," he started, "but it's important to remember that you don't owe anyone anything. Not the cops. Not the press." His eyes gathered an intensity that I couldn't recall seeing before. He stared at the wineglass in front of him, twirling it around once as the claret-red liquid swirled. "Don't be afraid to make yourself scarce right now. Your privacy is something that's worth protecting."

A careful pause followed, then my dad said, "I couldn't agree more, Roy. And we appreciate you guys coming over today. Means a lot. Joan. Seriously."

They nodded at each other. I looked at Remy, sitting next to me. She leaned her head onto my shoulder and stayed there.

"Love you," she whispered, and I balanced my head on hers for a few seconds.

"So, who's ready for dessert?" Joan asked.

"Let's do it," Piper called out in a theatrical voice.

"Don't forget the ice cream we brought to serve with the cake."

Make yourself scarce. The phrase glowed in my mind as the night wound down. I realized I'd probably been too kind in replying to all the people who reached out to express their sympathy. I needed to conserve my energy for bigger things.

"When does Sandy get in?" I heard Joan ask my dad in the kitchen, referring to my mom, thinking I was out of hearing range.

"Some time tomorrow. Late morning, I think. First flight out."

"Okay. If you need anything in the meantime, don't hesitate to reach out, Ken. Anything at all."

Somehow, speaking with my mom for the first time in months didn't seem like so big of a task anymore. Not with Xander recovering in the hospital with *life-threatening head trauma*. Not with reporters knocking on our door with questions.

After we finished dessert, the twins each gave me one final

big goodbye hug. As soon as the door shut behind them, though, the house slid into the emptiest quiet, a brutal hangover from the bustle of voices filling up the space. Not even the emptiness that followed my parents' divorce could compare. My dad said he'd be watching a replay of the Rangers game he recorded on the living room TV. Did I want to join? But I couldn't imagine anything I wanted less.

Back up in my room, all alone, I listened to the echoing creaks of his footfalls on the floorboards, or the water running in the bathroom when he showered, or the TV's murmur from downstairs. Determined to take Roy's advice, to make myself scarce, I didn't call up my social media apps to search Xander's name like I had earlier in the day. I sprawled out in bed and put on an old sitcom rerun and tried to distract myself to sleep. When that didn't work, I decided I needed to take one more look.

I pulled the drawer open to find the cupcake box wedged inside, the pink cardboard warped and cracked along the seams. Sitting at my desk, I opened the box and reexamined the discount card inserted into the inside of the lid, smeared with swirls of chocolate and white frosting. In my rush earlier, I never removed it from its indented spot inside the lid. Never saw the back. But it occurred to me now that this was the one remaining place I hadn't looked. I took a second to breathe and brace myself, already nervous in my gut. Then I pulled the card out and flipped it over, and there it was: blue ink on the backside of the card, a wobbly scrawl immediately identifiable as Xander's hand.

There were only three lines of text—a shortened URL link, a username, and a password. And I wish I could say this heightened my frustration or fears of what I'd find. But a strange satisfaction came from the power I felt I had. Maybe this made me a bad person or something, but honestly, I didn't care. My mind saw a long dark hallway stretched out in front of me, the lights coming on one by one as I walked toward the end. I was in middle school, reading a Nancy Drew book late at night. Stepping right into her shoes. A young detective.

I grabbed my laptop and spread it open on the floor in front of me, lying on my belly as the white LCD light glowed in the dark. I opened a private browsing window, because I'm not stupid, then typed in the URL, which called up a nondescript, encrypted-looking website, populated only with form fields for the username and password. After entering them, a folder came up labeled "Journals 1-30." A list of thirty documents appeared.

I tried to fight the signals my body was sending me—chest tightening, stomach clenching, hands trembling over the mousepad. But the waves came on too strong. My stomach growled and burbled, creeping into my throat. Before I could click on the first document, before I could read one word, I needed to pull myself up off the floor. The wooziness robbed me of my sense of direction. The white-hot severity of a migraine, battering my head from all sides. Black squiggles in the corners of my vision.

I fumbled for the doorknob in my room. Twisted it open with one hand, the other pressed to my beating forehead. I reached the bathroom just in time to see my insides spilling into the toilet.

PART 2

15

XANDER'S JOURNAL

Tricyclic & Selective Serotonin Reuptake Inhibitor Withdrawal Day 1

My left armpit won't stop itching. My elbow too. I'm generally brain-dead and fatigued, itching all up and down my left side. Every now and then, my hands will turn randomly ice cold. Or my arms will get wobbly or bent into shapes unintended by science. Then come the brain zaps—momentary flickers of electrical activity like fleeting fireworks in my peripheral vision.

I am a scab ripped off, left out in frozen bluster, battered by the sucking nullity of it all.

I want to dwell in the idea that I have meaning. I try to think of being a busboy as the means to an end, but what end? Maybe it is simply who I am and who I'm meant to be. Maybe I identify too strongly with being a busboy.

"You look pretty miserable there," my coworker Jen told me yesterday, behind her sour breath.

How could you tell? The set of my jaw? The tired, defeated look in my eye? My hunched shoulders and apathy towards you and everyone else?

Chaos theory, in the most literal sense, can be useful. Nothing matters, so don't apply meaning.

One crucial thing I've learned: never listen to your parents.

―――――

Tricyclic & Selective Serotonin Reuptake Inhibitor Withdrawal Day 2

My mom works as an anthropology professor at the City University of New York and likes to pretend that being a liberal professor in a city college provides cover for the mistakes she's made in other parts of her life. Or maybe she really is that deep in denial.

Let's start with the decision made to not just marry my dad, but stay married to him in spite of the years of abuse he's delivered to our family. Imagine me at the age of nine, all of 75 pounds, stepping in front of my dad while he chased my mom down the side of the road. Imagine me sticking my leg out to trip him, the force of my dad's full-grown strides too strong for me to make an impact. He charged through my outstretched leg like it was a bug on his windshield, leaving me stunned and dazed and bruised badly on my shin. He didn't strike her when he reached her, not that time. But that howl, that beastly generational, "What the fuck is wrong with you?"

Apologies were made afterward. Reconciliations. She sent him off to Connecticut to sober up and think about what he did. But then she took him back, like she always did, too stubborn in her old-fashioned commitment to keeping the family together. Because that's how their parents did it. Despite the promises to never do it again, though, all the sincere-sounding apologies, he's only gotten worse.

There have been belt lashings, too many to count. One time he hit me with the metal buckle end. A heavy, coldish pain I never could have fathomed. Then there was the time last year when he told me to get up off the couch, get some fresh air and sunlight. I said no, and he returned to the living room with the belt, forming it into a lasso with his hands.

"You need to learn some respect," he growled, the belt propped on his shoulder like Paul Bunyan with his axe. "Maybe your mom is happy to put up with all this sulky bullshit of yours, but not me."

I looked at him and laughed, but didn't move from my spot on the couch. No longer scared.

"Laughing? Okay, Xander. Get over here."

He went to grab my shirt, but I was too quick for him. I wriggled free and got my hands on the belt, wrenching it from his grasp. Then, without thinking, I turned the belt on a nearby lamp, swinging so hard it made sparks fly. The cord ripped from the socket.

He stepped back, wide-eyed, and with my chest pounding, I roared, "This is my fucking house! Okay? You hear me? My house now!"

He snarled but stayed put, frozen in shock, and I threw down the bat and darted outside, where I first remembered the existence of air, the need to breathe. I sped away on my bike, slept at a friend's that night, but not before I heard my dad calling after me, "Good luck explaining this one to your mom! You better not come back here if you ever want to see your friends again, you hear me?"

I entered this world through no choice of my own. My mom wanted to have kids and my dad indulged her like some feral, unthinking boar. She's not all bad, either. She works hard and encourages me to develop my writing skills. She can be funny, even.

I can't quite blame her for not being able to see the future, that my dad would turn out the way he did. But I still look back at that day when I was nine—the bone-crunching impact on my shin, what he might have done if I hadn't stepped in—as the turning point between us. Her making us come back to live together as a family only taught us how to forgive what we never should have learned to forgive. As the only adult in the room, she should have done the responsible and compassionate thing, for everyone, and divorced him. Saved us. Protected us.

But whether out of fear or hesitation or weakness, she didn't. And we found more ways to forgive. And now, that turning point is scheduled to reach its final destination.

16

SAM

My Aunt Pearl sent catering—turkey and roast beef and pastrami, pickles and coleslaw, pumpernickel and rye. She cited an old friend who once found herself in the middle of a 'media shitstorm,' after it came out that her husband had been defrauding investors for decades.

"The hardest part was the meals," my Aunt Pearl said. "They couldn't show their faces in restaurants anymore. They'd get the nastiest looks, even from people they'd known for years."

The gesture was well-intentioned, if not congruous. Photographers weren't waiting outside my building, ready to snap my photo or sting me with catcalls. No one sought to incite an offensive reaction from me, framing me as the latest pariah. The only shitstorm happened inside the four walls of my apartment, out of the public eye, where it became apparent that I'd only escape by eating my way out.

"You don't have to hang around here anymore," I said to my mother, who was fingering the icing off a cupcake. "Audrey will be back shortly."

"How could I forget?" she said. "Your new family."

"Don't give me that."

"Forgive me for wanting to stay by your side in a time of need."

"Need has a shelf life, too, you know."

She sighed theatrically. I took a lush bite of my pastrami sandwich. "Fine. I'll get going then."

"What, would you like me to express my bottomless thanks for being with me today?" I was grateful, and I knew she knew it. In my way, I was saying thank you.

"Would it kill you?"

"We both know the reason you're stalling. You don't want to go back there without producing some mend in the fence."

"Forgive me for wanting to keep this family together. If I don't do it, tell me, who will? Not you. Not your father."

"You're right—exactly right. The problem is that you've drawn the wrong conclusion. Maybe you don't need to keep chipping and chipping away at something that isn't working. Maybe the answer is to stop trying altogether."

"I told you I'm not doing anything until you grow up and have a conversation. Accept some responsibility."

"Responsibility? I let my emotions get the best of me. I can live with that. I paid for the damage."

She snickered. "The whole thing? I don't think so."

"I'll do it, in time. But what about him? Will he ever accept responsibility for screaming his head off, waving his finger in my face like a crazy person? No. Because you've let him get away with it all these years. We've let him. It was what, two weeks ago that you called your own self a coward! Your words, not mine. I only pointed out the obvious—that you're scared of being a black sheep, that god forbid anyone in your family or circle of friends should have issues under the glossy surface."

A tiny flutter appeared in my mom's eyelid, followed by a single tear. I found the sight somewhat beautiful, like a drop of dew on an otherwise sturdy leaf. More remarkable was that no others followed.

"You are a pair of children," she said, frowning at me as if I'd received detention in school. "Stubborn children."

"If we are," I said, "at least I'm the one trying to work through it. I'm starting therapy, considering meds."

She snorted again. "That's not you talking. That's Audrey. Or that doctor at the hospital. There's nothing wrong with you, Sam. You're a good kid."

"So, I should do nothing? You're the one who suggested they prescribe me Xanax."

"These are extraordinary circumstances."

"And what about your circumstances are so extraordinary? It's like you hold me to some higher standard because you can't bear the thought of anything being wrong with me."

She let this one sink in, squinting off into the middle distance, but I was only getting started.

"And this is all to distract from the bigger issue," I said. "The vicious cycle. He's great and charming for weeks—just for long enough to lull you into a false sense of security. The worst part is that deep down, he knows that. He knows it's all a push-and-pull to see just how much you'll let him get away with."

That's when she stood. She'd had enough. She began packing up her bag with all her things, her water bottle and iPad and half-eaten fiber snack bar.

"Okay, Sam. You have all the answers. You figure it out for yourself."

My mom futzed around with her cell phone before dropping it back down into the bag with the rest of her worldly materials. I took little pride in lashing out at her. Sometimes, though, it was the only way to get through.

She placed a frail hand on my shoulder and told me she loved me, was proud of me. I nodded. Then came the sound of a key twisting inside the doorknob.

"Babe?" Audrey called out.

17

XANDER'S JOURNAL

Tricyclic & Selective Serotonin Reuptake Inhibitor Withdrawal Day 3

I'm journaling today because I don't have the energy to do anything else. I can't bring myself to log online or engage with anyone, I'm so viciously hungover and brain-dead.

Tomorrow, there will be moments of complete despair. I know they are coming, and I know I will be powerless to stop them. It's not impossible I could use them as fuel to do the thing I've been putting off. My end-of-life policy.

Walking by the pond earlier, I saw a young Hispanic boy catch a fish, reel it in, and present it to his mother. They both smiled at me.

If I didn't take moments like these to interact with other people, I might forget they exist at all.

Tricyclic & Selective Serotonin Reuptake Inhibitor Withdrawal Day 4

If there's one person I want to understand, it's Holly. She knows about my back pain and the doctors and meds and even my dad. The belt, the coffee table, the lamp. But she doesn't support my solution. Another barrier holding me back, maybe, on some subconscious level?

Our texts:

Me: *i just read something funny in a book*
Holly: *tell me*
Me: *"suicide is the only true philosophical question"*
Holly: *this again? i thought you were past that.*
Me: *just makes me think. Maybe it's the noble thing after all.*
Holly: *how could it possibly be? and what book is this?*
Me: *Julian Barnes. he talks about rejecting the "gift of life" since we never asked for it in the first place… no one ever understands that.*
Holly: *what? what don't people understand*
Me: *its like in third grade when kids used to call me autistic even tho I'm not. everyone wants to label everyone else—depressed, anxious, suicidal, whatever. but maybe my purpose isn't to be anything at all. maybe it's to be nothing. Gone. can't that be an acceptable purpose?*
Holly: *No its not like that. we're almost done with school. We'll have the chance to start over soon. and I know you and care about you. doesn't that matter?*
Me: *i guess.*
Holly: *i know you're just saying that, but you're not gonna get better on your own. you need help. we can go together if you want…*
Me: *maybe that helps me, but not them. Ending it is a win-win. it ends my suffering AND teaches them a lesson. it makes my life more important than just myself. they'd learn just how much they've hurt me*
Holly: *but it's not just that. taking your life would bring so much pain to everyone close to you. Me. your mom.*
Me: *my mom doesn't care as much as you think. she's too distracted with work. im pretty sure she saw a suicide thing on my computer the other day and didn't even say anything.*

Holly: *see? your mom knows you're in a bad place, but she knows you won't listen to her. and that she'll only make it worse, like the other week...*
Me: *that's exactly my point. why should she have to pay for more broken lamps? this would HELP HER in the long run.*
Holly: *no you don't have a right to take your own life. i won't accept it.*

I love Holly, I do. But sometimes, she just doesn't get it.

———

Tricyclic & Selective Serotonin Reuptake Inhibitor Withdrawal Day 5

Experiment number three of stuffing a pair of socks into the exhaust pipe of my mom's car. I am adjusting to the light-headedness, blurry vision, and headache. The fumes meandering into the car, burrowing in my lungs, stinging my eyes. I brought a bucket to vomit in this time. Right after I puked, I panicked, just completely freaked. I opened the door of the truck, gasping for air behind the King Kullen in Valley Stream. A good enough place to die.

Why the hesitation? Biology. Evolution, I guess. No one tells you it takes work. You hear that someone jumped, stabbed himself, hanged himself. What about all the fibers in his body screaming out not to do those things? The panic is the last, hardest barrier to overcome. The certainty isn't the question. It's my ancestors who programmed me to sprint from the cheetah chasing after me.

Another way? Drugs to dampen the sympathetic nervous system's response, but nothing that will distract me or make me happy like benzos. Sleeping pills maybe. Alcohol? Next time.

FOIL

Tricyclic & Selective Serotonin Reuptake Inhibitor Withdrawal Day 6

I'm okay enough with computers. I can take them apart and put them back together. I can manipulate the wires and circuit board with my set of miniature screwdrivers, the sour taste of carbon dust settling on my tongue. But now that I've started tracking my cousin Lance's whereabouts online, I think can use this skill for something like a purpose.

This isn't a purpose I ever expected. And I'm still not sure of the exact form it will take. I simply know that I have the opportunity now to do something epic. To bring some meaning to my worthless life.

It started the other night when I wound up at Lance's—another foggy, drawn-out night. I woke at the break of dawn to the blare of his cell phone going off. Lance remained motionless at the other end of the room, passed out on his floor-bound mattress. A couple of flies buzzed around him, his pants halfway down with his Boston terrier Garth sniffing his ass. The phone rang next to him, vibrating too, but Lance didn't budge. He kept snoring and mumbling and whimpering like a little pug. In my hungover state, I hobbled over to shut the thing off, to get some more sleep at whatever ungodly hour this was.

But then the caller's name drew my eye. Hart. He'd left a voicemail.

"Where are you? I need the code to the lockbox in the shed. I'm going upstate. gotta grab my shit."

I swiped over to his texts.

XANDER'S JOURNAL

2083? 2038? Pick up.

That's when I heard Hart's truck pull into the driveway, kicking up gravel pellets. He cut the engine, and I dropped the phone and bolted straight back to my spot on the couch, hearing Hart circle around and peer through the living room window. I kept my eyes as shut as possible, squinting to see past the flickering lids.

"Morons," he muttered.

I heard him spin around on his heel. I lifted my head to see the back of him walking away from the house, off toward the shed in back.

He spent what felt like hours in there. I kept watch, panting like a hungry rat.

When he appeared in the doorway, I drew back so quickly that I fell off the couch, slamming my tailbone on the hardwood floor. Lance let out some whiny gibberish, but he didn't wake up. I took another breath and crept up to the window, peering over the ledge to see Hart carrying the biggest gun I'd ever seen. Then he got in his truck, slammed the door shut, and sped away.

Tricyclic & Selective Serotonin Reuptake Inhibitor Withdrawal Day 7

My mom told me to journal every day for 30 days and I've decided in this instance that listening to her instead of ignoring her, like I normally would, is the most punk rock thing I can think of.

18

AUDREY

A yellow cab, catching sight of me, switched lanes and swerved in my direction. It nearly swiped an SUV trailing in the other lane before pulling up alongside me. The driver of the SUV honked as I opened the door to the cab. With my workout bag and backpack slung over each shoulder, I climbed inside and told the driver our address.

During the short, rocky ride uptown, I moisturized my hands and face to drown out the hesitancy of facing Sam. Notes of lavender and eucalyptus in my nose. How would he react to my lateness? What would I tell him? He may have been too preoccupied to even notice.

I took the time in the cab to revisit the problem of my new Instagram followers. Or maybe not a problem, at all, but an answer? Maybe one of the ways we'd exploit these fast-moving new circumstances for professional and/or financial gain. Too fast, though. I was getting ahead of myself.

For now I needed only to stage-manage my account, to delete posts I thought I'd be judged for most: One with several paper bags from different fast-food restaurants, the vestiges of a Saturday binge with friends. Another of my brother and his former partner that he asked me to delete, though I continued to insist he looked cute.

The next time I looked up from my phone, we were parked next to our building. When I reached the door to our apartment, a strange impulse came over me to knock, as if I were a stranger to our home. I pictured Sam inside with a whole team of handlers to tend to the drama. But I simply slotted in the key and turned it more slowly than normal.

"Babe?" I called out. The pet name came weakly from my lips, as if I were out of breath.

Sam rushed over to greet me in the alcove, an unusual gesture. He hugged me tightly and kissed my cheek, lips warm, as I set my yoga mat and bags down. He looked fine or normal. Other than the embarrassing swell of his lower lip—which he seemed overly conscious of, moving his tongue around—he seemed slightly harried, not surprising under the circumstances. The surprise came when we turned the corner to the foyer alcove to find his mom sitting at the kitchen table. A tight look of frustration stitched into her face.

"Audrey," she said, rising from her chair with arms open, drawing me into a quick hug and brush across the cheek. I smelled Beth's perfume, trailed by the familiar dank scent of the Reid house, smelling always like a wine cellar with too much old wood lying around.

"What a day," I said.

"Crazy," Sam said.

"Not in my wildest dreams," Beth said. She reached over and pinched his cheek like he'd hit a home run in little league, and he smiled sheepishly. She reached for her purse draped over the kitchen chair behind her. "Well, I was just on my way out. I'm sure you two could use a little privacy right now."

"You sure?" I said. It seemed strange that she wouldn't have stayed to debrief; she was never one to pass up an opportunity for gossip. That's when I noticed a layer of tension in the air between the two of them. Sam scrolled his phone instead of maintaining eye contact with either of us for very long.

"I've done my part," she said, smiling. "You can take it from here."

"Thanks, Beth."

Sam walked her to the door as I made a move to unload some clutter—papers, folders, old granola bar wrappers—from my work bag onto the kitchen table. When I heard them say goodbye, and the door snap shut, I spun around to confirm the look on Sam's face, the lingering discomfort of some conflict or another.

"Okay so…What the hell was that about?" I said to him. "I feel like I just walked into a funeral."

He shrugged a little. "She wants me to call my dad. And I would like to not do that."

"God forbid he should call *you*," I said.

"That's what I said."

"It's been how many months now since you've spoken?"

"Six or seven."

"And she thinks today would be the best day?"

"Timing has never been her strong suit."

"Amen," I said.

He reached his hand out and I took it, fingers threading through each other, twirling playfully. He hugged me and squeezed tight, planting a single small kiss on the back of my neck. Warmth rose from my chest. It felt nice to be home, back to our private embraces. I supposed that my hesitation to see him had been overblown. We had so much history, so many roots.

"I missed you so much," he said. We pulled back to look each other square in the eye. With his eyes moist and red, I could see how scared and vulnerable he'd been earlier, and I didn't know any response other than to comfort him.

"I'm here now," I said. "We got this."

We hugged again, and tears slipped from his eyes onto my

shoulders. I didn't feel quite like crying myself, despite being the one of us far more prone to doing so, but I certainly understood the reaction.

"Who knows if that bomb would have ever gone off?" he said. "Or if he would've had the balls to use the gun. But if he did, I would've been right in the line of attack. I'm not sure how long it's gonna take me to get over that."

"You can take as much time as you need."

He grabbed a paper towel roll to dry the tears, blow his nose several times. "We have all night to decompress. I'm thinking we should just shut our phones off, watch dumb TV."

"Speaking of, my dad sent me a pic of you on the news," I said, pulling it up on my phone to show him. "I thought about drafting an Instagram post on the way over, but I wasn't sure you'd be thrilled with the idea."

He snickered. My mind raced back to the attention I'd begun receiving on Instagram, new followers assembling by the minute.

"Yeah, no," he said. "Not yet. I saw you finally made your account private, at least."

"Getting new followers out the ass."

He smiled. Our private sarcasm. "What about Gelb and Amy coming over?" I said. "Seems like he's dying to see you."

He shook his head. So much for celebration. He was in wet blanket mode, for reasons I could only pretend to understand.

"And Chinese?" I said. "I felt like that would be a given tonight."

Sam looked towards the kitchen. "My Aunt Pearl sent enough cold cuts to last us a week."

I glanced at the platter on the kitchen counter, pastrami and turkey and salami, all encased in a clear plastic dome. It didn't look very appealing to me, even if on our modest combined income, we never passed up the opportunity for free food.

"You might be happy to know that they assigned me a therapist earlier," he said.

"Oh, great. How did that go?"

"Wait. They prescribed me something, too. Ativan. I'm sure I could use it right now. Do you mind if I run out to the pharmacy?"

Outside, shades of a pink and orange dusk penetrated the sky. I didn't mind him evading my question so much as the awkwardness between us. Why did he always make everything so much more convoluted than it needed to be? Today could never have only been about one thing—an uncomplicated heroic act on his part.

"It's fine," I said. My clothes felt stiff, restrictive, all of a sudden. "I need to get undressed, anyway."

He smiled, wiping away the final remains of the tears. "I haven't been out of the apartment in hours. I could use the air. Do you think I need to wear a disguise?"

I ignored his half-hearted joke, noticing my stomach grumbling with hunger. I never got the chance to eat a real lunch. "Just hurry back, okay? We don't need to pick at Pearl's cold cuts. After all this, I'm still ordering myself a damn egg roll."

19

SAM

I needed river air. My spot. After picking up the prescription and a bottle of seltzer to wash it down with, I headed east. I walked two avenues to a small patch of wood park benches, where brown leaves crunched underfoot and the wind slapped my cheeks, slapped some sense into me. I gazed out over the rough, grayish water, bits of froth built up along the edge where the surf met the stone. Further south, I made out the U.N. building, windows lit against the backdrop of early nightfall, reminding me of Hollywood Squares. I'd made this observation before, during a previous session on this bench, one of those times when I came to contemplate the big decisive life questions. I came because I thought I'd get clarity—what the good-looking people on television received when they went to look out over bodies of water and think—but on most occasions, I came away with little more than windburn and a runny nose.

Sometime later I realized that the Hollywood Squares were never white. They started out blue, and sometimes changed to red.

The wind was still quite unpleasant.

"I'm so thrilled you called," Gelb answered, his voice clean sounding, inviting.

"Don't worry, I'm not calling to hang out."

"How are you doing, man? How are you feeling? On top of the world?"

I wasn't sure if I should tell him what he wanted to hear or answer truthfully.

"Not quite," I said. "But I'm fine, feeling fine."

"Have you seen the comments on this blog post?" he asked. His ADHD-riddled mind was too adrift to notice my reluctance. "I already talked to Nick about booking The Horse. I think we'll be able to fill the place out this time."

I didn't like the image that rolled into my mind—being trotted out like some circus act, appealing to the lowest common denominator. I minded it. But the image didn't last long. I needed to talk to him about something else.

"I thought I should let you know that the cops found your prescription on me earlier."

A pause. He really seemed to stop and think. "Okay? And they give a shit?"

"No, I don't think anything will come of it. But they tried to use it as leverage or whatever, to see what I may have known. And Audrey doesn't know that you'd been giving me them. But I think, technically speaking, there are certain legal implications for each of us right now."

"Sam," he said.

"Yes."

"This is what you're calling me about right now?" He let out a deep, cutting laugh. "This should be the least of your concerns. You did something *freaking heroic* earlier. Cops in New York City have absolutely no interest in tagging a few guys who let their friends borrow pills—"

"No, I know."

"Do you, though? Because for someone in that position, you sound quite paranoid."

I remembered the specific set of feelings that flooded me inside the locker room earlier, the vow I made to come clean. When the cops questioned me, they showed how they could rinse me of my freedom in the blink of an eye. My goal now was to not make that happen. And Gelb represented the first step.

"Either way, I want to return the other bottle," I said. "I have something else now, anyway. It's the right thing to do."

"If you say so," he said, unconvinced.

"Good. I'll keep you posted on timing."

After we hung up, a bitter gust of wind brushed up against my face. It kissed my cheeks and stung my ears, but didn't bother me as much this time. I realized why only once I stood. My legs felt like oatmeal, my smile plastered up against my jowls like settling concrete. I felt an odd floating sensation on my walk back to the apartment, a giddiness I couldn't recall from any of the times I took Xanax. I imagined the manufacturing process behind the tiny white pill I'd swallowed, the legwork behind this sensation. Mounds of granulate reduced to powder, pressed tightly together, tablets gliding across conveyor belts and then coated, scored, cut. All this so college kids could crush them back into powder to snort, anyway.

I didn't need this mass-produced, designer-drug sensation to know that Gelb was right about me being paranoid. Then again, it didn't hurt either.

20

XANDER'S JOURNAL

Tricyclic & Selective Serotonin Reuptake Inhibitor Withdrawal Day 8

It doesn't surprise me to learn that Lance has a large cache of weapons. He'll flaunt them out in the open sometimes, trying to impress his new ex-military friends like Hart and Deertick—dip-packing, neo-Nazi types who go to the polls to intimidate voters and generally stir up shit. Lance himself has been joining them lately to patrol liberal rallies and pass out literature about the Second Civil War. Packing heat in case it ever goes that way.

Still, there's one part I can't get out of my head. Knowing he's upstate fishing, I just went over there again to make sure I didn't dream it. I slipped inside the shed and peeled back the curtain that obscured the safe. I tried the two padlock combinations that Hart mentioned in his texts. When neither worked, I tried more permutations of those four numbers—2-8-0-3—and finally, on attempt four or five, it opened.

There were four guns total—a handgun and sawn-off shotgun among them, and two M15 rifles—but none of the guns captured the intensity of my attention like the vest. It didn't look like much—beige and pocketed—a few janky wires dangling and some C4 cartridges sewn into the pockets. My heart thrummed with excitement as I grabbed it and tried it on, adjusting to the weight around my shoulders and neck, like these dumbbells that made me hunch forward.

As I paced around the Shed, growing more and more used to the exhilarating heft of live explosive all around me, I knew this was information I could do something with. The only question was: How? And when?

———

Tricyclic & Selective Serotonin Reuptake Inhibitor Withdrawal Day 9

"Sabotage." "Rat."

These words fly high in my consciousness as I monitor Lance's activity online.

I might have enough to act on already. But Holly has offered up a different suggestion. Holly, of all people, has come up with a plan containing some purpose. A plan and a purpose and solution in one.

She told me to infiltrate. Sabotage. Rat 'em out.

If I believed in God, I would have to thank him, or her, or it. Thank you, god, for bringing me Holly.

———

Tricyclic & Selective Serotonin Reuptake Inhibitor Withdrawal Day 10

Writing in my journal sometimes makes me feel like a retard spray painting a wall, like a toddler skipping a rock across a pond, so awed by the fact I was able to introduce movement into the world.

———

Tricyclic & Selective Serotonin Reuptake Inhibitor Withdrawal Day 11

She moves from one side of the stage to the other, carrying two loose diamonds, a dead chipmunk, and a boa.

She ties the boa around her neck, and it flows in a winding path behind her, but it's not in her nature to be seen. She likes to watch others more than she likes being seen.

The clutch of spandex is tight against her breast. She laces up her slippers as electricity courses through her like little kids bustling on a playground.

The lights dim, a spotlight on her flushed face. A cello plays and she leaps.

21

AUDREY

I watered the plants around the apartment, tidied up. Anything to distract me from thinking about Sam's failure to disclose his golf plans that morning. How strange he'd been acting in the apartment. I could let this go. Couldn't I? Despite our unblemished history of *radical honesty* with each other, I could forgive a tiny fib. Right? Of the many hats I wore for Sam—girlfriend, confidante, best friend—I suppose you could say caretaker was the one that filled me with the most meaning. Or maybe it was the most familiar.

I took so much pity on Sam for his unstable relationship with his family that offering my family's compassion came as a kind of sacrament. The weekends we'd escape the city to my parents' house in Westchester. My dad sharing career advice with him and connections to his business network. The ski trips and Caribbean beach trips, all on my parents' dime—there wasn't any reason for Sam to feel guilty about accepting their love and generosity, even as I knew he did. There wasn't any price for him to pay, internal or financial or otherwise.

And yet the pity I took on him came with a price tag—for me. My compassion for his struggles, my stubborn devotion to that puppy-love summer when we met, blinded me from just how capable he was of dragging us down. The more I turned a blind eye to it and simply pressed on, the more I stood there right next to him, shovel in hand, plowing the ditch to new unseen depths.

That night, with Sam out picking up his medication, this denial manifested in my hunger for Chinese food. My drug of choice. I placed the order over the phone and during the wait could only think about the savory warm explosions of flavor. Having skipped lunch, I was so ravenous that when I heard a knock on the door to our apartment, I could only imagine it to be the food arriving. But when I opened the door, a man and woman stood in the entrance, introducing themselves as members of the FBI. Confused, I took the woman's outstretched hand into mine. She flashed me her badge that said Agent Ramirez. The other, Agent Bender, hefted Sam's golf clubs inside, positioning them against the wall in the foyer.

"We just came to drop these off," he said. Perfume battered the air when Agent Ramirez swept past me. "And we'd like to follow up with Sam about a few things, then answer any questions you guys might have."

Agent Ramirez looked around, squinting. "Is Sam here?"

No, I thought. Sam was hell knows where. "He just stepped out to run an errand, I think."

"You think?"

I remembered the Ativan. "No, yeah. He did. Can I grab you guys water or anything? We have a Keurig, too."

"We're just fine."

"Grab a seat on the couch. I'll text him, I'm sure he'll be back any minute—"

"Sounds great."

I retreated to the kitchen, out of sight, where my exasperation pitched higher and higher. What was taking Sam so long? How was I supposed to entertain these people? Any secrets he may or may not have had were fine as long as they didn't interfere with my simple need for peace.

The intercom on the wall blared, shaking me out of my skin.

"Hello?" I answered.

"Food here," the doorman answered.

"Oh. Right. Send it up."

I met the expectant eyes of the officers sitting on the sofa. "You know, dinner time. Chinese."

"We can come back later if that's better for you?"

"No, it's fine. I ordered a ton of food. Enough to feed us all."

After another knock at the door, the delivery driver handed me the bag, and as soon as I reached the kitchen table, I ripped open the mix of plastic and wax paper. There they were: the noodle shells I'd been craving all day. I dunked one into the pool of duck sauce, brought it to my lips. I was so hungry I didn't care how I must have looked to them, stuffing my face.

Joining them on the sofa, I said, "He responded, saying he's on the way back. I'm sorry."

"Please," Agent Ramirez said. "No need to apologize. How are you holding up so far?"

Out of habit, I just started talking. I retraced the moment my principal pulled me out of class to relay the news, how I could hardly speak to my students, even in the short span of time. But I soon realized there were only so many ways for me to express my disbelief. I told them I was looking forward to getting back to my routine, to the tiniest bit of normalcy.

"I don't do well with sudden change," I said, gnawing on a spare rib, some task for jaw to take on.

"Very few people do," Agent Bender said. A violent urge to cry descended on me. I wasn't sure I could keep it together anymore. Not with these strangers in my home, these police officers exerting their will over me.

FOIL

When I heard Sam's key twisting in the door, finally, it filled my lungs with much-needed breathing room. I stood and hugged him in the doorway, pretending all this was normal.

"What took you so long?" I asked him, keeping my tone non-judgmental.

"Sorry. I needed some air. My river spot."

If Sam was surprised by the sudden appearance of two FBI agents in our home, he made no sign. I watched his glassy eyes flick to the golf clubs in the foyer. He walked over and actually counted them to make sure they were all there. Other than the nine-iron he'd put to use earlier.

"You have a river spot?" I asked him under my breath as we stood at the table, out of range of the agents sitting on the sofa.

His eyes seemed to look everywhere but mine. He approached the scraps of food, picked at them. If he stopped to look at me, he might have noticed my desperation. But he was already out of it from the drugs, sluggish, his pupils the size of dimes.

"Where I've been going to think," he said.

"You've gone there once."

"Guess what, Sam?" Agent Ramirez called out.

"Do I really have to guess?" Sam asked. He looked very amused with himself, appraising his swollen lip in the mirror over the bureau.

"The city has offered to buy you a new set of golf clubs."

"That was my doing," said Bender. By way of explanation, he pointed his index finger in the air and smiled. "I figured it was the least we could do. I mean, Cobra irons from 2002? I had to look up the year."

"They were my dad's. Hand-me-downs."

Sam joined the two officers on the sofa, casually, as if they were old friends here to watch a movie. He even kicked his feet up.

I grabbed another barbecued spare rib, lacking any other source of comfort.

"Sorry if I'm being rude," I announced, "but I just couldn't wait any longer. The offer still stands if you guys would like to dig in."

Bender stood and walked over and fixed himself a plate.

"How'd the talk with Dr. Speer go earlier?" Agent Ramirez asked Sam, very concentrated on each other, as if they shared some secret language. "You set up with everything you need?"

"It went well," he said.

Uncomfortable with the perception of eavesdropping on them, I explained to Bender how it took me months to find the place that had both the quality and delivery speed I needed. But out of the corner of my eye, I kept watch over Sam and Agent Ramirez's increasingly private conversation. They watched some video on her phone before standing to meet us at the table.

Sam rose from the sofa and came over and grabbed the largest noodle shell in the carton. He dipped it into the orange-pink goo and fit the whole thing in his mouth before chewing it down quickly, forcefully, like a child with his pacifier. He looked at me, and out of some ancient instinct, I knew to hand him my fork. He shoveled the rice and chicken up toward his face, hunched over the table with crumbs raining down on the plate.

"She wants us all to talk," Sam said with a half-full mouth.

Bender took another bite, wiped his lips with a napkin. We went back to the gray L-shaped sofa. On top of the leather ottoman was a tray with a ceramic bowl, a gray stick of sage jutting out over the edge. Beside the bowl was a small, spring-top jewelry box. Inside the jewelry box was our weed.

"Are you the type of people who believes everything you read?" Agent Ramirez asked.

"Yes," I said. All eyes shifted to me, and I gestured with

my hands to deflect the attention. "No, not me. Sam. He reads every goddamn article there is."

"Sorry that I follow the news?" he laughed. I took the unspoken insult on the chin. I'd never be as worldly or well-read as him.

"No," Agent Ramirez said. "I didn't mean it like that. It's just that a lot is going to be written and said over these next few days. Much of it will be positive. Already is. But people may also try to defend this guy in a whole series of strange and unpredictable ways. If anyone, and I mean anyone, sends you a threat of any kind—a letter or a phone call or so much as a Facebook message—you should feel comfortable reporting that to us."

The history of what we were involved in rose high above us, above Sam, who seemed to derive a certain importance, enough to make him happy. He knew all the right questions to ask.

"How do I differentiate between a threat versus empty rhetoric?" Sam asked.

"We're monitoring the public social media channels," Agent Ramirez said. "But if you'd like to give us access to your profiles, we can monitor the private messages as well. It's unlikely that anyone associated with Xander would be dumb enough to message you directly, but you never know."

"I'll sleep on it," Sam said.

"Good."

I shifted in my seat to look at the darkened Manhattan streets outside. Truck horns sounded in the distance, commuters trying to get home. Frantic nightfall. I felt glad to be at home. I'd be happier once we were alone.

The agents walked us through some formalities—best ways to get in touch, business cards, direct phone lines. I nodded along but didn't make out much more than a few of the words. I'd gone inward, out of the present, so far away that I needed to compose myself in the bathroom. Would I confront him tonight? Not just about the golf lie, but his behavior in general—the drugs he was on right now and had been taking more and more, as if I didn't notice. The selfishness. The dying of our spark. I sat on the toilet with no real need to pee. How could I hold my feelings in any longer? Maybe the drugs would soften the blow.

When I returned from the bathroom, Agents Ramirez and Bender and Sam were exchanging handshakes in the foyer. Sam grooved the door shut behind them.

"Can we talk for a second?" he asked as I stood in the doorway of our bedroom.

"I thought...I thought you didn't want to yet—"

"No," he said as we sat down at the kitchen table, and I felt my shoulders sag with relief. Even if we might've hit a rough patch, there was still trust between us—the old trust.

"Is it weird to feel guilty right now?" he said.

"What? It's been what, six hours since it happened," I said. "You can't possibly—"

"Expect to process it all right now, right?"

"Of course not."

"Of course not."

A photo of us on the bureau caught my eye—drawn into a kiss, impassioned in sepia tones. Sam designed it for me as a Valentine's Day gift years earlier, and no matter how much Sam's friends made fun of him when they came over, I kept it proudly on display.

"In some ways, it makes perfect sense," he said. "It might as well be another work assignment I can't take any pride in."

I stared into the welter on the table: haphazard trails of lo-mein, picked-over wax-paper bags. "These professionals can help you, Sam," I said, a slight rasp coming out in the vowel of his name. "There's only so much we can do on our own. There's only so much *I* can do."

He'd shut his eyes, stuck.

"Promise me you'll go?" I asked.

He looked up at me, nodding.

"I was so scared earlier," he said, hands creeping towards mine on the table, "when they locked me up inside that room. Not just about the possibility of never getting out, but about losing you. I couldn't fathom it."

Our fingertips pressed together. "I know," I said. Even if I could see the pain in his eyes, the shattered-glass look of a fall from windy heights, he seemed to acknowledge that maybe we were ready to pick up the pieces. Maybe there still was time to get our future back on track. The slightest shimmer of light, peeking out from beneath the door.

We hugged, heaving, hands caressing each other's backs. Once we kissed, it seemed to snap us back into something like a routine. Garbage removal, dust-busting, the pungent smell of household cleaner in the air.

He filled me in on the rest of the day. He told me about the sounds that came out of him, Xander Shine, the screams. He confessed to the appalling thrill he got from driving a 9-iron into his skull. He talked about the locker room and hospital and some guy named Rust, who may have saved his life.

"Were they really considering making you stay at the hospital tonight?" I asked.

"Unclear. I think they couldn't figure out why I did it. How I did it. Someone like me."

"You know my dad loves your temper—like when you'd go to play golf with him and miss a putt and go, *Really, Sam?! Really?*" I did my crude, exaggerated impression of Sam, hands waving all around. "He says you'll always be there to protect me, no matter what. Who knew that all along, he was right?"

We laughed a little, and I thought back to the only time that Sam put his temper to work on my behalf. We'd spent the night bowling with a few other couples—one of those bowling alleys where they dimmed the lights at night. Disco balls and glow-in-the-dark pins. Toward the end of the night, after we finished bowling, we stood around the bar, where a guy with a goatee wouldn't stop staring at me. Sam went up to him and said, "Want me to send you some photos of her, to make it last longer?" The guy reacted by shoving Sam in the chest. They grabbed each other by the head and neck, but neither of them got off a clean punch before Gelb stepped in to break it up.

"And what about work?" I asked. "Does Claire care that you lied to her about golf? If they fire you, I think it's a good thing, honestly. Maybe it's the push you need to get the hell out of there."

"Oh, I didn't tell you?" he said. "I'm thinking of quitting. I may start a charity."

"A charity?"

"A charity. Think about it," he said. "This guy, Xander, he has Asperger's, right? People are already blaming it on that—mental illness. So, what if I started raising money for autism research?"

"Hold on. Slow down. You want to be bringing yourself *more* attention right now?"

"Only if it's positive." Was it possible? Was Sam really on the verge of something big? "There's never going to be a better time than this, right? It takes two minutes to start a GoFundMe. Hell, I can set it up tonight."

He fetched his laptop from the bedroom, filled with a proactiveness I seldom saw in him. A future seemed to align before our eyes—appearances on *Ellen*, person-sized checks from celebrities or large corporations, charity golf tournaments. Maybe this would be the spark that reversed our fortunes, after all.

"My new Instagram followers!" I said. "They're going to eat this up."

He didn't look up from his computer. Probably didn't even hear me, with his inability to divide his attention. So I left him and poured myself a glass of Pinot Noir. On the TV, I turned on one of my murder-mystery shows. I ground a small nugget of weed up between my fingers, packed the small glass pipe. I lit the weed with the lighter we kept inside the jewelry box, inhaled as smoke bathed the air. I lit a sage stick, too, drawing it towards my face as instructed by the healer I sometimes visited named Thelonia. She had dark features and plump hands, a mole on her cheek surrounded by a soft tuft of hair. She lulled me into deep relaxation as she mined my past lives—a welder in medieval times, a Jazz Age druggie—for lingering residues that could be affecting me today. Dark energies interrupting my sleep, growing worse and worse by the day.

I was circling the sage over the pressure points in my neck, just like Thelonia showed me, when I heard a small gasp come out of Sam. He looked on in pale-white horror.

"What the fuck?" he asked. I lay the sage back down in its clay dish.

"What? We need to ward off all the evil spirits we can right now. The 4chan and Instagram creeps."

"That lighter. Have we always had it?"

"This?" I held it up to the light, the yellow reflecting brightly. "I think Nina Chandelier left it here during book club a few weeks ago. I don't know about you, but I'm enjoying myself tonight. Our off day tomorrow."

Sam stood there, frozen in place over me.

"It's the strangest thing," he said. "I saw him use a yellow lighter earlier, just like this one."

"What?" A pause. "Stop it."

"They told me they never found it. But I saw him with it. I swear. He brought it out of his pocket and even flicked it with his thumb a few times. Do you think I fucking *hallucinated* that?"

I flung the lighter down on the tray as though it were on fire. "You're bugging me out right now. I don't even want to touch it."

He sat down next to me, grabbed the lighter, and inspected it in his hands like some fragile historical artifact. "I'm surprised you let Nina Chandelier over here. With her cigarettes."

"Do we need to report this to the cops?" I asked.

"Do we?"

"It's scary. But kinda cool, too, you know? Like one of my shows."

He looked at me. I looked at him. Then we started making out. Like in one of my shows.

22

HOLLY

How was I supposed to sleep? The racing questions alone would have been enough to keep me up. My mind churned as I shifted on the bedspread, laptop propped open to read the journals. Pain dug into my hips from the lack of movement.

C'mon, Xander. There's still time. Snap out of it.

He hovered like a shadow as I read the partial answers written in his journals. A fire seethed inside of me and wouldn't go out, no matter how many times I turned my computer off, then on, then off again. Even in the dark, the pixels skewered my vision with lingering haloes of light, each time I closed my eyes.

The more entries I read, the less confident I felt in my decision to withhold my knowledge of them from everyone. They'd discover these journals, sooner rather than later. They'd see my name mentioned there as something like Xander's muse. The breakup, his final push. Then again, the part of me that hated the media's misguided portrayal of him thought to take on the challenge. How long would it take them to prove me right? The victimless nature of Xander's actions meant I had time. I could say I was too distressed, too scared and naïve, to offer my story as evidence for fear of implicating myself. Wasn't there some law about that?

Reading entry after heartbreaking entry, a more immediate idea occurred to me: Lisa. Xander's mom could provide a kind of off-ramp for me, if I could find a delicate way to alert her to the journal and plans. She'd vouch for me. Or, if Xander could speak, he'd clear my name. Earlier that day, I thought it was too soon to visit. But now I saw a mutual benefit, a reason more substantial than a check-in on the state of Xander's health at the hospital.

It must've been after 4 am by the time I finished reading, by the time I settled on the decision that I should pay Lisa and Xander a visit at the hospital tomorrow. Once I closed my computer and turned off my headphones, I lay in bed and heard many familiar sounds pouring in from the outdoors: winds whistling, owls hooting, squirrels scampering, the more eager birds rising from their slumbers.

At one point, I heard a man's reedy voice outside. Our neighbor, Jae Li, drove a cab and was always coming and going at odd hours, talking on his cell phone to family back in Korea. On the night my mother left my father for good, an ambulance came to his house. Mr. Li lived there with his son, wife, and 87-year-old mother, who needed to be rushed to the hospital after having a non-fatal heart attack.

The ambulance arrived much earlier than the time that my mom told us she was leaving, before she finally decided she'd had enough of my dad's shouting at her, packed up a small bag, and went to stay at my aunt's across town. But I never forgot the way the blue and red light seemed to fill up the entire world that night. As if we were under an alien invasion, as if we gave Mr. Li's mother that heart attack. All the arguing between my parents had seeped through the wood in our walls. Shot over like a laser to their house, pushed her over the edge. In my head, I knew this wasn't how it all went down. But it comforted me to see it as a natural cause and effect.

Because to see it as pure coincidence would have made me feel even worse. Actions had consequences. And even if the consequences came to those who didn't deserve them, tough break. The red and blue ambulance lights flashed in my dreams to remind me.

I may have caught an hour of sleep before the first hints of early morning light came trickling through the window shades. My head throbbed, eyes heavy and crusted when I opened them. The sunrise meant I'd need to get ready for school, to brace myself for the onslaught of theories and finger-pointing I could avoid at home in bed.

The stares from people who never bothered to look my way. The students and even teachers who tensed up around me—it soon became clear to me that my name would be tarnished, just by association with Xander. Not that this was anything new. As soon as we grew close over the summer, I knew I'd be the object of confusion, scorn, derision. But I never could have anticipated so much outright hatred, returning to school the next day.

23

SAM

A more self-aware person in my position might have been wracked with night terrors. Flashbacks to the incident, Rust, and Xander Shine. Fever visions of his smooth skin and bloodshot eyes. All the grisly, sickening violence.

But as soon as my head hit the pillow that night, I passed out. I *dreamt*. As a rule, I think that people who talk about their dreams are painfully self-involved. That's why I feel entitled to share this dream I had.

A wooden slide had been installed on the side of a mountain. An alpine slide that scaled the whole country, with a black-and-white portrait of a celebrity featured at each stop along the way—Michael Douglas, Lady Gaga, Charles Grodin (young), Charles Grodin (old). The slide covered thousands of miles, and the key to making the whole thing work was that it stopped in San Diego. It had a name, too. Atticus. People knew about Atticus, there were rules and customs around it. Some rode Atticus for fun or to get where they were going more quickly, and the best part was that Atticus really worked. An old, leathery-skinned gentleman ran the operation. He convinced you to take Atticus because everyone liked slides, and everyone liked portraits of celebrities. Once you arrived at your destination, people might ask you how you made such good time and you said, "Oh. I took Atticus. Haven't you heard?" And then you had more time to find the flavor of seltzer water you liked at the grocery store or speculate about who was cheating on their partner. The leathery-skinned gentleman presided over Atticus like a riverboat operator from an old book. He never left, but always wore sunglasses, and spoke in a stern way that made you trust him.

I didn't often have dreams like this. Nor did I put much stock into the meaning of my dreams in general. But once I woke up the following morning, something became very clear.

The leathery skin, the sunglasses, the stern speech—they obscured a fact I'd been hiding from the day before. It was as though he'd aged 30 years and spent all that time on a beach in Hawaii. How hadn't I seen him right away? Gelb, the riverboat operator. Reincarnated from mythology. Gelb would be the one to help me cross the river.

24

XANDER'S JOURNAL

Tricyclic & Selective Serotonin Reuptake Inhibitor Withdrawal Day 12

"The Ramones are the only true American rock band."

I sat and listened to a rangy guy named Deertick speak these words last night. He's one of the guys involved in the homoerotic militia cosplay with my cousin Lance. They've been having me over to hang with them in his backyard, drink and smoke and gather around the fire pit.

"What do you think of the Ramones, Xander? Deertick asked me. "Do you like them?"

I shrugged.

"Does the kid not speak?" Hart asked my cousin. He paced around the fire in a sort of tweaked-out, wrestler's waddle. The flames made his cross eyes glint, shadows over his gnarled cauliflower ear.

"He's cool. Let him be."

"Pussy," Hart said, because I still wasn't offering my opinion about the Ramones or speaking to anyone at all. "Queer."

"He's not queer," Lance responded, chuckled.

"What if he is?" Deertick asked him.

"I don't know. I don't like hanging around queers. Or Jews for that matter."

Lance coughed.

"What are you scared of?" Deertick asked Hart. "That he's gonna kiss you? Or that you'll like it?"

That's when they charged each other. Fucks and shits and grappling. Deertick slapped Hart once in the face—not even a punch, just an open-handed slap that rang out like a gunshot and felt more insulting because of it. Hart landed a few body shots himself. Then Deertick put Hart in a headlock and bashed his ribs in with his knees twice. Hart was quickly spitting blood out of his mouth, dotting the yellow-brown grass.

They hit a stalemate. They pawed at each other like baby cubs, fell to the ground, laughing and ripping each other's shirts to reveal garish tattoos, all dragons and chain-links.

The Ramones got their name because of a nickname Paul McCartney once gave himself. Paul Ramon. They are a true American rock band in the sense that they make unapologetically narrow music, but the truest and most American thing about them is probably the fact that they're all dead.

XANDER'S JOURNAL

Tricyclic & Selective Serotonin Reuptake Inhibitor Withdrawal Day 13

I just started hitting myself in the head with my fists. Hard. I fell on the ground, hyperventilating, thinking about going into work in this state, thinking about suicide all the time.

Large buildings, crashing my knuckles through glass. Murmurs of plans, ideas, whispers. The great illogic of pain is that it begets more pain. The bug-bite itch.

Is medicine failure? Maybe I'm not entirely fucked.

My boss Jen has given me an assignment she calls The Taxonomy Project. It involves taking inventory of the beer in the walk-in refrigerator and re-categorizing the drink menu. Thinking about doing the Taxonomy project makes me want to tear her scalp off with my bare hands.

Have I ever woken up in the morning knowing what it's like to feel fully rested? My current capacity for sleep is unimaginably great. Inside, I am little else but gunk.

―――

Tricyclic & Selective Serotonin Reuptake Inhibitor Withdrawal Day 14

When I was twelve, I caught a frog in the driveway and stabbed it with an old and rusty knife my dad kept in the garage. He used it to slice up the roots in the garden, clearing out room to plant his squash. After I stabbed the frog and it lay there, dying, out came a smell so strange and bad it's impossible to describe. Though if I ever smelled it again, I'd identify it immediately. And then I would vomit.

―――

FOIL

Tricyclic & Selective Serotonin Reuptake Inhibitor Withdrawal Day 15

I've never felt more disposable than Holly just made me feel, so capable of being tossed away like the flick of a bitten-off fingernail.

This after what I could only describe as our connection. We kissed, she kissed me on the cheek every time we kissed.

Now, after a little disagreement over what I should do about my treatment, she sped away from me on her bike. She didn't like the idea of me driving around late at night, like a gumshoe detective in an old movie, pumping exhaust fumes into my lungs. The hard part is, I can't blame her. Not in the slightest.

If life is ultimately cruel, brutal, and disappointing, is it still important to have moments where we pretend like it's not?

Tricyclic & Selective Serotonin Reuptake Inhibitor Withdrawal Day 16

Light off a bald head, facial hair like an early twentieth century tyrant. Eyes like fool's gold. He walks with a hitch in his step. He has a gap between his teeth that occasionally makes a sound like the whistle of early boiling water.

Can you hear their delicate screams?

Tricyclic & Selective Serotonin Reuptake Inhibitor Withdrawal Day 17

I'm afraid I've let on too much with Lance. It was just the two of us tonight, roasting marshmallows and playing games on our phones, passing a bottle of vodka back and forth between us. I hate to admit it, but I don't mind him so much when it's only the two of us. He's still a moron but the horseshit, hip-hop persona slips away. He becomes more like the person I remember from my childhood, playing Nintendo in my basement, eating the good pears my mom would keep in the fridge. Less concerned with ranting about government overreach, putting on a show of machismo for his new friends.

"Can I ask you a question," I said at one point.

"Shoot."

I thought about what it was like to watch Remy act sometimes, the raw power she could summon in contrast to her sister Piper, who might have been a more technically proficient actor but less vulnerable. "The stuff you post online. The meetings with Hart and Deertick. That's mostly just talk, right? You're not really going to do anything?"

A half-interested smile. "Oh, we're not going to *do* anything. But we're prepared to defend ourselves in the event we're under attack. A possibility these Antifa shitheads seem to want to threaten every day. Anyway, what's up? Why are you asking?"

"I don't know. You know. I'd like to defend myself, too."

He spit, nearly laughed. "You're sixteen for Christ's sake. You're a book nerd. You got a future ahead of you. Enjoy your youth, bro."

I'd anticipated this, disliking how he held himself above me despite being only a few years older. "I might be young, but that doesn't mean I can't see what's going on." Here I paused dramatically, and he looked at me. "'Cause I think you guys are right. The more this country remains under the thumb of our liberal oppressors, the quicker it's going to hell."

He blew out the flames that engulfed the marshmallow on his skewer. "Now *that* I won't argue with."

We sat for a few moments listening to the crackle of the kindling, a cold fall breeze rustling through the trees.

"What about your little lady?" he said. "Heather?"

"Holly."

"Does she know you're into this stuff?"

"No, no. I keep her out of it." I didn't like the line of questioning. I wanted him to know as little as possible about Holly.

"Do you think you'd ever seriously risk your life for something like this?" I asked him.

He whipped his neck and stared me down as if I'd offended him. "Pardon me?"

"Say you're at one of these rallies and shit gets real serious. Do you think you'd stay and fight? Or do you think you would run?"

Lance looked off into the distance, mouth uncorked as if he'd never given the question any serious consideration. But then something shifted, and he seemed to become very solemn, grave almost. "When was the last time you saw my dad? Your uncle."

I recalled a Thanksgiving when my mom forced him to come. "Two years ago. Thanksgiving, I think."

"Yes," he said. "Exactly."

I stared at him, maybe squinted.

"After my mom passed, my dad did what he always wanted to do. He cut and run, started a new life for himself in California." He gesticulated wildly toward the house. "Sure, he pays for this place, but that's just so he doesn't have to deal with me, so he can have less guilt about meeting up with hookers in the middle of the night or whatever the fuck he does out in L.A.. So, if you're asking me if I think there's anyone or anything worth living for, the answer is no, my friend. I'm all in. Ready to die, as they say."

Lance placed two marshmallows on the end of his skewer, but with his hands shaking, he stabbed his index finger, drawing a drop of blood. "God damnit." He sucked on his fingertip to stop the bleeding and shot me a quick, shameful glance before darting inside. I grabbed the skewer and placed a marshmallow on it and dipped it into the flames, watching the white erupt red and then turn to pink and black. I blew on the flames at the end of my skewer until they died, soft little plumes of gray smoke drifting outward.

Taking a bite, sticky and hot and sweet between my teeth, I saw Lance's silhouette passing between rooms inside the house. His words confirmed what I already suspected. He was just as broken as I was inside, just as abandoned and cut out from the world. Some way or somehow, that feeling would come rushing out of him. And I was maybe the only one who could stop him.

PART 3

25

SAM

Hi Sam, this is Dr. Speer from the hospital yesterday. I'm thinking it would be a good idea for you to come in to see one of our trauma specialists today. We have some openings this morning if you're able to make it in. How's 10 am? I really do think it would be best if you made it in. I'll look forward to hearing from you. Thanks.

Audrey and I sat in bed the following morning, listening to Dr. Speer's voicemail and agreeing that I had nothing to lose, nothing much better to do. We came up with a plan. During my return to the hospital, Audrey would catch up on her shows. Afterward we'd meet at our favorite diner nearby. We'd celebrate by eating, because that's how we celebrated. Certainly, at the very least, a chocolate chip waffle would be in order. A key ingredient to our plan.

As Audrey showered, I held the phone in my hands and dialed. I waited through three rings, then a fourth. I feared having to leave a voicemail, derailing our plan. Then, I heard the voice on the other end, one I hadn't quite called by accident.

"I'm coming over," I told Gelb.

SAM

"When?"

"Half hour."

"You wanna go to brunch?"

"What? No. I told you yesterday. I'm coming to give you back your pill bottle."

He chuckled distractedly. "Oh, right. That. Sure."

Audrey was still in the bathroom by the time I finished dressing. Blow-drying her hair, completely nude. I crept up behind her and wrapped my hands around her waist. In the mirror I saw how my lip had swelled up again overnight. I took two Advil from the cabinet then kissed her neck and shoulders, which were warm and smooth, oily almost. We stood still for a moment, hands intertwined, gazing deep into each other's eyes in the mirror. How does desire hit? For me it's always chest-level, flutters of air that skitter up from the lungs and fill the throat and sometimes the eyes. I saw then what I almost never permitted myself to see. To name it is foolish, degrading. The future, the past—the barest and most vulnerable form of her, the most confident, hair clumped like when she'd emerge from the swimming pool at her parents' house. I couldn't believe I'd ever allowed myself to betray that sight, that I'd ever attempted to. I knew what I had to do now. The small steps I needed to take to redeem myself.

I found the pill bottle inside the plastic storage container under our bed, pocketed it, then went to the front of our apartment to the coat rack. I dropped the bottle inside my breast pocket before putting on my coat and saying goodbye.

I took the First Avenue bus for the twenty-block ride uptown to Gelb's apartment. On the way, I stopped at the bagel place on our corner, the only bagel place I knew of that stayed open 24 hours. You'd often see yellow cabs parked outside late at night, along with livery cabs and various other tinted-window vehicles, which led Audrey to speculate that they sold drugs from out the back. Not that they ever offered us any.

There was a short three-person line inside, late-morning commuters in peat coats and plush sweater vests. I ordered my cream-cheese bagel and grabbed a copy of *The New York Post* from the newsstand.

Too Close for Comfort, the headline read, across a photo of the crush tumbling out of Penn Station. *Questions swarm over how a Queens teenager escaped detection when he carried a bomb inside Penn Station yesterday, and why it took a local commuter, Sam Reid, 26, to bring him down.*

On top of the photo were two smaller ones—on the left-hand side, a cropped photo of me from the newscast; on the right, him, Xander Shine. The sensationalized juxtaposition caused me to freeze with disbelief all over again. It brought to mind some otherworldly video game battle. The charities and television appearances my imagination so easily conjured the night before wouldn't fall into my lap, as if I were sitting on the couch, a video game controller in one hand, a joint in the other. They required planning, logistics, emails, phone calls. My jaw socket hummed with the craving for a Xanax. Everything seemed easier on it, more attainable. Making dinner seemed easier. The resistance that came with starting a project at work melted away.

"Holy crap," said a nasal voice to my left. "That's you, isn't it?"

"What? No. I mean, yeah. Yes."

"I read you lived around here. Unbelievable. Just unreal. A real hero right around the corner. What do you know?"

He held out his hand to shake and introduced himself, Steve Gold. He had dark crow's feet under his eyes, gray hair. I blushed.

"Did the president call you?"

I chuckled. "No, not quite."

"DeBlasio?"

"He did, yes."

"Wow."

SAM

I expressed my modesty, my disbelief, until the guy from behind the counter called out my order. He didn't recognize me, which signaled the start of a very Manhattan-like dichotomy. There were those who'd recognize me, and praise me. Everyone else couldn't care less.

The bus took ten minutes to arrive, followed by steady traffic up First Avenue. I caught up on the news on Twitter, the mentions of me rolling in at a diminished pace. There was even some news that didn't involve me.

When I arrived at the lobby of Gelb's building, the doorman asked me to confirm the apartment number before ringing up. I paused. Then I heard her voice, the panic and shock in it.

"Sam?"

The hairs on the back of my neck stood on end.

"Sam, what are you doing here?" Audrey said.

I turned. I saw the look on her face—the lines dug in over her eyes, the frown, the glare.

"I," I stammered. "What are you doing here?"

"No, Sam. What are *you* doing here?"

26

HOLLY

@MichaelDavenport
1/x DEVELOPING: Inside the Queens high school of yesterday's bombing suspect, questions are swirling around Xander Shine's inner circle. Did friends know about his plans? Push him to act due to bullying?
8:14 AM - Oct 24, 2018

2/x "If there's anyone who knows about his motive, it would be them," says one source, whose identity remains anonymous due to age. So far, none of Shine's friends have come forward with information. But more is certain to come to light in the coming days.
8:16 AM - Oct 24, 2018

I pulled up to the park where we met every day during our lunch break. The four of them were already sitting on the rocks—eating and vaping. Teddy, Hal, Piper, and Remy each looked appropriately solemn when our eyes met. Remy handed me the white paper bag at her feet, a satisfying lightness to it in my hands from my hot dog inside. I noticed I still had little appetite. Whether for hot dogs or cupcakes or the finest Italian meal the city had to offer, it didn't matter. I hungered only to sift through Xander's journals, to hunt for more clues.

Everyone asked over and over how I was doing. I assured them, over and over, I was fine.

"So, I heard that reporter knocked on your door last night?" Teddy said after a while, making us all sit up a little straighter. Teddy was a restless, pushy person, always tormenting Xander for his acne or weight fluctuations or transition glasses. Sometimes it seemed like we were only all there for his entertainment, so I didn't appreciate the line of questioning. He may have been as responsible as anyone for driving Xander to do what he did the day before.

"He called my house, too," Hal said. Frustration in his tightened lips. Michal Davenport's profile pic flashed before my mind. His close-cropped shrub of curly hair. Thick slab of teeth. "Obviously I'm not saying anything. My dad said he's ready to wring this guy's neck."

I watched the breeze carry a small pile of leaves across the tennis court.

"It was pretty much nothing," I said. I sat. The rocks felt jagged and cool against my legs.

Teddy took a drag of his Juul, looking surprised. The tip of the vape glowed blue against the gray. Remy looked up from the script in her lap, memorizing lines for the new play they were putting on. Piper plucked at her eyelashes.

"I mean. Do you think the cops are gonna question us?" Teddy said. E-mails had already gone out to all our parents, the school doing damage control, assuring everyone they were taking extra precautions to ensure security on school grounds.

"Yeah, should I be, like, flushing my stash in case I get a visit from the cops?" Hal said.

Wide, worried looks passed over Piper and Remy's faces, as if this might endanger their pristine, Ivy-league track records.

"No," I said, letting out a small laugh of disbelief. "From what I've heard, they're digging into Lance more than Xander, since he was the mastermind or whatever."

"Unbelievable," Remy said, regardless of how many times we'd all expressed the same sentiment at my house the day before.

"What I still can't figure out," Hal said, "is how Xander ever got himself mixed up in something like this."

We exchanged a shrug of mutual recognition, still making our way out from under the shock of what we experienced together on the field trip yesterday.

"I'm not all that surprised," Teddy responded. He picked up a tennis-ball-sized rock from the ground, stood, and tossed it back and forth between his hands. Other than Piper and Remy, who shared one, Teddy was the only one of us who had his own car. I remembered one time he got pulled over for running a stop sign. We had several open bottles of alcohol in the trunk. But when the cop approached the car, Teddy transformed into a much older, calmer version of himself—all head nods and sincere eye contact. *Yes, sir. No sir, my deepest apologies.* The cop let him off with a warning.

"Xander always marched to his own tune," Teddy went on. "He always thought his shit didn't stink."

"C'mon, Teddy," Piper said.

"No, I'm serious," Teddy said, his face pinched and red. He threw the rock up in the air, tracing a high arc before landing with a clunk on the pond. I remembered how Xander did the same thing the last time we were here. This must have been how boys expressed their innermost feelings when they couldn't find the words. "Maybe you guys have this romantic view of him—his lectures and philosophizing—but I saw right through it. He had a real dark side that I was always afraid of. Not that I thought it would amount to this. But he's always had *school shooter* written all over him—"

"You don't know what you're talking about," I heard myself say.

"Oh? Enlighten me. Sounds like you know more than you're letting on."

Would I tell him about the journals? On some level, he may have understood. We were all so hungry when our group first formed freshman year. Teddy liked to write, too, which may have been why he felt so threatened by Xander. But no one could match Xander's talent, flair. He was the first person to make me feel like my flaws could be strengths, my self-pity a tool for harnessing my art. One time when we came here to Golden Park, he told me about a screenplay he was working on called *On Golden Pond*. It was a Transcendalist take on twenty-first century high school life and in the hands of someone else, that might have sounded so corny. But Xander spoke about the play without shame or fear.

"Our only obligation right now is to make bad art," Xander said, his first time using a term that turned into a catchphrase for us over text: #badart. "Then one day, maybe ten years from now, maybe we'll create something worthwhile."

It was a hot summer day in July. Xander laid his head on my shoulder. I ran my hands through his hair. The canopy overhead provided cover, sun cutting through the leaves and shade thrown over the lawn. In the distance, a man and his greyhound dog circled the pond. Beyond them, a mother breastfed a newborn, and a druggie slumped over the staircase railing. But the man and his dog had this wiry spirit that I felt an immediate urge to sketch. Xander jotted down notes furiously in his notebook. We were hungry for knowledge and each other. We turned to look shyly into each other's eyes and every now and then, kiss. He trembled each time I kissed his cheek. He tasted sweet and bitter, like beer. The only scary part was when Xander would flip, abruptly, and grow distant. But I'd be lying if I said I didn't find it exciting sometimes, reminding me of the troubled figures we learned about from history. Van Gogh and Hemingway, Woolf and Plath. As embarrassing as it is to admit, I sometimes thought we were teetering on the brink of something—whether greatness or harm—that maybe the harm would be sacrificed for the greatness.

"Xander wasn't trying to target any of us," I told Teddy, looking him dead in the eye. Everyone else stared at us as if we were spotlit. "Or anyone."

"Well, the facts don't really seem to back that up," he answered, not missing a beat. "Unless you know something the rest of us don't?"

Here I had it, a chance to confess. Confide in friends I was supposed to trust. But I clung to the ongoing advantage of knowing things they didn't. I still hadn't finished reading everything. I may never come forward in the end. That would be my right.

"I know he wanted to get Lance in trouble," I said. "That's all I know."

"Bullshit."

"For fuck's sake," Hal cried. "This is our friend. Possibly dying in the hospital. And this is how you're speaking about him?"

Teddy shook his head and paced, seething but having the good sense not to say more. A thick cloud of vapor trailed his jumpy movements. I wanted him to leave. He always talked merciless amounts of shit behind Xander's back, sometimes to his face. What kinds of petty things did he—*they*—say about me behind my back?

"I'm sorry, Holly," Hal whispered to me. He looked grim, frustrated, sullen. It wasn't fair to him, either. He'd faced just as much horror as I had yesterday. He may never get to play another meaningless video game with Xander. He may never even see him face-to-face again. None of us might.

"It's okay," I said to Hal. Out of sheer instinct, some

desperate desire for comfort, I reached out and grabbed him by the hand. A tear slipped out of his eye.

Teddy spat and stared at Hal. "So much for respect. Now you're making a move on his girl—"

"Enough!" Remy said, her tone strident. Teddy frowned. We listened to Remy, always a notch more mature than the rest of us. "We can't let this get between us. Please."

We accepted the silence, chastened. Already the group was tainted by jealous crushes—Teddy and Piper, Remy and Hal—the end of our senior year looming with yellow menace. A gathering storm.

Teddy tossed another mid-size rock into the pond at the park, concentric circles rippling out from the splash. This was exactly what Xander's actions looked like, except the ripples went deeper and wider than the pond's flat surface could ever reflect. If Xander was the main blast center, then each of us were the ripples—his mom Lisa, his sister Paige, me, my dad, our friends, their friends—concentric circles of friends and family flung out like astronauts in space, spinning and entirely alone. Everyone so disoriented we were vomiting inside our helmets.

I couldn't believe how stupid I felt for thinking our love would ever amount to greatness. The death threats my family later received, the candy bar wrappers left in my locker—those were one thing. Scary, but empty. But to sit there and watch our group of friends gradually dissolve over the next few months—that part would upset me for years.

27

AUDREY

I never expected Sam to lie about something so small as an appointment with his therapist at the hospital. But such is the nature of lying: pull out one card and the whole house comes crashing down.

"I needed to drop something off before my appointment," Sam said in the lobby of Gelb and Amy's building, lying outright through his teeth.

"He says to come up," the doorman cut in.

I forced a smile at him. I kept my voice down, as shocked and ashamed as I already felt. But the anger was rising higher, swirling in the back of my throat. "Tell me the truth. Right now. No more lies."

"Lies? he responded, cheeks washed red. "Plural?"

I glanced down at my wristwatch. "It's 9:55. You never run late to anything. Unless you magically rescheduled—"

"I—" he cut me off. His eyes darted to the windows and the doorman and back. "How did you make it up here so fast? And why?"

"I took a cab. I wanted to talk to Gelb."

"But…why?"

I looked down at my fingernails, the two-week old polish

chipping off. "I had a gut feeling you were lying. And that turned out to be spot on."

He gesticulated with his hands, deflecting. "Can we sit? Talk somewhere? We can talk. Right? We can always talk."

"The elevator is around the corner," the doorman told us.

"We know!" I said, more sharply than I intended. "Thanks."

I walked towards an unoccupied section of sofas and chairs in the lobby, gold trimming along the edges of the upholstery. Sam followed me. He sat in a chair, and I took the sofa with its garish gold trim and stiffness from lack of use. I couldn't fathom the thought of my breakup happening anywhere so public as the lobby of a lavish Manhattan high-rise. But here we were, committing to it.

"It's not just your lie about your golf plan yesterday, or even this morning."

"What, then?"

Another pause. I stared at him, hesitating over whether to say it.

"I really don't know what you're talking about," he said.

"Xanax." The word blackened the space between us. He looked down at his feet. "Amy told me Gelb's been giving you pills. She said it's been getting worse. That's why she told me. And that's why I wanted to talk to him."

He flinched, punch-drunk. "So, you've been sitting on that, too? It's not just me here. You're supposed to be watching your shows right now, if I'm not mistaken."

"Don't," I snapped. "Don't you dare. You're not the only one who knows how to put on an act, you know."

My teeth were grinding, jaw locking up. "We've never lied to each other once in our relationship. And now I find out about two in two days? How is that supposed to make me feel? How could I possibly not suspect that there's not…more?"

"I know, Audrey," he said, looking down at his hands in shame.

"I can't believe you thought I'd never notice. You'd have one glass of wine and start slurring your words, then pass out on the couch."

"That's exactly why I came here today. I got spooked by the cops sniffing around my golf bag and our apartment. I actually came up here to return the pills to him."

"No," I said quickly, watching the corners of his mouth crease. "You're lying again, I can tell. You're a terrible liar."

After a lengthy pause, he said, "This time I'm telling you the truth. "

"I don't care," I said, fury unloading off my chest. The pent-up force of months-long resentment, exploding all at once. "All the time work I've put into helping you—helping *us*—and this is what I get in return? The job searching, urging you to consider therapy. You've made a complete fool out of me. You know that?"

Tears rushed down my cheeks, slipping silently off my chin. I couldn't look at him anymore.

Sam hung his head. Cradled it in one hand propped up on the armrest of his chair. "It's all been extremely tough these past few months. You know that."

"No. That's not how it works. Not anymore."

More painful silence. A young couple that we might've known strode by with their small white-and-brown dog. We angled our backs away from them, trying to shield them from all the ugliness assembled in our faces.

"I'm so sorry, Audrey."

I shook my head. "I figured one of these days, maybe you'd come to your senses and come clean. Maybe you'd owe us that much. But for you to make up a whole story, to lie about going to therapy of all places, that's where I have to draw the line."

"You're right, Audrey—one thousand percent right. It could be a stumble, if we wanted. You know that."

Trembling, a hand over my mouth, I tried to collect my

breath. Why was he jumping to the conclusion that it was over? Was that what he secretly wanted? We sat across from each other, burning up in our skin, lost and pathetic.

"Honestly, I didn't even mind the Xanax at first," I said. "You were doing something, at least. Your moods were getting better. Our sex was getting better. Why would I say anything if our sex was getting better?"

He shrugged, looked off in thought. The image of us staring at each other in the mirror that morning entered my mind. The final sanctity that existed between us. The sex the night before, our final goodbye. He brought this on himself, sabotaging us before our eyes.

"Do you remember The Bens?" Sam was saying. The red in his cheeks had abated somewhat.

"Pardon me?"

"The band."

"You're bringing up a band right now?"

"For some reason, I'm remembering when you sent me a song by them. *Bruised*. It was that first summer. We met for drinks in the city. I'd broken my nose, remember?"

I nodded but wasn't sure why. Of course I remembered, but inside I resisted him trying to wrest control of the conversation.

"I was on the train when you sent it. I remember listening and being flooded with all this emotion, looking out over the bright green-and-blue seats, the smell of someone's McDonalds nearby. They were the saddest lyrics too—*love just leaves you bruised*—but in that moment they were the most uplifting. Because you knew exactly what they meant, and so did I. What was that? What *is* that?"

I looked off through the window of the lobby, eyes squinting from the bright. An old lesson came back to me, an even older name.

"I know what you're doing," I said. "I know you're trying to get me to remember the good times. But here's another name for you—Lacy Hafner. Do you remember her?"

"Your high school friend?"

"Yes. We were so close, Sam. We did everything together—dance, swim. *Attached at the pigtails*, my dad used to say. Now, it's been five years since we've talked."

Sam sighed, shoulders stooped to make me pity him. But I would not take the bait.

"Lacy became really overbearing. Her dad was out of the picture. Her mom couldn't control her drinking. It got to where my parents were helping her out with her car payments, just so she could finish community college."

"I didn't know that. Why didn't you tell me?"

"Because it was really hard, and it still is hard. But just because something is hard doesn't mean it's wrong." We locked eyes. I recalled the toll that Lacy and her family took on me. I was so preoccupied with trying to solve Lacy's issues I could barely sleep. When I did sleep, I'd wake up some nights with my nails digging into my scalp, growing itchier and itchier the more I scratched. The only way to break free, I learned, was to let go. "Sometimes, when I think about it, I don't think I've ever actually wanted you to change. I've wanted to keep you right where you are, to take care of you without ever fully making you better. That's what makes me feel important. But it's never allowed me the space to grow into anything more than that."

I saw him mashing his lips together, a mix of pain and anger in his eyes, whether from the cut that resided there or my stern words, I couldn't know. I only knew it reminded me of the worst side of him, the temperamental side my dad got to know on the golf course with him sometimes.

"Is that a line your therapist fed to you?" he asked, quaking at the sound of his own words. "How long have you guys been rehearsing this conversation? I should have known when you went to go run your little errand yesterday. You couldn't even drop everything to come home during an actual emergency."

I looked away again, head shaking. I refused to indulge this smear of my therapist, a raspy-voiced, middle-aged woman named Tina who had my best interests at heart.

"Everything is on your terms. Every goddamn thing in our relationship." I wouldn't hold back anymore. I couldn't. "You take up all the space. You get all the attention. For the past year, it's felt like I've been the only one fighting for us. And now this? You're right, I should've pulled the rug out months ago."

The silence, at last, delivered us some truth. The unjust reality that had become of us. I knew for certain we'd never recover from this. We so rarely fought or argued that this was equivalent to an atomic explosion at our core, taking out our legs and heart and shaping everything else to come.

"You're always so quick to judge," Sam said, "but if you cared so much, you wouldn't be doing this. Not right now. It's all so much worse than you know. Are you aware of the real reason I haven't been speaking to my dad for the past five months?"

"What?"

"The night you were away and I went to Long Island. I told you about the fight we had. The part I didn't tell you about? I went down to the garage after, and I shattered the window of his car."

I recoiled, tears forming in my eyes once more. *Another lie*, I thought, but had sense enough to keep my mouth shut.

"Every day since then, while I'm at work, all I think about is just…ending it." His face screwed up; tears filled his eyes. "What about this is worth it? Tell me."

The red wrath in my mind settled into a milder pink. "You need help, Sam. Professional help. This isn't healthy or fair to me. I can't do this anymore. Don't you get it?"

My voice broke. I couldn't think of anything else to say.

"You don't give a shit. You never gave a shit. My family is completely dysfunctional. They don't know how to behave like humans. You're all I have. And now you're taking that from me, too."

"I'd argue you did that to yourself."

He grimaced, stood.

He turned his back to me, but then spun around to say one more thing.

"I hope you're happy. I'll wind up dead because you were too stupid to see this isn't the time to be making rash decisions."

All my defenses engaged, I hardly processed his words. Only fought back. A small scowl unfolded over the corners of his mouth, and he started walking away. But not before I called after him, not caring who heard anymore. "Let me guess? Another empty promise."

28

XANDER'S JOURNAL

Tricyclic & Selective Serotonin Reuptake Inhibitor Withdrawal Day 18

My mom is substantially older than my dad. She was married once before, to a professor nearer to her age, but they never had kids together. By the time she broke it off with the professor, she'd already begun ushering my dad back to her office for hand jobs—so impressed by the play he wrote in which he broke the fourth wall, a technique she'd later say he acted as if he invented.

Before my dad left, he would sometimes take us out on my grandparents' boat on the Connecticut coast. Jellyfish and crab and sea glass, waking up to find sand crusted in the hollows of my ears. He'd take me out early in the morning to catch striped bass and scup, talking about fishing and the sun and how I shared his boyish curiosity for things.

"You're so different from your sister," he said, "it's scary."

A crisp day in June. I was eleven. "Is that a good thing?"

"Good and bad," he said. A bass caught my line and dove out of the water. "Oh, a big one. Reel it on in now."

I followed his instructions, but the fish kept swimming out, so my dad swiped the rod from me and did it himself.

When he got the fish aboard, he grabbed it violently and said, "See, me and you, this is what we're like. We swim out. We gotta wriggle and squirm. Even if we know it won't really change anything in the end, we still need to do what's in our basic nature."

I didn't know exactly what he meant by that, but I recognized something complimentary in it. With summers off as a high school English teacher, my dad could afford to spend these weeks at my grandparents', and my mom would join us for the weekends. We'd play checkers at night but never for very long, as if he'd used up so much mental energy during the daytime that he had no choice but to pass out at 7 pm. That and the glass of scotch at his side.

My mom kicked my dad out of the house several times for his drinking. She'd send him off to Connecticut or a friend's to sober up. I could always tell when they were having problems because the ice cubes wouldn't come out as thick as usual from the tray in the freezer. Or she'd leave papers out on the kitchen table, clothes dangling on the backs of chairs. When I'd ask her about them, she'd say, "A tidy home is evidence of a feeble mind."

How do you act around your family when you know you're about to leave them?

My dad's back from Connecticut now, but I wish he would've stayed there with his secrets and alienation and pain, which all have the same smell as mine, foul and old at the center. I wish I wasn't around to see him sulk or impose his rules, like making me leave my room at least once a day. It's worse than if my mom had simply found someone new. In that case I might still have good memories of him, versus the shouting and splintered, bug-eyed stares we have now. The orders and belt lashings and the dumbass nickname he has for me, Cave Dweller.

Do I wriggle out? Or am I simply haunted by the sight of that fish fighting for its life?

Maybe some people really are better off drunk.

———

Tricyclic & Selective Serotonin Reuptake Inhibitor Withdrawal Day 19

Sometimes I think I want my death to sow total confusion. Not the deaths of innocent lives or even bodily harm like I've long fantasized about. For example, in middle school, I used to imagine the satisfaction of kidnapping this kid in our class, Conner. He was the one who started a rumor that I still showered with my dad, of all things, as if I'd ever dream of getting anywhere close to my dad. On the day I found out, I remember letting my imagination run wild. I pictured hauling him off somewhere dark and decaying, an old cellar where you couldn't hear his screams. In this fantasy I'd hog-tie him, and burn him maybe, and stuff an apple in his mouth. I'd inflict small but increasing amounts of pain. A set of medieval tools spread out before me.

Now, I just want to see him sweat. That's the only thing that might imbue my death with the slightest bit of meaning. That and spoiling whatever germ-brained plans Lance might be making with his friends.

Then again, why do I feel the need to be meaningful in my death? Sometimes I don't. But at other times it feels like the only bargain I have left to make for my mom, Holly, Hal. So that they don't have to attend my funeral and think, *another senseless teenage suicide.*

29

SAM

Storming away from Audrey, I couldn't believe how quickly we'd unraveled into this pissing match. How much worse it might have been if we weren't in a semi-public space. The gold-gilded confines of Gelb and Amy's lobby filled me with fresh revulsion. I wanted to burn it all down.

I exchanged a quick glance with the doorman, circled around the desk, and punched the button on the elevator. When I arrived at Gelb's apartment, I knocked on the door and someone I'd never seen before answered. He wore a beige t-shirt with a wolf printed on it, two sizes too small, and a headband made of a shoelace.

"There he is," he said. He offered me his small, limp hand, the shoelace holding back his oily curtain of hair. "Sam Reid, the Penn Station hero. Have we met?"

I stepped past him and into the belly of the apartment, where the blinds were half-shut and a lingering, damp scent hung in the air.

"Who are you?" I asked. "Where's Gelb?"

"I'm Ainsley," said Ainsley. "Gelb is ritualistically puking."

I'd say that Ainsley didn't smile when he said this, but it

was more like he almost never stopped smiling, like his whole life existed just on the brink of a laugh.

"Sam, is that you?" Gelb called out from beyond the bathroom door. "I'll be out in a second, buddy. Just hang out with Ains, okay?"

"Okay," I called back.

Then came the sounds. Feral and nightmarish, like a wild boar suffering from a stomach virus.

"He'll be fine," Ainsley sighed. Still smiling. "This is his first drink."

"Drink?"

"Oh, you're uninitiated, too?"

I stared.

"Shamanic healing," he said. "Ayahuasca tea. The brew of the heavens."

He lifted his chin to indicate the stovetop, where a sludgy brown liquid sat smoldering inside a saucepan. More violent retching rang out from the bathroom.

"Would you like to join in the ceremony?" Ainsley asked me. "There's more than enough to go around. I'll be heading back to Mexico at the end of the month."

"How do you and Gelb know each other?"

"We met at the airport in Salt Lake. Long layover."

Ainsley sat cross-legged on the couch. He spoke in a smooth, breathy lilt like he was caught between eras, like Fred Melamed in a Woody Allen movie if he couldn't disguise the fact he was born in 1992.

"So, tell me something, Sam. What's your opinion of coincidences?"

"Coincidences?"

"Coincidences. The cosmos."

"I have no opinion of coincidences. Is this one of those questions you're asking me just so I'll ask you?"

Now his smile grew, so that it actually seemed real. "Well. Aren't you?"

SAM

I shut my eyes. I wanted him to go away. Gelb might've been encountering visions of sixteenth century papal proceedings, or kaleidoscopic intergalactic space missions, or god himself. What a mistake I'd made coming up here.

"What's your opinion of coincidences?" I asked. I stood to grab a beer from the fridge and drained half of it in one sip.

"Easy there. Pace yourself. It's got some twists and turns."

It wasn't uncommon for Gelb to grovel before these trust-fund types, with their pet alligators and drug habits. This was his line of work.

"At age nineteen," Ainsley said, "I traveled to Europe with my friend and sometime bandmate Harry Kaminov. He was a small but ferocious man, Harry, a drummer, and a good one. You can teach any old ape to play guitar or bass—take Gelb, for instance—but drummers are a different story. You can't teach rhythm. You can't teach moxie. Harry still had his long hair back then. I loved that hair. We spent the summer playing street music, busking. We didn't sleep in a bed for three months. We ended up in Greece, Corfu, sleeping on the beach in a bamboo hut. We performed in front of the Pompidou, in Paris, and met all these street and circus performers, sharing food and filled with all the vim of our youth."

"Sounds thrilling."

"I had a mini acoustic guitar at the time, a travel guitar, I think it was a Martin. All Harry had was a djembe drum and a glockenspiel. But like I said, Harry was the type of man who could get asses shaking with a piece of a straw and a rawhide."

"I don't like that you're referring to him in the past tense."

"What? Oh, no, Harry Kaminov is very much alive. Don't worry about that. He's a periodontist."

"I'll be just another minute!" Gelb called out.

"Is he going to be okay?" I asked.

"He'll be fine." Neither of us spoke for a minute. Ainsley

FOIL

took the time to remove his shoelace headband, shake out his curls like a model emerging from a swimming pool. Without the slow-motion effect, he looked like a rabid, overweight squirrel.

"One night in Corfu, Harry and I were walking through town and we came upon a little music shop, just off the esplanade. There in the display window was a Fender Squier Strat, gleaming from behind the glass like a crown jewel in a museum we visited. It wasn't any Squier, either. It was this deep, brilliant blue, with hints of sea-foam green, unlike the standard-issue powder blue you see around here."

I felt my hands needing to peel the edges of a cardboard coaster on the coffee table. Jaw worked up into a clench.

"Now you're with me," Ainsley continued. He slipped another shoelace out of a sneaker sitting on the coffee table. He wrapped both shoelaces over his head and cinched them. "A Squire Strat just like yours, from the pictures that Gelb showed me."

"You want my fucking guitar?"

"Easy now. Let me finish the story. It's got twists and turns. Now Harry Kaminov knew how much I wanted this guitar. He promised me that once we saved up enough performing, we could put the money towards it. Heart of gold, Harry, one of the best. Then one night without my knowing, he bought the guitar! All on his own. He brought it back to the beach for me. Do you believe it? I was so happy I could have kissed him. I did kiss him, later, but that's a different story. Needless to say, this was cause for celebration. We drank, we dropped beans, laughed endlessly into the wee hours of the morning. Then take a guess what happened when we woke up."

"What?"

"The guitar was gone. Some Slovakians lifted it from our hut and got the hell out of dodge."

"Tough break."

SAM

"Now I don't consider myself an overly sentimental person, but when Gelb told me you were coming over—*the Sam Reid, the Penn Station Hero*—I got to thinking. Maybe some cosmic strands were aligning. He told me that you hardly even play anymore. So, I figured, what could it hurt to ask?"

"It hurts to ask. It hurts a lot."

"You say that now, but I happen to know something else about this guitar of yours—that it was handed down to you by your uncle, the late jazz guitarist Raymond Reid."

For a moment, silence. "And you think that's going to make me *more* inclined to sell it to you?"

"Maybe not. But what better way to honor your uncle's memory than to keep it in business? The same guitar *Barn Cat* was written on. *Electric Rigaloo*. My bandmates and I are laying down some psychedelic tracks, man. You should get involved. Let me play some for you."

That's when Gelb opened the bathroom door. He looked like he'd gotten out of a very hot bath—skin pruned and pale everywhere except his cheeks, which burned in high red circles.

"Are you sure this is good stuff, Ains?" Gelb groaned. He fell down on the far end of the couch from us, his eyes asquint and fluttering.

"Oh, I'm quite sure. I drank last week."

"I'm not seeing anything. I feel like when I was eight and had such a bad case of the flu that my legs were completely paralyzed. Even my dick and balls are shriveled up."

"Not everyone hallucinates their first time," Ainsley said. "Your digestive system can break the DMT down instead of sending it to your brain. Particularly if you're not used to it. *Caveat emptor.*"

"Gelb," I said. "Do you think we can speak in private? Would be best, I think."

"Ainsley doesn't bite," Gelb said. "Anything you say is in confidence."

Ainsley turned to me and pointed at Gelb with an outstretched arm, an open hand. "Gelb. He is my son."

"Michael," I said, calling him by his first name, making the atmosphere go cold. "It involves Audrey."

"Jesus. Why didn't you say anything?"

"I was trying."

"That reminds me," Gelb said. "She texted me saying she was stopping by? I didn't get why you both needed to text separately."

I hesitated. "Yeah…"

"Ainsley," Gelb said. "I'm sure you can find some friends brunching at Le Parker Meridien, yes?"

Ainsley moped, stood. "Sam," he said, handing me a business card with his number and address. "It was good seeing you. Consider my appeal, sleep on it. I'm prepared to make you an unusually generous offer for that guitar."

He moved like a slug toward the door, gathering up his belongings in a single, drawn-out motion.

"Gelb," he said, pointing, still smiling that not-happy smile. "I love you."

"I hate you."

"I love you?"

"I love you. Scoundrel. Now get the hell out of here."

Before leaving, Ainsley turned around and bowed to us.

"Who's the pedophile?" I asked Gelb, who wrapped a moist gray hand towel around his face.

"Ains? Ainsley Gantz. We met at the airport in Salt Lake."

"He looks like Jed Bickle."

Gelb laughed. "A little. Jed is fatter, though."

"Jed lost thirty pounds last year."

"You know what I mean. In spirit."

"How much do you have him on the hook for?"

Gelb sighed. "Do you know Tinactin? The athlete's foot spray."

"Tough actin' Tinactin?"

"*Touch actin Tinactin*. His grandfather discovered the active ingredient, Tolnaftate. I've read more about that stuff than I can tell you about. They have their money tied up at Wells Fargo, which, as you know, has been going bust ever since the fraud charges. So, they're looking to invest somewhere else. It's a slow reel, but I'm closing in."

"Aren't you supposed to be on a two-week break from work right now?"

"Prospecting never sleeps, my friend."

Gelb went to stand, but his center of gravity didn't quite cooperate. He wobbled, then fell onto his back. He let out a high-pitched laugh, more in line with a shriek. His shirt curled up to reveal red stretch marks along his stomach. Through his sweatpants I could make out the outline of his shriveled-up dick and balls.

"Are you sure you're good?" I asked him.

"I'm fine. I can handle a dud."

Gelb lay flat on his back with the cool compress over his face. His burly chest rose and fell like it was being pumped by a piece of medical equipment. In a slow whisper, he began counting. *In for five...Out for seven...One...In for five...Out for seven...Two.* I waited for him to finish. He'd subjected me to far worse diversions and escapades through the years. A mindfulness practice was more palatable than needing to drive four hours to pick him up in Massachusetts because his car broke down.

After he uttered the number twelve, he used non-numbered words again.

"So, tell me. What's going on with Audrey?"

Where would I start? How could I begin to tell him what happened with Audrey? I was turning the words over in my head—*bad, nothing good, a breakup? a break?*—when he sat up and looked me dead in the eye.

"Sam, your eyes. They're all red, puffy. What happened?"

I didn't have to say much, it turned out. Gelb noticed right away. That's what made it rush out of me—my eyeballs, my nostrils, my teeth. Gelb's picking up on it made me sob like a lost little puppy.

30

XANDER'S JOURNAL

Tricyclic & Selective Serotonin Reuptake Inhibitor Withdrawal Day 20

"Come join the human race, bro," Teddy said to me the other night at Hal's.

Teddy is too easy a villain, too comic book. With Hal it's different. We've taken on a new hobby together, vexillology, otherwise known as flag design. We've been frequenting a subreddit together and two weeks ago, I came in second place in the monthly contest. Good enough for us to make a real-life flag out of the design.

The theme was art déco, which isn't a topic I knew anything about before doing the research. The theme before that was lunar regions and before that was South African Provinces. The dimensions of a flag—the strength contained in that simple rectangle—seem to suit my eye. It's like, have you ever seen a billiards player lining up a shot? There are the shots they have to think a lot about, getting the angles just right. Then there are the easier ones they could sink in their sleep. When I get going, I come as close as I've ever known to a flow state. I can see each shape fit neatly into that rectangle, the patterns flow out from the central layout, the color themes emerge like fruit picked off a tree.

When Hal comes over, we'll sit across from each other with our laptops propped open and an hour on the clock, sprinting to the finish. It doesn't become interesting until the halfway point, when our eyes burn from staring, our faces contort and minds languish. As a rule, with twenty minutes left on the clock, we get high. Terrible worlds open to me when we get high—brimstone and everything subtly imperfect. With five minutes to go, Hal will get this look on his face—this doleful, droopy look like Jesus in his dying moments on the cross. After we finish and compare notes, I'll stay up all night tinkering with the design, observing all of my fractionally missed opportunities, vowing to be better. The part of me that likes myself would call this determination. The other part of me would call it deep need.

Because it's not that I'm finding happiness from thinking with words and complete sentences, but from not thinking at all. I'm tapping into a fuller detachment from conscious thought.

I've shared none of this with Hal. He's never shared how vexillology makes him feel, either. But the thought of us sitting there together in front of our computers gives me some momentary pause. Maybe we don't need to share any thoughts or feelings to recognize the value of participating in a shared activity. Some might call this the delicate nature of male bonding. A more female part of me longs to tell him I appreciate the simple fact of his presence, when so few others seem to offer me anything close. But we never use words like these in front of each other, and we never will. And this fills me with the same profound sadness I feel when I come across any new disappointment in my life.

XANDER'S JOURNAL

Tricyclic & Selective Serotonin Reuptake Inhibitor Withdrawal Day 21

This is very likely going to be my last journal entry. Things are moving fast now. Too fast.

Lance and co. are preparing to travel to DC next week to protest a Black Lives Matter march. It's notable to me that their protests don't ever focus on fighting for change, or advocating for much of anything. Instead, they line up against change, obstruct anyone working to achieve the tiniest shred of progress for their communities.

I can't stand the thought that I waited too long to cut them off. That one more armed conflict took place that I could have stopped.

The websites are lighting up in anticipation of a coming clash. Buses are being organized. They're really thirsting for it. There's talk of hotel packages.

"Anyone going armed needs to be prepared to overrun law enforcement."

"Nothing is going to happen unless we MAKE it happen."

"The world is watching and they're laughing at us, laughing at our country."

"1776! Resistance is victory! You are victory!"

Last night, I lifted the vest from the Shed at Lance's. Stowed it under my bed. The field trip to the museum tomorrow feels like a nice touch, wholly unanticipated, a way of confusing everyone all the more about my motive. A signal to Conner, Teddy, anyone else who's ever crossed me: Tomorrow marks the culmination of what's been building up inside of me for far too long.

I have all the materials ready now. The flammable little concoction I made, sealed in a plastic bag. The lighter. The gun. The vest.

I used to be so scared of dying. But now all I can think of is the relief.

31

SAM

The tears quickly gave way to manic fits of laughter. I could always count on Gelb to laugh with me at all the best things—like what would happen if a nuclear warhead fell straight on top of your head? Would there be anything left of you for your parents to bury? Any recognizable DNA speck? Could you place a DNA speck inside a coffin and bury it? Another one: A man in Bangladesh had trees growing out of his hands. His tree hands were going viral. Nothing like this would ever happen to us. We were invincible. We knew everything about everyone. We hated everyone.

We took tequila shots and ate Xanax bars. We went to a hookah bar. Then we remembered we hated hookah bars. We went to a strip club. Then we remembered we hated strip clubs. America was a lie our grandparents told us to keep us from becoming communists. America was *Fake News*.

When we got back to Gelb's apartment, we drank more tequila and smoked more weed and ordered chicken parm sandwiches. I fed my oblivion with violent hunger. My blood pulsed. My mind became one with the self-perpetuating force of the doped-up alcoholic stew.

We invited Ainsley back over to join us for a game of *Risk*.

Waiting for his arrival, setting up the game, I told Gelb about a long-forgotten letter. In our waning days of college, an old-time record producer named Arthur Schottenheim had written to Gelb, asking that we re-record our demo. I intercepted the letter before Gelb ever learned of its existence. I stowed it away at my parents' house, underneath a history paper I'd written, above a Thomas Pynchon novel I never understood.

"Hey Gelb," I said, knowing he couldn't hurt me anymore. Nothing could. "Have I ever told you about the time I fucked you over?"

"Is this different from every day that you fuck me over?"

"No. This is real."

Gelb stilled for once. He set down his can of orange soda. A string of mozzarella cheese hung down from his chin like Halloween webbing.

"Arthur Schottenheim. Does that name ring a bell?"

He hesitated, pondered. Then his eyes started bulging out more than they normally did, which was a good amount.

"My cousin's guy, the one from that little record label?"

"Yes. I went back to pick up some things a few weeks after we graduated. He'd written to you, asking us to get back in the studio, but I never told you about it. I buried that goddamn letter, man."

Gelb's brow furrowed. "Are you kidding me?"

"I'm not kidding you. I'm sorry, bro."

I maintained eye contact with him, determined to stand my ground. I'd have it out with him, if need be. I'd eviscerate him. Now that I no longer had to cover my tracks, I felt like I could confess everything. Tell him how selfish he'd been over the years. No one else could ever be right around him. His work schedule took priority over everyone else's, but if you ever backed out of a plan, you were dead to him. Even when he swooped in with his advice on how to advance my career, he never considered that I might not want to hear it.

I was getting ready to tell Gelb all of this, that no one else ever had any room to breathe around him, he sucked up all the air. But then something else happened. Something stranger. Gelb stared me down for another second or two—his nasty, bug-eyed stare, the one he used to intimidate opponents from back in his high-school wrestling days—set to launch into one of his famous diatribes. But then he belly-laughed.

He laughed deeply, poisonously.

"I've known about that letter for years," Gelb said, pinching the bridge of his nose and wiping at his eyelids.

"You have?"

"We all have." The red in his cheeks melted away. He laughed because he was an American. And America was bullshit. "Arthur called me, like, four days later, asking if I'd gotten it."

"We were all waiting for you to own up to it," Gelb said. "Even Wren."

"Wren."

"We knew it would never amount to anything. Then I guess we all forgot. What made you think of that now?"

A good question. The incident, the breakup—they led back down to some source I struggled to locate. But then it hit with the force of a true revelation. The lies I told, the obstacles I imposed to remain in one singular, fixed position—they signaled all the ways I hurt myself. Music was one. Work was another. The withholding and self-victimization at all costs. I was an American, through and through. You didn't need to be a genius to see that the country was killing itself. School shootings, blood lust on Twitter, craven politicians on all sides. In stopping the psychopath who targeted Penn Station yesterday, I became the latest, tired example. My impulse to brutalize Xander Shine came from the same self-hatred that animated him.

"I don't know," I told Gelb. "Nothing."

My vision swam. I needed another tequila shot. I took a

rip of the bong Gelb kept on the coffee table, then checked my phone. Dr. Speer had called again. He left another voicemail asking if I still had the availability to come in. For the first time, I felt I could open up to someone—about myself, my job, my relationships, my family. Audrey had called, too. Just to check in, maybe?

No. Her mom had come in to keep her company, to console her, she said in the voicemail. They were having trouble connecting to the Wi-Fi.

When Ainsley showed up, entering in his smooth cocksure manner like a television illusionist, they told me about their ideas. They were forming a punk doo-wop band called The Amazon Shopping Carts of the Recently Deceased. They were writing a play about a skirt-chasing frat guy who'd yet to come out of the closet. Once we settled into playing *Risk*, The Game of Global Domination, they told me how they were starting an Instagram page where they'd interpret rap songs on the ukulele.

"You're not the first to come up with that idea," I told them, seizing Congo.

"Bullshit," Gelb said, battling Ainsley in North America.

"It's not even the first time *you* have come up with the idea. I came over here a few years ago and you were playing *Get Low* by Lil John on that little child toy instrument."

"Woah," said Gelb, holding his hands up in defense. "I forgot you were the serious, music-making man of our generation."

"I still like it," said Ainsley.

"Tell Sam he should get on Instagram," Gelb said. "You'll have triple the following of anyone we know."

For a moment, Ainsley looked off in a facsimile of deep thought. "Instagram is to modern-day society what horses were to the Native Americans when the Europeans showed up," Ainsley said. "You know it's going to spell death, somehow, but you have to ride along anyway."

"Anyone want to do a J?" Gelb asked. "We still have another hour before Amy gets back."

I checked the clock. It was after 3 pm. We'd done our job, wasting the day away.

"I don't do drugs," Ainsley said.

"I thought you're a Shamanic healer," I said. "I thought you *drink*."

"Yes," Ainsley said. "That's what got me off drugs."

"I'm a hero," I told Ainsley drunkenly. "That's what got me off drugs."

Everyone found this terribly funny.

Ainsley rolled the dice, snapped up one of Gelb's territories in eastern Eurasia. Gelb had lost his focus. He couldn't unglue his face from his phone for more than two minutes at a time. The game was toast.

Ainsley offered to lead us in a guided meditation. We declined. We couldn't Dominate the Globe forever.

Gelb sat staring into his phone, scrolling limply, gnawing on a rope of gummy candy. If I was the American, Gelb was America itself. Would he ever realize that he'd never outrun his own appetites? That the drugs and the Ainsleys led only to his unraveling. I thought to ask him—confess that I still pillaged him for his appetites, same as ever—but not in the presence of his glazed-over eyes, slurred speech, and cell phone video games.

I told him I needed to leave. He hardly looked up from his phone, offered me his soft fist to pound. Outside, dusk was falling. I walked downtown.

Faces brushed past me, obscured or quickly illuminated by streetlamps, storefronts, headlights. Between sideways glances, I moved further and further south, down Second Avenue, until I reached the bridge. I looked up at the yellow-brown arches, the support beams, and rusted-out suspensions of the 59th Street Bridge. Viewed from the window in our apartment, the bridge seemed manageable, a Lego set. But up close you're nothing, too tiny to register.

There were so many ways to imagine a suicide happening. Slipping in front of a moving train. Overdosing. But the trope of the bridge always stood out to me. In high school English class, I used to get some satisfaction from dreaming up my funeral in the journals our teacher would make us write at the end of class. I basked in the theoretical shock of my closest friends and family gathering to attend the ceremony on a drab, cold day. More recently, I'd remember those journals and think, how amateur. How vain to imagine your loved ones huddled around your gravesite, weeping and saying that now that they've had the chance to dig up your unfinished ramblings and songs, revisit them in the light of your premature death, you really were some misunderstood genius.

I knew I didn't have the heart to climb the bridge. I hadn't done the research. But from two blocks away, in the shadow of the bridge, another option unfolded like a songbook before my eyes: our apartment building. The thirty-story roof.

Inside the lobby of our building, I nodded and waved to the doorman, thinking too much or nothing at all about how it always had to be like this. Whenever those subway trains roared past me, or I looked out over the ledge from some vertiginous rooftop, I held the fear responsible for holding me back. How often had I wished to eliminate that hesitation with drugs. Now that I had, I made the goal as singular as possible. My nerves didn't fuss or fight. Determination crowded out any distraction.

I hit the PH button inside the elevator. An older woman and her massive, unmistakable sheepdog joined me.

"Can you hit six please, love," she said in a British accent, offering little in the way of eye contact. I nodded and obliged her request.

On the ride up, the possibility of running into Audrey crossed my mind. I leaned my head up against the wall as the air seemed to leak out from the small space. What would I say to her? I recalled our argument that afternoon. I was so bad at lying to her that in explaining why I went to Gelb's, to return the pills to him, I couldn't even tell the truth without seeming like I was lying. The same used to happen in high school when I'd come home from a friend's, and my mom would ask if I was high. The simple line of questioning made me squirrelly, smirky, unable to look her in the eye. Even though I was dead sober, my jumpiness under interrogation made her only more suspicious. Add that to the list of broken behaviors I exhibited, too numerous to consider fixing at this point. What other choice did I have? I wasn't meant to survive this world. Not with my peculiar brand of disordered brain activity.

Inside the elevator, I shifted back and forth with the impatient certainty that once I reached our floor, fourteen, the door would open to Audrey standing there. She'd see the look on my face, know something was wrong, and I'd lose my mettle. I couldn't lie to her anymore. I'd break down, tell her my plan. The next thing I knew, I'd be strapped to a gurney inside a mental institution.

"So long," sang the old British lady when the door opened on the sixth floor. I lifted a hand in her direction, grimaced. The dog tugged her down the hall and out of view. I held my breath as the door shut and I rose higher. The fourteenth floor passed in a half-second of pure relief, followed by pure dread. The door re-opened on the top floor, and I found the staircase that led straight up to the roof. When I opened the door, a forceful gust of wind repelled me, swept through my hair and across my skin. A firm reminder of the battle I was up against. With some further relief, I saw no one occupied any of the benches or common spaces on the roof. I circled the perimeter before settling on a corner that looked out over the bridge. A small alleyway separated the high-rise directly to the east of our building. I reached my hand out to touch the five-foot-high wall. A simple push-up required to hoist myself up onto the ledge.

That's when his voice tore through my mind. The voice at the heart of it all. There with me the whole time but never louder. Propelling me and somehow stifling me at the same time.

"Would you like me to send you the list of writers with law degrees again?" my dad said that night. The night that changed everything. He and my mom had me surrounded in the kitchen of our home, which was the only place we could talk. The only place we could scream at the top of our lungs and sling dishware at close range. The open space and yellow lighting were prime.

"I should have never listened to you," I told him, clutching my hands together under the table. They felt separate from the rest of me, alive on their own, my fists vibrating against the fabric of my pantlegs. "I should have left for Austin with Abe."

"Back to this again?" he sing-songed to me, a mockery. The words burst from him with all the enthusiasm he usually reserved for highway road work, raging from behind the wheel of his Mercedes. All that money and still feeling like the world had it out for him. "Back to Mr. Guitar Player? Mr. Idealist?"

"At least I'd be doing something I believed in!"

"Fine, Sam." He leaned over the table, jabbed his finger towards my face. The back of my neck prickled. I hardly felt the weight of my head. He paced between the door and sink. "You know everything. Why should you listen to your father? I've only gotten along for sixty years in the world."

He left the room. My mom whispered, "Your father is doing what he thinks is best for you." She leaned toward me, the skin around her mouth so tired and thin that the smear of pink lipstick left on her front tooth seemed even more jarring and sad. I felt sorry for her, wished she'd had a better life, taken better care of herself. I wished she stopped sneaking her cigarettes late at night, as if we didn't know. But I didn't want to do what she did, give in to my father's tyranny.

My mother said, "He's offering something generous—an education." And then her face twisted, growing ugly like my father's so often was. They were the team, I remembered. I was the outsider. "And you have the gall to throw it right back in his face?"

"That's another thing!" my father's voice came from the doorway, startling us both. "You're done, Sam." His words seemed to rattle the thin-paneled wood walls. "Consider yourself cut off. Or maybe you can let Audrey's family take care of you. The way your moron friend Gelb does with his girlfriend's rich parents."

I didn't have time to think before I was on my feet. I charged toward him. Glaring at his bulging purple forehead veins. Breathing in his putrid aftershave.

He thrust his index finger in my face, actually touched my cheek. A sliver of spit hung at the edge of his mouth. My heart was pounding. I couldn't feel my feet. He said, "Just like the world had no room for a mediocre guitar player."

I jerked my fists forward, stopping just short of his head. He flinched.

"Fuck you," I shouted.

"You want to hit me?" he said. "Do it."

I cocked my fist back. He raised his arms, fists ready.

"Sam!" my mom shrieked, her chair clattering to the floor behind her. She would throw herself between us if she had to. "Sam, stop!"

But then I pulled back and rushed out of the kitchen. Down the stairs to the basement, through the door to the garage. The black paint of my father's Mercedes shimmered in the uneven light, part moonlight through the row of small windows, part the flickering single bulb on its frayed cord. I opened the side door and walked outside, into the crisp night air, towards a messy stack of Belgian blocks sitting abandoned by the end of the driveway. Without thinking about it—without a thought to consequence—I picked up one of the stray blocks, its bulk cool in my hand. And then I was back in the garage. With his car.

My chest pounded, insistent and in control of me.

I drove the brick as hard as I could into the driver-side window. But it didn't break. The glass wobbled and dented, a small white scratch appearing on the surface. Then I used two hands. I dropped the brick straight down into the glass, which shattered instantly this time, leaving behind a sprinkling echo of sound. For good measure, I kicked off the side-view mirror, watching the electrical wires slide midway down the side door, dangling pathetically. My breath came hotly. I strode back out to the driveway and stood there, panting, holding the brick against my chest. The night air met my head and cheeks and brought me little relief.

Five months of silence followed. The silence somehow worse than the shouting. Every day, I fantasized about ways out—jumping out of a window at work, for total dramatic effect, or all along my 30-minute commute, tripping into an oncoming subway train. Inside my apartment, with the bridge beckoning from our window, there were days when all that held me back was Audrey. She didn't deserve to be haunted by her boyfriend jumping off the balcony of her apartment for the rest of her life. And yet as one door closes, another one opens, they say. Yesterday proved I could make good use of my anger. I could end human life. The breakup today marked the final level of the video game. An answer, an explanation, a merciless lesson to my parents—*you did this*. Purpose in the neatest and calmest sense of the word.

Would my window ever be more open than this? The material world had little to offer me anymore. Not after I'd become a literal hero yesterday. It was only downhill from there.

Cars stalled and turned and sped down Second Avenue. A

truck's horn blared, startling my heart, but I put my head down and touched the lip of the ledge. My whole body trembled. I cried, screamed. I cried some more.

To punctuate my parents' guilt, I pulled out my phone and sent them $500 on Venmo—around what I believed I still owed for the damage to the car. Then I turned my phone off, for what I believed to be the last time.

I looked over the top of the ledge, down to the street level, where tiny pedestrians passed back and forth over the concrete. Nine point eight meters per second squared: The acceleration formula from high school physics lurked in some strange fold of my brain. Wary of killing someone else from my fall, I moved several steps south. I screamed again and spread my fingers out over the surface of the ledge, cool and rough in my hands like sandpaper.

Always a strong climber as a kid, boundless energy committed to playground monkey bars, I summoned that spirit to hoist my body up onto the four-foot-long ledge. My knees buckled as soon as I stood. The wind buffeted my skin, threatening to do the work for me. I turned as slowly as possible to face west, back to the uneven blare of cars and trucks and teeming life.

Finally, with my hands behind my back, wind threading through my fingers, there was nothing. A tiny ledge underfoot. A world of void behind me, the smallest slip separating me from my destiny.

32

HOLLY

I changed into a simple outfit to visit Xander's mom at the hospital: blue jeans, white tee, gray hoodless sweatshirt. I resisted the blacks and reds she might have associated with me and Xander. It had still only been 36 hours. Going over there to sit by her side, share memories, sob, and wonder why—I didn't want to look silly.

In the car with my dad, I thought of how we used to gather with Lisa in their kitchen, trading gossip about our friends, college essays, and standardized test scores. Lisa became a motherly presence for me in the absence of my own, I'll admit it, the only one capable of softening Xander's moods with her wit. She sometimes picked us up from school to study together at his house. One day, she allowed us to dye their cats' fur purple and green, the three of us doubled over with laughter the whole time. She was always recommending books for us to read, old movies with Robert Duvall, and the strange part was we actually liked them.

I knew her thoughts on Xander would be smart, clear-eyed, free of judgment. Maybe she would even help me make sense of what happened—some better explanation than anything my parents or friends offered. Still, as we rounded the street corner, nearing the gray columns and rotunda of the hospital, worry dropped down into my stomach: How much did she know about his involvement with Lance? How much did she want to know, really?

My dad stayed in the car waiting for me. The hospital didn't intimidate me. Tagging along with my mom as a girl, I'd grown used to their rhythms. The antiseptic smells and ghostly reminders of death lurking as she shuttled me back to her office, handing me crayon sets and picture books.

When I arrived at the fourth floor waiting room, I saw Lisa sitting in a corner with Paige, Xander's sister. I breathed in the familiar hospital air—thin cover to the urine and rot—and stepped inside to check in with a nurse. Paige gave a little frown, looking me over, greeting me at the glass enclosure. Her eyes darted past me, wary of onlookers.

"I'm so sorry, Paige," I said, noticing the dark circles under her eyes, vivid in the light. "I don't know what else to say. I can't…I know how you must—"

"Don't," she said. "Don't pretend you know what we're going through. My mom wants to talk to you. But if I had a say, you wouldn't be stepping foot anywhere close to here."

I sighed, took it. I wouldn't hold anything against her, as awful as I knew she felt, as volatile as I knew she could be. Cut from the same cloth as Xander. I pressed past some empty chairs. Lisa looked up from her phone to greet me with moist, tired eyes.

"Holly," she said, standing. "Come here."

She embraced me, I knew she would. It took everything in me not to melt into a puddle in her arms. "You've always been so good for Xander."

She drew back and looked at me. She said, "I don't want you to feel the least bit guilty."

"I just want to know what happened."

She gestured towards the chairs. "Come. Sit."

But I couldn't. Glued to the spot, stuck inside a memory—

the last time I went over to Xander's house. Xander and I were watching a movie in the living room when Xander's dad Russell came in to grab a snack from the fridge. He'd just returned to living in their house again, and the white light from the fridge cast his face in a jagged triangle, a startling new shape that seemed to haunt Xander. His whole mood soured in the presence of his dad—less touchy-feely, more uptight and distant. "Paige, my mom, me—we were in a fine place," he said after his dad went back upstairs. "And now she has to let him back."

I looked at Lisa inside the hospital.

"Where's Russell?" I asked her.

Her teeth clenched, knowing how it might look to hide anything from me. "We agreed it wouldn't be the most productive for him to be around right now. Too fresh, you know? The dynamic is too new."

I nodded but said nothing.

"I'm really glad you decided to stop by," she said. "Even just for five minutes, it helps to have people on our side. Everyone lining up against us. We need to be strong right now."

Fear isn't an emotion I ever expected to see in Lisa. She managed her family and career responsibilities like a trained juggler—an inspiration, aspiration, for young women like me. Even now, she spoke with so much self-assurance that it took me some time to notice that she was anxious, eyelids fluttering and hands fidgeting with her phone. Her words seemed hopped up—drug-induced, maybe.

"How is he doing?" I said. My voice sounded unnatural to me, like I was reading the newspaper out loud, a girl's voice.

"I can see you want the truth," she said, stilling to look down at her hands.

"Yes."

"It's not good, Holly. He's not responsive. He's having these seizures."

The words hit me like a fever. Sweat rose along my head and back. The worst of my gut fears confirmed: Xander was gone. I'd never get the chance to speak with him again. No one would.

"Are you okay?" she asked me. "Please, sit. You're looking pale."

I sat, feeling the slightest bit more anchored to the world, relief to my wobbly legs. "Can I see him?" I asked.

"I don't think that's the best idea."

I could only shake my head, look away into the vague middle distance. If I saw any of myself, I feared I might be a completely different person under there.

"They're telling me he's already lost over sixty percent of his brain activity, a number of key cognitive functions."

Multiple new Xanders crossed my mind: Xander shriveled up and wheeled around in a wheelchair. Xander speaking out of the side of his mouth. Xander deprived of his reading and writing, a useless vegetable. An even worse fate, somehow, than him dying.

"I can't even believe I'm saying it," she said, the tears rolling down her flushed cheeks, her breath catching, "but they've already asked me to consider pulling the plug."

"How," was what I said. I don't know why, but she seemed to understand.

"He must have been feeling so completely desperate. He had nowhere else to turn."

"Lance," I said. "Xander never even liked Lance, he's never gotten violent once."

"He'd stopped taking his meds. And he always wanted to be part of something. He must've just…snapped."

I turned my head to see a smattering of others in the enclosed glass room, exchanging leery glances with me. I felt so tunneled speaking with Lisa, I'd barely noticed them.

"It's hard for me to believe that he would've put his suffering on anyone else," I said, sighing at the thought of repeating myself. "Maybe us—maybe he would have committed suicide one day, I don't think either of us would have been completely surprised by that. But this? Innocent lives? No. It's not him."

"You wouldn't believe the fights we've been having lately. Unlike anything before. We argued about all sorts of things—politics, fascism, civic responsibility. And you're right—I didn't think he'd turn to violence, at least not so quickly. But he was deeply troubled. From the way he talked sometimes, I thought maybe we'd receive a visit from the FBI at some point."

"What? When?"

"These last few weeks and months. You know how he can be—I'm sure he didn't want to involve you."

"It's so cruel. I feel like we could clear this up in half a second if he could just fucking speak."

She composed her thoughts. "I've been thinking that, too. But then maybe, maybe also…not?"

"What do you mean?"

"I would give anything to have one conversation with him—to ask why he had to go down this road. But then I remember that he never listened to me to begin with. Maybe hearing him say he had every intention of doing what he did, maybe that would hurt more than the ambiguity. We can't take responsibility for behaviors we can never change."

Her words hung around for a few seconds after they left her mouth. They shot through the hospital air with real determination. Real truth, too. This was information I knew I could do something with. I had no other choice.

Looking out over the ER—patients being hauled in and out on gurneys, doctors cutting through the crowded corridors, some displaying good humor as they went—I realized I never could have changed Xander on my own. He wasn't ready to see practical solutions. Only escape plans.

But was Lisa responsible? Part of me wanted to yell at her, sitting across from me as she beat back the tornado of messages on her phone. I felt sad for Lisa, that she could have so easily imagined Xander doing something like this. I knew better. The very facts I was reading in his journal confirmed it. Anyway, I knew this: all parents did wrong by their children at one point or another.

Suddenly I felt silly for changing into my normal jeans and sweatshirt, anticipating she'd feel the same way I did. She was always too blasé with him, too forgiving. She didn't want to push him over the edge. And yet, here we were.

Lisa looked up, past me, to a figure behind my head. I spun around.

"You're not going to believe this," Paige said with her phone in her hand. She wore a look of complete befuddlement. But I had zero reaction whatsoever to what came out of her mouth next. "The guy who stopped Xander yesterday? Sam Reid. His family just filed a missing person report. No one can find him."

33

AUDREY

My mom and I were getting ready to go to my brother Taylor's apartment, to huddle with family as solace to the heartbreak, when I felt my phone vibrating in my pocket. A photo of Sam's mom and dad and dog, Jenkins, appeared on the screen. It was so unusual for her to call, I felt I had no choice but to answer.

"Hello?" I said tentatively.

"What happened, Audrey?" she asked me, cracks of crisis all along her voice.

"I'm sorry, what?" I answered, as my own mom looked at me, confused.

"He's missing. Michael told me about the breakup, but no one else has heard from him for hours."

My heart was thumping, and I was disoriented. My feet being sucked into an all-powerful rip tide. She'd used Gelb's first name, Michael. No one ever used his first name. Not even parents.

"Have you heard from him?" she asked.

I decided I needed to not make this a big deal. Not now. At least I needed to try. "No. Not a word. Why would I?"

"So let me get this straight. You thought today would be a

good day to do it?" she said, a pleading fragility to her tone. "You couldn't have just held on for a few more days?"

I took a moment to think. "There are aspects to our relationship that you don't know about, okay? And I'm not comfortable discussing them right now."

All I heard was her grunting, panting, maybe even crying on the other end.

"I'm sure he'll turn up soon," I said. "He's probably just napping or something."

"Well, he's not at the apartment, so where else would he be doing that?"

"I don't know. Anywhere."

Before I could get another word in, she said, "They were considering keeping him overnight in the hospital, you know that?"

"I do know that," I said too quickly, hearing the defensiveness in my voice, the same as with Sam earlier.

"And Gelb? How many drugs did they take?"

"I have no clue. I last saw him in the lobby and he seemed fine, sober—"

"You know what?" she said. "I don't even want to know. Gelb texted but won't pick up the phone. That tells me everything I need to know."

A pause hovered on the line. How would I explain myself to her? Did I need to justify breaking up with him today? Sam didn't think twice about lying to me, repeatedly. Why should I be held to a higher standard?

"I tried everything to help Sam," I told Sam's mom. If I didn't hold back from telling Sam the truth, why back down from his parents? The very people responsible for shaping him. The ones more responsible for his pain—and, by extension, mine—than anyone else. "But this simply isn't my mess to clean up anymore."

"Is that right?"

"Yes. It's yours."

"Oh, wow," she said. "Len is right. You really can be a bitch sometimes."

There was nothing left inside of me anymore, nothing besides my own self-preservation. I pulled the phone away from my ear, smashed the red end button on the phone without saying goodbye. Anger boiled in my veins. My own mother sitting next to me looked like she wanted to ask what happened, but a part of her already seemed to know.

34

HOLLY

Honestly, I was mad. There were two other people who'd interacted with Xander in the immediate run-up to the incident: Lance and Sam Reid. Now, one of them had gone missing.

"We're about to pass that ice cream place you like on Flatbush," my dad said from the driver's seat. My eyes stared out the window—a flat gray day that never seemed to get started—refusing to look over or engage much at all. "Want to make a pit stop?"

"I'm fine."

"Okay, then."

We kept driving, back toward the house, where I could get back in bed and read the rest of Xander's journal entries. I knew my dad was doing his best. And I didn't know if Sam was involved or not. Frankly, I didn't care. I only knew that his disappearance meant he couldn't share anything he may have seen, heard, known.

"I guess this is a bad time to tell you that your mom called again," my dad said, and it took all my strength to keep from screaming. I'd shut off the notifications on my phone by then. I'd learned my lesson from the tweets and text message speculation, the facts spiraling just like Ms. Duprey had warned us about. If I had seen my mom calling, I would have lost it. "She's staying at the Radisson across the park. She wants to speak with you. Despite what you may think, she does have good advice in these situations. Most of the time, anyway."

When my parents first separated, I had just turned twelve. I embraced the newness of pinballing between their houses on the opposite sides of the park. I treated it like a game. Sure, there were tedious parts—two sets of toothbrushes, backpacks, the berry conditioner I liked—but I'd take that over their shouting matches and broken promises. Nights culminating with my dad pulverizing his old hockey equipment in the garage.

As I got older, I rode my bike the four miles that divided them. I slept better, too, less worried about waking up to an argument or my dad waking me in a gruff voice just to tell me I'd left the television on. It surprised me sometimes how vivid my dreams became during that period—lifelike tableaus of sound and color that I often sketched. Beach scenes with our friends, trips to Europe with Xander, the frightening thrill of being lost in a corn maze. Meanwhile, my mom climbed the ranks at the hospital, earning her finance degree. The separation gave her the space she needed to focus on her career, and it's not wrong to say I gravitated to her more than my dad for this reason. She started seeing someone new, a teacher named Pat who treated her with respect, who listened and didn't resort to name-calling. They rented a house together on 212th Street, where Pat would ask me about my friends, even after I told him I didn't have any. Sometimes he'd leave a palette knife or set of graphite pencils in my room. My mom would help me pour the acrylic. My dad never understood. That's what made her leaving for San Francisco so hard. How was I supposed to account for the sudden loss of my mother? My only stable life force. She knew it wouldn't have made sense for me to come with her, to uproot me from my friends with only a couple of years of high school left to go.

Maybe it was petty of me to hold a grudge against her. Stupid for turning to the comfort of late-night trips to get dollar-menu fries, chicken tenders, chocolate shakes. But being aware of a problem and addressing it are different. Sometimes that's the widest gap of all.

"Maybe we'll catch the hockey?" my dad when we arrived back at the house.

I looked at the distressed green leather couch, the ottoman and bureau with old photos of the two of us, the Ikea-bought oil paintings in the living room. A single painting of mine hung on the far wall, a surrealist portrait of a woman in heavy makeup at breakfast. Spilled milk defying gravity, rings of cereal spread scattershot over the canvas. A favorite of my mom's, though she requested it stay here in New York with me. Perhaps to liven the place up.

My dad let out a half-sigh, half-grunt when he took his seat on the couch. Never one to suffer his chronic knee pain in silence. Again, I reminded myself he was doing what he could. This simply wasn't his territory.

A lump began gathering in the back of my throat. I didn't want him to see. I went straight to my room, cracked the door shut behind me. With my back against the door, I let it out. Hard. Molten tears down my cheeks, chest lurching up and down, slumped down on the floor.

Because, really, how was I supposed to trust anyone anymore? Over just a few years, my parents blew my life wide open. Now my best friend had attempted to commit a violent act that may have implicated me, leaving only the most cryptic traces of an explanation. This when I did all I could to help him.

I grabbed the phone, left with nowhere else to turn. My hands shook with hesitation over the keypad. But I had no other choice. I was too unsure of the ways of the world to know what to do. I'd tell her about the journals Xander had shared and ask for advice. I needed an adult. Because it wasn't about not wanting to speak with her anymore. It was about admitting I needed to.

She picked up on the first ring.

"Oh, cookie," my mom said.

35

AUDREY

My parents huddled around the sofa at Taylor's apartment to vent, brainstorm, ask why. The boundless compassion of my family, rushing to lend the tiniest bit of order to the chaos. But even if they offered me a lifeboat for the roiling seas, it was a rudderless and motor-less oner. Our hands grasping for sails that were always either too firm or too slack.

Vibrations kept surging through the leather of my handbag, resting by my left foot on the ground. Multiple calls from Gelb. Texts from Amy. My closest friends since college, pleading with me to call them back. But for what? To make them feel better? They'd push me closer and closer to regret, even without saying as much. I couldn't. I would not fall for that.

"Sam seemed so good over the summer," my mom said, busying her hands with a couple of colored pencils on the ottoman. "He told me he couldn't wait to go skiing again."

"You know how hard I tried," my dad told me, eyes agleam, half-moons under them. We'd been talking in these circles for some time. "I saw so much of myself in him. We met recently to discuss his new job prospects. I took that as a good sign."

I went to speak, but my voice broke for the eleventh or twelfth or hundredth time. Each hour that slipped by without word from Sam was another hour we feared the worst. I knew that breaking up with someone meant cutting them out, emotionally, but I still imagined the sorting out of apartment logistics and clothes and furniture. Once the dust settled, maybe we'd even sit down for coffee and a more grown-up conversation than we'd had yesterday. Some healthy closure. It never occurred to me that I'd never see or hear from him again. The growing possibility hit me with unfathomable sadness. So many tears spilled out of my eyes that I found it surprising any time there were more. But there they were, each time, my throat and lungs scorched.

"Audrey," my dad said, taking my hand. "You know I love you more than anything. And I still think he's gonna turn up. But no matter what he did or where he went, it has nothing to do with you. You know that, right?"

I looked at Taylor, sitting on the far edge of the couch, a gray hoodie pulled low over his eyes. It was one of the few times I can recall my younger brother being speechless. Taylor loved to rib Sam for his quirks—his gastrointestinal dysfunction and compulsive handwashing and sheltered Long Island upbringing. Sam, to his credit, always took the potshots in stride, only to remark in private how obvious it was that Taylor was projecting his own insecurities. But inside the apartment that day, anchored in place on the couch, gritting his teeth, limited eye contact with any of us, Taylor merely sat there. Far away in thought. He didn't offer any witty retorts to our verbal spats, like he so frequently did. Like I honestly wished he would have. Because seeing Taylor shut down brought me back to the darker times from his past. Most recently, during his senior year of college, he stopped going to class for two weeks, barely got out of bed. My mom drove 21 hours straight to pick him up.

"Taylor," I said. My voice jolted something in him, and he looked over at me. "You alright there, bud? You look like you're seeing ghosts."

He blinked. My handbag shook, then stopped. Then vibrated again.

"What? Tell us."

He sighed. "There's one question I keep coming back to in my head. But I'm not sure we're ready to have this conversation."

"C'mon," my dad said. "Stop screwing around, Taylor. Speak straight"

"Is it possible that Sam's disappearance is connected to this bombing suspect somehow?" No one responded or said anything for a moment. Immediately, my thoughts jumped to the yellow lighter from our apartment, glowing in my mind. I recalled Agents Ramirez and Bender, paying us a visit, laboring to fit the puzzle pieces together.

"Think about it for a second," Taylor said. "We already know Sam was making up these strange stories. What else could he have been up to behind Audrey's back? For all we know, maybe he knew this kid in Penn Station."

"Are you crazy?" my dad asked.

"It's not outside the realm of possibilities."

"I hate to be the one to break it to you but, little Sam Reid from Long Island was not involved in some underground terrorist plot. That much I can promise you."

As they went back and forth, I felt a weird sort of instinct to defend Sam. Despite what he'd done to me. I knew my dad was right. Taylor was descending into conspiracy-level thinking, as if he were up late watching his own little movie. Sam had nothing to do with Xander.

"Sounds like more white-washing to me," Taylor said.

"What?" I said.

"Why are we all taking so much pity on him?" The room seemed to grow warmer, damp, deprived of air. Finally, Taylor was getting down to the heart of his feelings. "He never knew how to treat Audrey right. I saw it from a million miles away. How did you ever even see a future with him?"

"Taylor," my dad said sternly. A spasm spiked from my back to my right hip. The gray of my dad's beard glinted in the light. I knew I was in no condition to return to the classroom tomorrow. I thought about the growing stretches of time I'd have to miss at school and even some of my students, Baron and McKenzie. If the subs would know which of their demands to cater to and which to ignore. I may not have had my boyfriend or our shared home, but unlike Sam, I had purpose. Others relying on me. "You can speak ill of Sam all you want. But I won't let you talk this way about Audrey. She did absolutely nothing wrong here."

Taylor peered at me from under his hood. "You always could have done better, Audrey. If one good thing comes out of this, it's that maybe you will."

"Are you done now? Is it out of your system?" my dad said.

"I think so."

"Good."

I knew Taylor liked to play the bully. But deep down he wasn't lashing out because he thought that little of Sam. With his moody, Freudian fixation on all of life's un-answerable questions, Taylor understood Sam all too well. The two of them were always far more alike than different. I did so much through the years to help Taylor, it ate me up inside. The late-night calls, the babysitting. I'd do anything for Taylor, as flesh and blood. Sam, on the other hand, I didn't need to babysit anymore. That I was more certain of than ever.

36

HOLLY

It was a short bike ride, just across the park, to the Radisson where my mom was staying.

"Do you want me to drive you?" my dad asked.

"Nope," I told him, buckling the strap on my helmet. I slid my laptop into my bookbag. This was between me and my mom now.

"There's something you should know before going over there," he said. The lines on his forehead deepened, so I gave him the space to think. "When your mom left for San Francisco, I thought everything would change. A brand-new start for us all."

"Dad," I said, drawing out the sound in characteristic frustration. "Now?"

"Yes, now. I've never said this, but I feel like it's important to tell you how wrong I was. Change takes work, and I was too wrapped up in feeling sorry for myself to put in the work. And I'm sorry."

I looked down, as if the eye contact threatened to vanish me. Every atom inside of me told me to run. But he kept speaking.

"The issues between me and your mom were our issues—

separate and more complicated, probably. Not that I've minded spending the extra time with you. Not at all. I love having you around. I just think I didn't quite know my own limits. So maybe it would help to know you're not crazy for feeling the way you do towards us."

There was no stopping the tears that slid out of my eyes. The surge of heat in my face.

"Thank you," was all I could say. He corralled me, squeezed my left shoulder. I turned and went to collect my bike in the garage.

Rounding the corner of my street, I recognized my dad's words for all the things they were, all at once. A confidence boost. A recognition of past mistakes and present shortcomings. A kind of growth.

I whipped past some cars lined up in gridlock traffic in both directions. I concentrated on the two interconnected tasks before me: the words I'd share with my mother and the act of pedaling, navigating potholes and wet leaves as if one fueled the other. As if the harder I pedaled, the clearer I could see what I wanted to say, what my dad had the good sense to confirm for me. *I know I've been acting rash, immature maybe, but that still doesn't mean I think you made the right decision.*

The simplicity of my focus shrunk the world. I was so consumed by our looming conversation that I seemed to forget the existence of my surroundings. I imagined squirrels scurrying across the sidewalks, pockets of leaves arcing up from piles on the ground. But I didn't seem to observe any of these things until I felt a bolt to my heart. My name being called. A voice from somewhere on my periphery.

"Holly Palmer! Where you headed?"

My fingers splayed out and jammed on the brakes. I craned my neck to the right, from where the sound seemed to come, a pocket of kids sitting on the rocks by the pond. With dusk falling, their faces were hard to make out. But as they waved me over, I recognized Teddy. I matched his voice to the one that first called my name. Drew and Conner surrounded him. They passed a joint or cigarette back and forth. A few of the girls came into focus: Annie Felton, who only lived a few blocks away, whose house we'd sometimes end up at when nights turned aimless. Emma Blakely, who started dating Conner after he and Piper broke up. Seeing her made me realize, for the first time, how strange it was to find Teddy and Drew hanging out together. They'd been fist-fighting enemies some three months earlier.

"Holly, how are you doing?" Annie called out, her voice soft and inviting.

I couldn't help it. I was too non-confrontational. I parked my bike, unstrapped my helmet and hung it over one handlebar. The signals in my brain told me to keep riding the path out of the park, but I didn't. I pictured them mumbling behind my back, calling me out. Teddy reporting back to Piper, asking what was wrong with me. When I pulled up, I hung back a few feet, silently saying that I wasn't staying to hang out.

"I'm doing okay," I said to Annie, as sincerely as I could. "Thanks for asking."

"Any updates on Xander?" Teddy asked.

My mind flashed back to the hospital, the shock and suffering in Lisa's eyes. I looked down and shook my head, confirming what they already seemed to know. The news had been traveling. He likely wouldn't make it through the night.

"I'm really so sorry," Emma said. She sounded earnest, perfectly nice, and I thought how this was a type of skill certain people seemed to gain at some point: the ability to sound interested or caring or thoughtful when they didn't mean it. At least not any more than a centimeter below the surface.

"You want a hit or two?" Teddy asked, perhaps as something to fill the awkward space. He knew I didn't smoke. "It might help take the edge off."

"That's okay," I said. I thought about my mom waiting for me at the hotel, a thought that put me in no rush to get there. What would it be like if I stayed? Got high, blew off my mom, turned my phone off. Forgot about the radically altered state of my world. If this were a different day, I might have talked with Emma and Teddy about the next set of ACTs coming up next week. Who would get a football or basketball scholarship. Who asked the dumbest questions in math class. But nothing was the same now.

"I'm running late to a tutoring lesson anyway," I said, not wanting to reveal the plan with my mom. Not wanting to acknowledge anything about my mom being in town. I grabbed the handlebars of my bike, swiped the kickstand, and made a move to leave.

"Wait a second," Teddy said. I tried to hide my exasperation. Teddy, always so happy to be the pest. To unfurl his little bumble bee stinger, to get you to swat him away.

"What subject are you getting tutored in?" Teddy asked. Annie's eyebrows flew up in interest. A sly grin crept over his mouth, as if he saw straight through my lie. Now he only had to pick at it. "You're like, one of the smartest kids in school. What could you possibly need help with?"

"Calc two," I said. His mouth puckered, as if tasting something sour. "Just brushing up."

I didn't wait for his reaction. I turned my back on them and walked the bike a few paces before getting on. I pedaled away from the pond, back towards the main path and out of the park. By then, it was almost fully dark. I powered the bike with all my manic, woozy energy, winding through streets I could have navigated blindfolded. More than ever, I looked forward to college next year, envisioning the campuses of the small liberal arts colleges I'd visited: Upstate New York, Massachusetts, Connecticut. Old gothic-style buildings surrounded by manicured lawns, frisbees and baseballs suspended in air. A chance to *start over*. Join like-minded others, interested in art and books and not the dull, never-ending cycle of drama that consumed Teddy and Conner and Annie Felton.

Outside the hotel, several blocks from the park, I latched my bike to a street parking sign, clipped my helmet around the strap of my backpack. A set of automatic doors swung open when I reached the entrance. The bellman greeted me with a wide smile and wave. I saw my mom waiting at a table by the bar in the lobby, looking at her phone through a pair of glasses low down on her nose.

The over-complicated mix of emotions swelled inside of me, heightened from my run-in with Teddy. A scraping in the back of my throat like knives. I tried to think of the good times: Friday-night trips to the movies, pawing at a tub of popcorn, our own huge sodas, Raisinets for my dad. Broadway musicals when we could afford to go—*The Lion King* and *Man of La Mancha,* Disney on Ice—and never a lack of food on the table, a dreary Thanksgiving or Christmas. And there were my parents, checking in on me every thirty minutes the night I got my tonsils out. Always paying too much attention to me or none at all.

"Sweetie, come here," she said, rising from her chair when I reached the table. She wrapped her arms around me—smelling like herself, like perfume and coffee and rainfall. I returned the smallest trace of a hug. My eyes locked on the carpet, a pattern of beige and brown and blue lines of varying length and width. The lobby bore the trappings of cheap, modern hotel décor—navy blue and sea foam green wallpaper. Light gray stone fireplace, geometric red Eames chairs. I hated it all so much.

"Tell me what's going on," she said. I looked up at her and she smiled, as if to draw me out of the numbness that had overtaken me. I could feel my face muscles working to maintain my scowl. Up close, she didn't look very different from the last time I saw her, save for the extra crease or two at the outer edges of her eyes. "Or you can just sit and brood. That's fine with me. I have nothing but time."

She folded her arms and reclined in her chair. That's what snapped me out of it, finally, her casual sarcasm in response to anything that was supposed to be serious.

"None of this would have happened if you'd never left," I said with the fury of a two-year grudge built up inside of me. I watched her shoulders and head slump to one side, like a dog being led to its cage for chewing up the furniture.

"I might've never started hanging out with someone like Xander if things had ever been *fucking normal*."

Her left index finger shot up into the air, as if preparing to spit a cutting retort back at me. But then she took a breath. Collected herself.

"I can't tell you it was wrong for you to see him," she said, the veil of sarcasm gone from her voice. "Lord knows we've all liked the wrong guy at one point or another."

A tiny sigh flowed from my chest. Which only made me feel worse, like she was winning in calming me down.

"None of this is your fault, you know that, right?" she said. "I don't care how close you guys were. I don't care if he told you every detail of his plan ahead of time. Or even if you thought it was the right thing to do. You could never have stopped him from doing what he did. He'd made up his mind."

"No," I said loudly. Xander's journal entries blazed in my mind. How did I ever think I could trust her? "Please stop talking!"

Two tables over, a pair of men in dark suits turned their heads to look at us.

"What?" she said. "What's going on?"

"You don't know the first thing about him. Or us. Please stop pretending you understand!"

"Okay, okay, Holly," she said, looking genuinely hurt. "I can see how angry you are."

"It's so much more than anger! It's…bullshit."

More concerned eyes on us, including the receptionists behind the desk near the entrance. But I didn't care anymore. Not about the saliva leaking out the side of my mouth. The fire in my throat. The endless tears down my cheeks.

"Sweetie, please, can you just lower your voice a little? Or we can go to my room."

"He's the only person I've ever gotten close to," I said, in a lower but still harsh tone. "And now it's taken from me. It's over! He's dead, probably."

"I'm so sorry, Holly. That's all I can say. I know how hard it must be."

"No, stop saying you know! Stop doing that thing where you pretend like you understand when you really, really don't."

She nodded and looked away. Resigned to being my punching bag for the evening. In a strange way, this was what we needed, how our family worked. Only a full tear in the fabric could make us take a good long look at the pieces, strewn over the floor, and hold the frayed scraps up to the light. We were talking again, in other words, even if we were fighting. The talking meant the opening threads of a new fabric, a new series of conversations.

"I guess I should have expected this," she said. "Tell me. What are you needing right now? Space? A few days off from school? I'll stay as long or as little as you want."

I thought only of the most irrational responses: I needed a time machine. The magic to erase years of pain and frustration. A way to not obsess over all the flabs or folds of my body. A way to transport to a week, two weeks earlier, when I could have done something, anything, to stop Xander.

"I don't know," I said, looking out over the expanse of the lobby, guests sipping coffee or tea, cutting into their food. "There's nothing you can do."

She frowned, seeming to understand. After a drawn-out

pause, she said, "What was it that said you needed to tell me, by the way?"

"What?"

"On the phone. You said you needed to show me something."

"Oh," I said, remembering for the first time. Had I really planned to confide in her? The idea seemed so foreign to me now. I couldn't imagine gathering the strength to explain how Xander had not only brought me to see the weapons he'd used yesterday. He'd passed me the evidence, spelled out clear as day. Sent me his journal entries.

"It's nothing. Honestly. Something related to school. I don't want to get it into it now."

"Holly," she said impatiently.

"What? It's not a big deal. I don't want to talk about it right now. Can't you respect that for once?"

She shook her head, looking off, defeated. Then it occurred to me: I didn't need her to know what to do. The right thing to do was with me all along, written out in the magenta sticky note my dad had passed me, recorded in a photo on my phone. There was a more objective audience out there, one that would help me clear my conscience, lift the burden of secrecy weighing down the laptop inside my bag. I needed to go to the cops, I realized, with or without her. I needed to tell them everything.

37

AUDREY

As a means of distraction, my family remained helpful. Free food and the hum of life. Small talk to pass the minutes between the updates, or lack thereof, on Sam's whereabouts. Amy texted to say Sam's mom received a call from the police. They were *escalating the case*, whatever that might have meant. But still nothing on where he'd gone.

I noticed the control I'd ceded over my own thoughts. The expressions of hope that I couldn't make stick. Amy and Gelb texted to assure me it would all work out still. Lots of heart emojis, *I love yous*. Some big misunderstanding that would come to light soon enough, they suggested. We'll all look back, someday, and laugh.

But I don't think I wanted to hear anything that might help. *The fire extinguisher is on the wall*, everyone seemed to want to tell me. *It's right there within reach. You can grab it at any time you want.*

But I think I just wanted to see what it would be like, for once, to burn up in the flames.

Away from all the repetitive conversations, from somewhere in my peripheral vision as I looked out over the

Manhattan skyrises, squiggly lines seemed to call out to me. Sam could never wrap his head around the side of me that believed in spirits. But here they were, arriving on my doorstep. Could I latch onto what they were saying?

When I turned my head to view Sam's disappearance from a different angle, I felt less surprised than what I expressed to my family. In a strange way, it made perfect sense. By acting so rash, he could reclaim his victimhood, make people worry about where he'd gone. A role far more familiar to him than hero. We'd always had conversations about how he wanted out—which I always took to mean the city, the hustle and bustle—but which now seemed to signal something darker. And what did that mean for me? What could I *do* now that I couldn't before?

I don't know if I thought about my response to these questions as much as I responded out of some primal calling to be in motion, rather than sit still. Pacing in my brother's apartment. Scampering to the refrigerator to stare at the expired butter and teriyaki sauce. Then, telling everyone I needed to pick up my birth control prescription from the pharmacy.

"Do you want company?" my mom asked. "I don't like the thought of you being out alone right now."

"It's fine. I'll take an Uber there and back. I could use a few minutes to gather myself, anyway."

"Okay. What should we do for dinner, guys?"

Out on the street, the fresh air brought me stunning clarity, as if other people suddenly became interesting to me for the first time. I handed money to each panhandler I passed on the street—multiple paper bills—without bothering to check the denominations. Inside the corner bodega, I struck up a conversation with an elderly man who asked me if I could recommend any of the Irish stouts in the display case. When I said no, he told me he didn't know why he asked, few people drank them anymore. But there used to be this bar down on

Mulberry Street that served the best draught and if he ever found it again, he could die a happy man. I wished him luck in finding the stout and bought a pack of sour straws and two Kit-Kat bars.

After walking north for five blocks—noticing the green scaffolding that covered what felt like seventy percent of the buildings—I took the first bus that arrived next to me, submitting blindly to the direction it took me. I powered my phone down, climbed aboard, and paid with my MetroCard. I didn't talk to anyone. I eavesdropped on the conversations—a weekend baby naming, a dentist appointment shrouded in some mystery. It didn't take me long to notice we were heading east, traversing the bridge into Queens. The recognition didn't strike me as immediately profound. I felt fine about entering Queens, as good of a place as anywhere.

In between stops—Cross Island Parkway, Bell Boulevard—I seemed to see straight into my future. There was another guy hovering around somewhere. We'd marry and have two baby girls together, that much was clear, and when we were in our fifties, we'd divorce. I spent another 20 minutes or three hours on the bus. The next time I paid any attention to the stop names, I heard the word *Bayside* announced by the driver.

If you asked Sam, he probably would have told you I'd never picked up a newspaper in my entire life. But I'm not dumb. I read about Xander, where he lived and spent his time. By traveling there, I felt like I might uncover the clues that would unravel the mystery behind Sam, too. I might learn something, in other words.

I exited the bus on the outskirts of a park overlooking the Long Island Sound. *Golden Park*, the sign read. And this felt right. I'd find a bench to sit on and think. The answers would come to me, steeped in golden light.

I knew how far I'd strayed from the lie I'd fed my family, grabbing a prescription at a nearby pharmacy. I could only think of covering it up with another one: *Stopping by Gelb and*

Amy's, I texted. *They were begging to see me. Will text when I'm on the way back.*

I drew breaths from the base of my lungs and took a few bites of the Kit-Kat bar in my pocket. A part of me longed to do what Sam did: leave it all behind, make everyone worry about me. But that's what separated us. I saw how exhausting this was already—the delicate, narrow dance of maintaining several lies at once. I wouldn't allow this version of myself to exist beyond today. No matter how strong the urge, I would never become this.

The park's expanse widened upon my entrance—rolling lawns with sad, brown and green patches of grass, weathered tennis courts in the distance. I walked the footpath towards the courts a quarter of a mile before settling onto another bench, set back from a small pond and backdropped by a rock wall. A group of teens circled the pond, eating hot dogs and drinking Gatorade. Bayside High students, perhaps? A couple of them took turns inhaling a boxy vape pen, blowing thick clouds of smoke into the dusk-laden air. I shuddered at the thought of getting so close, observing Xander's classmates in their private habitat. I remembered the false paranoia that came with being in high school. The fear of being watched every second of every day by parents and teachers and tutors. The desperate thirst to escape.

I took out my phone. My brother had texted to see if I needed anything, but not with any urgency behind it. Not yet. My family knew I needed space. I told him all was good, I'd be back soon. I clicked over to Twitter, remembering some passing developments I'd read about Xander and his high school.

@MichaelDavenport
2/x "If there's anyone who knows about his motive, it would be them," says one source, whose identity remains anonymous due to age. So far, none of Shine's

friends have come forward with information. But more is certain to come to light in the coming days.
8:16 AM - Oct 24, 2018

I made little meaning of these facts when I first read them. Perhaps just some recklessness and gross insensitivity on the part of the reporter. But when I pulled the thread up again, a slew of new replies emerged.

@f0rmansking11 that whole group can't be trusted. Hal, remy, teddy, Holly.
@bsideroll288 oh yes, have you looked into her? holly palmer??
@michaeldavenport she def knows some shit no one else does.
@f0rmansking11 yup. bitch is crazy. her and Xander are thick as thieves. Emphasis on thieves.
@michaeldavenport DMs are open. Message me.
@jsack345 lol. shes crazy but. you really need to doxx her?! tough
@bsideroll288 dude. her bf tried to blow up a train station on a field trip. sorry not sorry.

I didn't spare a moment to think before I was opening up google, typing 'holly palmer bayside new york.' Halfway down the page, I came across her Instagram profile, though it was private—a grainy picture of her wearing sunglasses. Straight brown hair, baby fat still in her cheeks. I did a bit more digging online, which led me to an anonymized Tumblr blog. I could only conclude it to be hers. Gothic-themed, hand-drawn sketches peppered between the words. Short reviews of new music by emo bands. Vague mentions of a character named X throughout the page. His thoughts appeared to overwhelm hers—*X says not to worry, X says their music is trash but I still like it, here's some new flash fiction from X*. Two paragraphs about a character named Chloe performing a one-woman play titled *Marrakesh*.

I flipped back to Twitter to look at the headshot that ran alongside every other tweet about him. When you looked past the dark strands of hair dangling into his eyes, he didn't look so scary or unloved, even. There was humanity there in his light green eyes. He hardly fit the profile of the typical school shooter you heard about, far too often, on the news. He had friends. A girlfriend, possibly. There was more to the story, that much I sensed. Would this Holly Palmer know?

The facts being reported still didn't add up. Why did Sam see Xander carrying that yellow lighter and why did the cops dispute him on it? Why did Xander have that bomb on him in the first place? Could he and Sam have known each other, after all? I didn't have any of the answers, but Holly might.

I remembered the feeding frenzy that overcame me in the cafe the day before. A wet kind of nausea began to stir inside my belly. Was I any better than that reporter, Michael Davenport? Here on my little mission of personal discovery. Prying into the lives of teenagers.

I paced back and forth. I switched my phone off. Enough.

I walked and walked, filled with the need to empty myself out. At the far end of the park, a stone archway overlooked the highway and Long Island Sound. Bikers and runners moved at varying speeds on the path that separated the bustling highway from the water. A somewhat unexpected and beautiful vista, even at dusk: a sea of small white boats, docks, foamy waves. I envied the simplicity of all these other lives seen from afar. How nice it would feel to ride a bike somewhere right now. Leave my phone behind, get lost in nature. I'd do a triathlon if it meant never needing to think about any of this again.

But of course: impossible. I knew I needed to turn my phone back on. And I knew it wouldn't be good when I did.

The string of voicemails and texts from my family,

appearing as soon as I switched the phone back on, confirmed what I already seemed to know. All hounding me to call them back.

My mom picked up the phone. Something shifted—a twitch in my spine, a spasm through my hip. My body reacted without me.

"My god, Audrey," my mom said, nearly out of breath. I heard the commotion in the background, the rest of my family huddled around her. "Where have you been?"

"My phone was charging in the other room," I said.

"They found him."

"What? Where?"

"The alley behind your building," she said, as calmly as a person could say something like that. "He's gone."

"No."

A monumental queasiness in my stomach. A lump in my throat. Tears streaming down my cheeks.

"It's all over. He must've jumped," she said, her voice breaking now. Only my mom could deliver the news. No one else in my family would be able to get the words out. She barely could, as it were. "I'm so sorry. Please come back to Taylor's."

The softness of her voice brought me the smallest comfort, however short-lived.

"Audrey, please," my dad said, taking the phone. "Where the hell were you?"

I thought quickly. "So many people have been reaching out," I said. "I needed to take a break from my phone."

"You can't give be giving us a scare like that," he said. "Not when all of this is happening."

"I'm coming back right now," I said.

When we hung up shortly afterward, all the pipes inside of me burst open, the rushing waters too powerful to escape. He'd actually done it. The unthinkable. He'd fallen to his death from the roof of our apartment building.

FOIL

I hugged myself, curled up into a ball. I sobbed so hard, so viscerally, I tipped over on the bench. The waves of pain grew stronger and violent in their consistency. I prayed for the tiniest shred of mercy. Unlabored breathing. But nothing came.

38

HOLLY

A twisted part of me enjoyed the privilege of being the one Xander trusted to protect his final words. The journals lived with me, in secret, where no one else could pry, leer, corrupt. Maybe that's why, on my way to see the agents at the downtown Manhattan field office, I so severely questioned my decision to hand-deliver them his journals.

I rode the F line from Queens in a shaky, dimly lit, older-style subway car. Hard, orange-and-brown bucket seats. Sticky speckled floors. Passing from Brooklyn to downtown Manhattan, early evening, I felt the certainty arising that as soon as I made it aboveground, I'd turn right back around. Home. The comforts of home never seemed nicer.

Overhead, the orange-lit circles on the map dwindled from three to two. Two stops left for me to decide.

What was I hoping to accomplish, anyway? Maybe I'd clear up the story for the cops and at the trial. But for what? Xander hadn't exactly earned the benefit of the doubt. He put people's lives at risk. Did it matter that maybe, actually, he *didn't*? That Lance and his crew were the only real target? Any logic I'd applied earlier fell short. Why volunteer? Why risk being implicated alongside him?

No. I simply would not go through with this. I would go home, make myself a peanut butter and jelly sandwich, a tall glass of chocolate milk, and wait for the storm to blow over.

A fresh flurry of passengers shuffled between the train and platform at the next stop. I stayed seated at one end of the car, no one in the seat next to me. A stooped homeless man occupied a whole bench at the center of the car. All the new passengers averted him, including the larger, middle-aged woman who took the seat next to me. The flab of her hips pressed up to my leg. The doors closed, and I didn't move a muscle.

No sense in turning back yet. Perhaps being underground had clouded my thoughts. I needed to stand outside the building, in the fresh air, to know what was right.

We pushed forward for another minute or two—violent hissing and clanking of the train over the tracks. Then we came to an abrupt halt. A conductor's garbled voice came over the loudspeaker. *Train traffic,* all I could make out.

Sighs and eye rolls. I tossed my head back, and some calm seemed to wash over me for the first time during the ride. Peace with my decision to conceal Xander's journals. Even the discomfort of the woman's skin touching mine seemed to fade slightly—I breathed through it.

I snuck a look at my phone, even though I didn't have service. Remy had texted. Her name popped up on the home screen, and I thought little at first of her texting. We texted at all times throughout the day. But then I saw the link preview of a reply to a tweet from Michael Davenport, of all people.

@bsideroll288 oh yes, have you looked into her? holly palmer??
@michaeldavenport she def knows some shit no one else does.

An invisible hand over my windpipe. Fire through my face.

I squirmed in the seat, legs unable to stop moving like a baby in her height chair. The woman next to me glanced at me as my restless legs drummed up against hers, so I stood and moved towards the doors. More texts from Remy unfurled underneath the link:

wtf. what the fucking fuck!!!
its conner and drew, I know it. those idiots.

How could they have known? Teddy, the only real answer, the missing link. He'd pressed me in the park earlier. He'd sniffed out the secrecy, the guilt, on me like the creature he was. *You don't know what you're talking about*, I told him.

Sounds like you know more than you're letting on, he shot back.

Teddy must have gone to Conner and Drew with his suspicions. Always eager to climb the social ladder, move blame away from himself—Teddy threw me under the bus.

Another text from Remy, arriving in rapid fire: *this is the same tw egg they used last year!!*

I recalled the cyber-bullying scandal that rocked the high school our junior year. A rash of anonymous Twitter accounts—Twitter eggs, we called them—had posted heinous, largely untrue garbage about our classmates. Xander, always an easy target. The most juvenile things you could imagine: Xander showered with his dad. Hal had lost one of his testicles. I'd been spared, thankfully, before the accounts were shut down. No one ever discovered the identities of the users, but everyone had their suspicions. Conner Day and Drew Stanton at the top of the list. They were on the field trip the day before—of course they'd take it out on Xander, me, anyone else they suspected and could bring down. They'd reactivated the Twitter eggs for this very purpose.

When I clicked on the link, the Twitter app opened an empty page with the spinning loading wheel, followed by a screen saying, *Uh oh, an error was encountered. Please try again later.*

I attempted to text Remy back: *just what i fkn needed right now.* The background color of the text bubble turned from blue to green. Then, a minute later, a little red exclamation point popped up next to the text—*Delivery failed*.

Groans flowed through the subway car. We sat motionless. One goddamned stop left to go. I thought of all the times I'd been immobilized underground on the subway—train traffic, police investigations, a sick passenger, which may have meant a dead passenger. Instagram videos would play for three seconds before cutting off. Every web page resulting in the spinning wheel of death. As New Yorkers we all dealt with this frustration at some point, but the stakes were never higher than today, never worse than me being the subject of the Twitter pages failing to load. It thrust me straight back to the day earlier, when Xander first disappeared. When I could hardly breathe.

I'd traveled the subway alone before, but now it felt like a mistake. A friend could have helped me pass the time, at least, disrupt the lack of airflow through my lungs. The suffocated rumination soon gave way to rising spasms of anger, defiance. If rumors were being spread about me, could I push back with the facts in my possession? My sole possession. The itch to fight churned through my belly.

Trapped underground, without service, it didn't take me long to flip back to my original position. A revived need formed to share Xander's journals with the cops. Because, why not? Things were getting too out of hand. I felt a certain amount of power returning to me. If people were going to say things about me, I at least wanted them to be true. I'd post them on Twitter myself, if need be. It wasn't about the shame anymore, the fear of blowback or repercussions. It was about protecting my reputation.

A jolt of electric force spiked through the train. We started moving forward again, as if higher powers were guiding me towards the right path, as if my prayers were being answered.

Even if I knew, then, that none of the journals would end up being made public, I wouldn't have cared. I was ready to fight back. Ready for battle.

———

The downtown Manhattan field office was all mottled browns, tattered seat paddings, charred linoleum floors. I checked in at the front desk, gave my name and information to the officer sitting behind a big plexiglass window. Then I found a seat in the waiting area, slowly realizing the agents weren't as eager for me to arrive as I expected. They were busy with other cases, real crimes, a whole city's worth of mischief on any given day.

Across from me, a twenty-something couple sat like they'd been waiting there a while. She didn't wear an engagement ring and maybe I was supposed to feel a certain way about this, but I didn't. It was just something I noticed. The girl reclined, reading a book and draping her legs over his. *Is this how we looked to others?* I wondered. Maybe we wore different clothes—hoods and piercings, dyed hair spilled over our eyes—but I couldn't deny how normal Xander and I must have seemed just three months earlier, holding hands down grocery store aisles. Riding our bikes to school or hanging in the park.

"Palmer? Holly Palmer?"

I looked up from my phone to find the face of the woman calling my name. Slicked back ponytail, rigid smile. She introduced herself as Agent Ramirez, then offered coffee or water, which I declined. My bookbag felt heavier than ever on my back. I disliked Agent Ramirez immediately. I wanted to get the conversation over with as quickly as possible.

She brought me through the metal detectors, followed by a hallway that led to the den of cubicles and offices. Plainclothes officers wore rolled-up shirtsleeves, pantsuits, khakis. When we arrived at her office, the first thing I noticed were two potted plants on either side of her desk, one a cactus and the other a fern. Pueblo artwork decorated the walls. Her partner, Agent Bender, stood up to greet me with a warm smile, much more demonstratively than she did.

"Can't tell you how appreciative we are of you coming forward to share information," he said, carrying a yellow legal pad filled with scribbled blank ink, arrows and circles. He sat perched on the edge of the dark wooden desk, she in the rolling chair behind. I dropped my backpack to my feet and took one of the two gray, stiff, armless chairs across from them.

"Every bit counts," Agent Ramirez said. "We'll try to make this as painless for you as possible. It sounds like you and Xander were awfully close, is that right? I can only imagine how tough these past couple of days have been for you."

I nodded, thinking how others sometimes described my speaking style as blunt. I'd spend days fixating on how I spoke sometimes.

"We're not, like, boyfriend and girlfriend," I said, feeling hesitant and childish all of a sudden. "But yes, he's told me things he probably wouldn't tell other people."

"We gathered that from speaking to some of your other classmates," Agent Ramirez said, and I resented the ideas of being a missing puzzle piece for them, a skeleton key. "But you can speak freely, you know? You can't get in any trouble by talking to us. You're simply another witness."

Agent Bender cleared his throat. "Would it help if we brought your parents in?" he said. "It's somewhat surprising for someone your age to come forward like this without your parents being involved."

"No." I shut my eyes, heard the paper of Bender's legal pad shuffling between pages. Was I strong enough to do this on my own? Did they think I was hiding something by coming alone? "The last thing I want is for them to be here."

I stilled my hands under my thighs, took in the stale,

coffee-infused air. Their stares crawled all over my skin, red-hot and accompanied by a rising nausea. I feared I might throw up into one of the potted plants next to Agent Ramirez' desk.

"This is all, like, so embarrassing," I said. "On so many levels. I'm not even sure my parents would want me to be here speaking with you."

"Right," Agent Ramirez said. "Home life. Always tricky."

So she did understand. I nodded. There was nothing to hide.

An extended pause followed, where I sat there see-sawing between all my conflicting thoughts. Then she said, "So what is it you wanted to share with us? It's okay to have doubts. But if you think this will help us, and everyone, get a clearer picture of what happened yesterday, then it's important to come forward with what you know."

My left hand drifted down to the zipper of my bookbag, containing a weight far heavier than I could ever manage alone. I leaned forward, unzipped the bag, and felt for the cupcake box, the discount card taped to the top. When I brought out the bright pink box, I saw their faces light up with confusion and amusement, almost, as if I were a kid wasting their time with toys. Why did I bring the box to begin with? I only needed the card. Why was I always making these humiliating, childlike decisions?

"Here," I said, dropping the box onto the desk. "Xander gave this to me right before he broke off from the group." Their eyes rotated back and forth to the box, me, each other. "I didn't really know what to make of it at first. Then late last night, when I was looking through it again, I found the card with a web address written on it. You can see it on the back there."

Agent Bender's hand darted to the card, flipping it over as his eyes widened.

"I was curious, obviously, so I visited the page and found

his journals there. I know I should have come forward and shared this sooner. It's just been complicated."

"Hey," Agent Ramirez interjected. "No need to apologize. We appreciate you doing it now. What have you learned so far from reading through it?"

"Well, the first thing is that he was never going to set off the bomb."

Agent Ramirez stiffened, leaned forward in her chair. "Sorry?"

"You'll see when you read it. He wanted to scare people, but really, he wanted to stop his cousin from ever using it. And Xander was…" My voice trailed off for the first time. Tears pin-pricked my eyes. "Xander is? Sorry, I don't know why I said that. I know he's still alive. Barely. Sorry, this is just all so strange."

"It's okay," Agent Bender said with fatherly compassion. I imagined him caring for kids of his own. "Take your time."

He handed me a box of tissues. I grabbed two and jammed them into my eyes sockets as hard as possible, as if I could physically force out the storm of confusion and hesitation rolling through my head.

Through all the phlegm in my throat, I said, "The truth is, Xander has contemplated suicide for almost as long as I've known him. Part of the reason we broke up is that I couldn't stand how much he talked about it—so brazenly sometimes, like he was threatening me with it." I felt my voice rising higher and harsher, approaching the same tone I used with my mom at the hotel earlier.

"That sounds really awful," Agent Ramirez said.

"Yeah, I don't know. I guess maybe I encouraged these thoughts sometimes. Or I sympathized. But I never thought it would come to this. Not in a million years."

Their eyes narrowed. Agent Bender spun the card around between his fingertips, then passed it to her. I thought back to the speculation on Twitter. How helpless I felt from the narratives being formed. Here, though, I had some power. I could put this all to rest. End the speculation. The final push I needed to come forward.

"In one of the journals, he mentions he got the idea from me. But all I told him is that he should turn Lance in for having something so illegal. Nothing about using the vest himself."

As soon as the words left my mouth, I regretted it. They wouldn't believe me. Why make excuses for something I didn't do?

To my surprise, an air of boredom seemed to come over Agent Ramirez. Like she wanted to get home, to her boyfriend or family. She brushed straight past my confession and put her glasses on, rolled in her chair over to her computer. She couldn't have cared less what role I may or may not have played.

"And is this everything?" she said, eyes glancing at me for half a second. "Any more evidence you want to share?"

I watched Agent Ramirez plug the web address into her computer browser. Guilt and regret pulsed through me. Had I betrayed Xander by sharing his journals? I knew how private he'd always been about his writing. He rarely showed me anything that wasn't in pristine, near-finished form. Then again, with him on the verge of dying, what did it matter? A dead person couldn't experience shame, or pride for that matter, in their work.

"It's all there," I said. On my phone, I saw my parents had both called and texted. At the hotel earlier, I'd told my mom I was going to meet up with Remy. They didn't take long to figure out it was a lie. A dumb lie. One call to Joan, or Remy herself, was all it took. Their texts peppered with concern, lots of question marks. I could not think clearly, had not slept for two nights. I should have chosen anyone besides Remy.

"It's going to take us some time to sort through all this," Agent Bender said. Agent Ramirez's eyes remained glued to the screen, scrolling through the pages. "You have somewhere to go, yes?"

My cheeks sizzled, realizing I'd been sitting there using my phone or staring off into space. A nuisance to them and their work.

"Yes," I said, standing and sweeping my bookbag over my shoulder in one motion. Agent Bender stood and reached for the door handle.

"I'll take you back out to the lobby," he said. "You're welcome to hang out there for a bit, to figure out transportation back to Queens."

"Don't worry," I said. "I'm fine."

"Thanks so much again, Holly," Agent Ramirez called out when I turned my back to leave. "You've done the right thing here."

I looked back at her, nodded quickly, then walked through the door. Later on, when I looked back on my decision to come forward, I felt less guilt than a more complicated shame in helping to clear Xander's name, even in the slightest of ways. His journals would come out in the court case against Lance and his crew, many months down the line, with me identified as the one to alert the cops. When I signed an affidavit for the official court record, I'd end up feeling like Xander's puppet, there to do his bidding. This when I've never been so sure he deserved such generous treatment. Not with everything he took from me.

Outside, with a slight spitting drizzle in the air, I looked up the directions to get home. I headed straight to the subway station and sent my parents my ETA. All through the forty-minute trip, I wasn't quite inside my body. I tried to lock into what Agent Ramirez said—*the right thing*—attaching the tiniest bit of relief to my decision, a weight off my shoulders. At least I didn't have to be the only one to carry the burden of keeping his secrets anymore. A certain amount of pride came from reclaiming control, offloading the weight, taking a step forward towards feeling better.

The relief didn't last long. When the conductor announced our train stop in Bayside over the loudspeaker, it meant only one thing: the next step would be to tell my parents.

39

AUDREY

When I think back on why I reacted the way I did over those 48 hours, this is what I come back to: I desperately wanted to believe that Sam still believed in the same magic I did. I wanted him to believe that everything would work out as long as you keep up your faith in the unseen powers of the universe. Sam liked to guess at the features our future children might inherit from us—my darker eyes or his lighter ones, my tan complexion or his fair skin. He liked to identify towns in New York or Connecticut that we might settle into as a family. A small ranch house loomed somewhere. Just enough property for the kids to run around and play catch, for us to bar-b-que on warm summer nights. Such conversations always kept my hope alive, even as I watched, from my front-row seat, the spirit turn dim in him.

Back at Taylor's apartment, once my family finished freaking out over my extended departure, I failed to locate this optimistic part of myself. Sure, I hugged my parents tight, picked at the sushi they ordered, spooned ice cream straight from the pint. But the only thing I can remember doing with any clarity is crying. I cried harder than when Sam told me about what happened at Penn Station; harder than catching him in the lie at Gelb's; harder, even, than when I recounted the blow-by-blow fight for my mom. I went into Taylor's bedroom, shut off all the lights, and swaddled myself with the duvet cover in his bed. Nothing was real anymore. I believed this. I'd wake up from the nightmare soon. This stretch of time where too much was happening at once, where time moved at both warp speed and interminable slowness.

It might have been five or fifty minutes before I heard my dad come in. He pulled a chair by my bedside and stroked my hair, watched me let it all out.

"Sweetie, you're going to come out of this so much stronger and better. I know it. I've already put a call in to Rabbi Milner."

"Dad, come on. Be serious."

"We can go together tomorrow, or not. But I know you've said he's helped before. Like when you fell for that Facebook scam and lost seven hundred dollars?"

"Are you really bringing that up right now!"

"Just something to think about."

I rolled over, turned away from him. Sam's voice wouldn't stop playing in my head. His goofy, high-pitched laugh. I could have easily imagined so many other futures for him. Part of me thought I was doing him a favor by breaking up with him, giving him the space to develop his music or writing. I could've imagined him moving to another city, picking his guitar back up, gigging in tiny dive bars. I could've imagined him earning just enough to make ends meet, an act of defiance towards his parents.

Except now, I was the girlfriend who pushed him to his suicide. And I had no way of processing that other than to cry and sulk and hate myself.

My family took turns coming in to keep me company, ministering to me like a wounded soldier in a military hospital. "You know how selfish this was of him?" Taylor said. Still paralyzed in bed, I curled up between a body pillow and a box of tissues. "Just the most unfair thing to do to you that I could possibly imagine. Not to mention his family and friends."

I couldn't hold his gaze.

"I know you're in shock right now, but I'm saying all this to make you feel better. So you won't blame yourself. Because you've done nothing wrong. You should know that."

I could only push the slightest amount of air out of my chest, muttering a terse *thank you.*

My dad left early in the evening. He drove back up to Westchester to feed the dogs while my mom and I stayed at Taylor's. The two of us huddled together in his full-sized bed to pass the night. Taylor took the couch. I'd be out of school another day, at the very least. The subs had my students send me handwritten 'get better soon' cards. I missed my students, plain and simple. I missed everything about my life before being thrust into the eye of the storm. Already it was bearing an ugly, impulsive side of me—a self-loathing, like what had taken hold of Sam—a side that, frankly, revolted me. How would I face our friends? The other teachers at school? Between the second-guessing of my decision to break up with him, the crying and my mom's snoring in the bed next to me, I don't think my eyes shut for more than a minute at a time that night.

I used to tell Sam, half-jokingly, that we were each other's one true love. But I understood now there was no such thing. Only a fool guided by faulty magic would believe that. Because the magic that once lived inside of me was dead.

40

HOLLY

"You did what?" my dad asked me, his voice rising in both pitch and volume. We were sitting at the kitchen table, the venue of so much hostility throughout my childhood. Night had fallen. My mom stood leaning on the counter opposite my dad, watching us. She looked more amused, if anything, than troubled.

"Why didn't you tell me about this earlier?" he asked before I could respond. "I asked if there was anything else you knew."

"I hadn't even discovered the journals yet," I said.

"It doesn't matter! Don't you understand I could have protected you? Now, it's all going to get completely out of hand."

"Ken, relax," my mom said.

"No!"

When he snapped at her, as he so often did, the veins in his forehead popped a striking purple. He stood, began pacing back and forth over the length of the kitchen.

"Sorry, but I won't do a damn thing until I understand why our seventeen-year-old daughter took it upon herself to go to the cops without our knowledge or permission. Is that so much to ask?"

His mouth slammed shut. My whole face burned. Why did everything always have to be so combative between us?

"I already told you," I said. "It was the right thing to do. And it'll help clear up the story, Xander's name."

"What about *our* name? You ever think about that?" he roared.

A hideous laugh rose from my lungs. "Look at you. You're pathetic. You don't even know what I told them yet!"

He pressed his fingers into the tops of his eye sockets, seeming to exert real force, though the adrenaline must have blunted the impact.

"How about Roy, Joan?" he said, still trying to get through to me. He didn't care to know what the journals said or didn't, what I told the cops or didn't. He only needed to exercise control over a situation that had slipped from his grasp. "Your friends Piper and Remy? What are they going to say about us behind our backs?"

"I don't care what they think."

His head whipped around. "Great, just great. We'll become the laughingstock of Bayside because you had to make a rash decision without consulting us."

He turned to my mom, pleading for support. "You believe this, Sandy? I mean, back me up here. This is ridiculous."

"No," my mom said, and I could feel my head twisting in surprise. "She had every right to share evidence and help the cops paint a clearer picture of what happened."

A surly grin overcame his face. "Perfect." Another pitched, hyena's yowl. "That's not the point, you know that? There were simpler, more private ways to handle it. I—*we*—could have helped her. We could have talked to a lawyer first. But no, god forbid anyone should act with any sense around here."

"I don't see why it's that big of a deal," my mom said.

"Of course you don't! Shocker. The bleeding-heart

Broadway singer is on the side of the terrorist high school kid. Brilliant."

"No one is saying that."

"I'm trying to stay calm, I really am." He stilled to look at me, lowered his voice. "I know you're on the brink of losing someone close to you. I'm just trying to help in the only way I know how."

We watched him backpedal towards the door with his hands up in a defensive posture. "You guys seem to have all the answers. You figure it out on your own."

He stalked out to the front porch, and soon faded from view. Plumes of cigarette smoke wafted over back toward the window. My mom smiled at me, but I wouldn't send her one in return.

"He'll get over it," she said. "I've seen him far worse than this."

I didn't know what to say to that.

"Anyway, it's not about right and wrong. It's about him feeling like he has control."

I stared into my phone, feeling the heat of her eyes on me. After another endless pause, she said, "But I meant what I said. I'm proud of you."

I shrugged. "Thanks. It was nothing."

I stood and went into the living room, collapsing onto the couch with my eyes shut. A minute or two later, I heard the rumble of my dad's truck starting in the driveway. He backed out, drove to who knows where. My mom joined me in the living room. She took the seat on the far side of the couch, began stroking my lower leg.

"Are you familiar with the term disassociation?" she asked quietly.

"Is this a test?"

She looked at me, a small smile drawn across her lips, seeming to recognize my sarcasm as a byproduct of her own. Suddenly, then, the smile vanished.

"I know you think we're the worst parents ever, but your dad had it real rough as a kid. And he coped by dissociating—just completely leaving his body and mind. His rage became a defense mechanism. He told me a few times, during our arguments, that he wished I was dead. Then he couldn't remember any of it afterwards."

My eyes scanned the living room. A bookcase took up the whole wall, its shelves filled with old hockey trophies or costume furnishings. An ancient, maroon-colored encyclopedia, a rusting knight's helmet. Then there were the memories: the night he slammed a dinner plate down on the kitchen table. It shattered into a thousand pieces over the placemat.

"I didn't know that," I said.

"You heard only a fraction of our arguments. We used to go into the car just so you wouldn't hear."

"So, what are you saying? You excuse his behavior?" I spoke too fast, felt too manic. "You're just fine with all of it now?"

"I'm not saying that. I'm saying that if you were in my position, you might understand why I chose to do what I did. You were still so young when we separated. It happened during that time he was between jobs. He snapped at me again for buying something. And I finally had enough. This job offer in San Francisco came along, and I didn't want you to sit around resenting him more than you already did. I figured it would be a chance for him to step up and be there for you."

I saw what she meant. You could argue we'd grown closer, me and my dad. Made it work, in our way. It wasn't like we fought every day. Not even every week. Only when we did, World War III broke out. I didn't like the thought of her plotting this all out in advance, working behind the scenes to fashion her idea of a better life for me, as if I didn't have a say.

"I wish I could do what you did," I said. "Pick up and leave. But I can't. I'm stuck here."

She grabbed my hand. "Come to San Francisco, then."

I shook my head.

"I've been thinking. Who cares about school? Or maybe you finish out your senior year. Then come stay with me."

"If only it was that easy. My whole life is here."

"Just something to consider. There are great colleges on the west coast."

And that was that. I couldn't consider her suggestion. Not yet. A blocked nerve in my brain would not allow me to fathom it. For the next two hours, my mom puttered around the house, taking calls or busying herself with chores. "Dirty or clean?" she said, holding up several items of clothing picked off the floor from my room. She ran two loads of laundry in the machine off the kitchen.

"Joan told me you had a nice dinner with her and the girls the other night," she called out at one point. When I offered little in the way of a response, she went on to talk idly about the man who sat next to her on the flight in from San Francisco, how he wouldn't shut the hell up for almost five hours.

After a while, my dad returned home. He didn't say much, didn't apologize, although he would, in time. Almost instantly, he followed my mom's lead in doing chores around the house—re-potting plants, taking out the trash. Things were calming down, I sensed, maybe even too quickly. The return to stability felt false, unfair. When I went to use the bathroom, I saw how depleted my face looked. So ashen and underwater. How long would I need to process what happened that week? How long would the pain linger in my bones, my joints, my eyes?

A text from Remy on my phone when I returned to the couch: *Heard you saw teddy and conner earlier. You good?*

A bubble of feeling in my chest, tears slipping from my eyes. Somehow, in the firestorm of grief and anger, one person wasn't going back down from the fight. I doubted Remy knew how much that meant. How much it would mean, in the months to follow, to be the one by my side. To stay up late talking about everything, or sometimes nothing, to be that anchor for me.

Thanks for checking in, I texted her back. *Just the boys being typical morons. I'm fine.*

At a certain late hour, my parents and I relented to our hunger, gathered in the kitchen to reheat leftover lasagna and pick at scraps of Joan's cake. Again, my parents knew better than to bring up the journals, police, or Xander. I'd fill them in on all the details, over time, but for now the three of us settled for talking about my after-school schedule the next day. An hour-long session on brushstroke technique with Ms. Duprey, followed by math tutoring.

A sitcom re-run played at a low volume on the small TV. The smell of decaf coffee brewing in the machine. For the first time in days, a normal type of quiet in the air.

41

AUDREY

I woke to the enticing smell of coffee. My mom and brother's hushed voices drifted in from the kitchen—another enticing prospect, on any other day, there to gossip about family and friends and celebrities. But I couldn't get out of bed. A fresh bout of surges through my chest, a rash of tears down my cheeks. My chest flapped with the feral energy of a caged animal inside. The pain was unbearable. My head knotted in places I hadn't known about before. Eyes so irritated and tight.

On my phone, I scanned Twitter. Some new reporting popped up: The city's chief of police held a short press conference where he admitted to the security failures and said they were investing money into tightening them. He expressed his gratitude that there were no fatalities. I remembered how the FBI agents who visited our apartment warned me against following the late-breaking developments so closely, as they often turned out to be unreliable. But the news seemed to give me some task to focus on, some grounding in an otherwise toppled world.

The reports reminded me of this recurring nightmare I'd had been having. I spoke about it with my therapist often—

FOIL

being behind the wheel of a speeding car with a broken brake pedal. Some nights, I'd wake my foot jamming against the footboard of my bed, attempting to press the brake pedal. Now, of course, I wouldn't ever wake up. I had command of the wheel, but none of the tact or knowledge needed to slow the car down.

I came out of the bedroom with my hair in a wild tangle, wiping crust from my eyes like a little girl. They looked at me with far too much pity. I saw Taylor scrambling for the remote to the TV, which was playing the local news. He quickly hit the power button, and the screen went black.

"Should we go for a walk?" my mom asked. She poured coffee into a mug and placed it in front of me. "Sitting inside and sulking all day can't do you any good."

"I don't know," I said, unable to remember another time in my life when I didn't even want coffee. In theory, at some point, I'd return to the apartment for some peace and quiet. And yet along with everything else Sam took from me was the ability to be alone there without worrying about seeing his ghost.

"C'mon," my mom said, stroking my hair, untangling some of the knots. "Just ten minutes, then we can come straight back."

I took a meager sip of coffee, nodded. The temperature had dropped overnight, so we bundled up in random winter coats from the closet. Even though it was overcast, I wore my sunglasses in the inevitable event that I burst straight into tears the moment we hit the street. The cool air soothed me, though, when we left Taylor's building and headed south toward Union Square. Fresh air in my lungs, the self-propelling force of putting one foot in front of another. My mom was right, of course she was. From that day forward, she came into the city every Monday night to stay with me, bearing a bouquet from her garden or the bodega on the corner. Without instructions, my mom knew what I needed wasn't my dad's sermonizing, or suggestions about which specialist to see next, but a shoulder to bury my head in. A soft-spoken voice cooing sweetly in my ear. A hand tickling my back.

At Union Square, we slipped between the street vendors and musicians and skateboarders, reminders of the city's epic, undying churn. We didn't speak much, not about anything significant. We walked further south for another five minutes, then another ten. We reached Washington Square Park. The famous archway blended into the light gray sky, keeping watch over the buzz of activity in the park below. Taylor led us to a favorite coffee shop on the perimeter of the park, where we picked out some pastries—a chocolate-almond croissant, a mango and walnut scone, a coffee each, whole milk and simple syrup. My appetite kicked up for the first time all day. I noticed the relief in my stomach as my phone vibrated with an incoming call. An unknown number showed on the screen, and maybe because I finally felt the slightest bit better, I picked up.

"Hello?" I said, catching my mom and brother popping their heads up to look at me.

"Hi, is this Audrey Brandeis?" said a man's voice on the other end. The coffee shop seemed so cramped and loud. I darted out the door. My mom and Taylor trailed behind.

"Yes, who is this?"

"This is Michael Davenport, *New York Post*. I know how hard this must be for you, but I'm calling to see if you would like to provide any comment?"

"Comment? On what?"

"Sam."

"What? How'd you get this number?"

"I know," he said sheepishly, as if he hated himself as much I did in that moment. "So does that mean no comment?"

My chest constricted. "Yes, why the hell would I want to comment?"

"Sometimes people want to honor a person's memory that way. You know, shape the narrative."

I shook my head back and forth in disbelief, watching as Taylor and my mom looked on with equal horror. "No comment and please never call this number again."

When I hung up, Taylor said, "The balls on these people! Unbelievable."

The call sunk me straight back into the pits of my despair. My mood shattered. I took a few steps back in the direction of Taylor's apartment, but my legs felt so heavy. Tears rushed down my face. I stumbled forward, and my mom cradled me in her arms. Taylor hailed a cab.

How unfair that this was the person I had to be now—this victim, wearing the stench of what Sam took from me. I was always the strong one in our relationship. Always there for Sam to lean on, to fend off his drawn-out anguish. Now I couldn't imagine being strong for anyone, ever, much less myself.

Taylor's bed felt like the only peaceful space I had left. I'd regroup, take as much time as I needed. And yet when I finally collapsed onto the mattress, my whole body tensed. The muscles in my lower back were being stabbed. My body in a state of frantic paralysis. I knew I needed to stretch, foam-roll, walk. But the effort required seemed huge, so far away from being attainable.

My mom left a bowl of popcorn and blue Gatorade on the nightstand. Every few minutes, I'd place a single kernel on my tongue. I'd let the salt seep into my taste buds, the texture moisten and wilt before dissolving completely. Beyond these tiny morsels of sustenance, there was no real hunger, just an empty mass where my stomach should be. I'd never been so robbed of my appetite before. Every night in our apartment, when the clock struck 9 pm, I'd cave to the urge to snack on anything we kept around. Potato chips, lightly salted cashews, semi-sweet chocolate chips. *Bottomless pit hour*, I'd call it.

Now I couldn't even muster an appetite. I would have preferred the heaviest food binge to this emptiness.

Holed up in Taylor's bedroom, I found myself drawn to watching documentaries that featured people facing far worse circumstances than I did. Kids born with brain defects, overcoming the odds by participating in organized sports. Human trafficking victims. These other horrific stories summoned within me the mildest appreciation for the privilege of basic shelter, food, clean water, air.

The next morning, during one of my now-routine Twitter checks, I saw the reason he'd called the day before.

@MichaelDavenport
BREAKING: Sam Reid, the man who stopped the #PennStationBombing suspect earlier this week, endured a fatal fall from the roof of his Upper East Side apartment building yesterday. It's still not clear what precipitated this tragic new development, but sources close to the matter confirm that Reid had been heavily impaired at the time. Family and close friends are mourning Reid's loss in private. 1/2
7:49 AM - Oct 25, 2018

"We're heartbroken and in complete shock," said Beth Reid, Sam's mother. "We can't imagine how this could have happened, but hope that everyone can respect our privacy during this extremely difficult time." Read my latest: bit.ly/qyt2r 2/2
7:50 AM - Oct 25, 2018

I wish I could say this made me shudder and cry, like almost everything else did. But my mind raced to the one person I knew this impacted more than anyone else. I didn't think before I picked up the phone to call.

"Audrey, hi. How are you doing?" Gelb answered. His voice sounded thin behind the typical rasp. "I've texted and everything."

"Did you get a call from any reporters yesterday?" I asked him.

"What?"

"I can explain in a second. But for right now I just need to know if a reporter called you."

"Yes. That Davenport guy."

So there it was, I thought: the final piece that would do me in for good. I'd never recover from Gelb telling him about our breakup. I'd be smeared, vilified. The girl who pushed the #PennStationHero to his death.

"And?" I asked, my voice and hands shaking. "What'd you tell him?"

"Nothing," he said. "I'm not dumb. I wouldn't say anything about your breakup at a time like this."

"Okay," I said, not sure if I should believe him, if I understood what it all meant yet.

"Why? What's going on? Are you sure you're okay?"

That's when it hit me. Sam's mom. If she gave the reporter a quote, she must have been the one to tell him about the drugs. Relief washed over me, even as I began to grasp the implications. By blaming the drugs instead of our breakup, Beth had spared me the blame. She laid the blame at Gelb's feet instead.

"Did you see what Michael Davenport tweeted this morning?" I asked.

He stuttered a few times. "Amy made me delete Twitter from my phone."

"Take a look. And then you might want to talk to Sam's family. I'm so sorry it had to come to this."

He babbled some apologetic-sounding sentences. Once we

hung up, I returned to scrolling that god-forsaken app. A growing number of retweets and comments had accumulated on the post, just in the few minutes we spoke on the phone. A spark that ended up elevating the story from local news oddity to national sensation.

Tight coordination ensued. Sam's family and Gelb and me all reading from the same script in response to reporters' questions: Sam's death stemmed from some youthful partying gone awry. He'd been drinking and taking drugs with friends, then slipped off the roof when he got home. An accident, we all said. A mistake confirmed by the police's toxicology report. Even if no one quite bought it.

A theory soon took off, suggesting Sam and Xander knew each other beforehand. Sam had helped the kid get into Penn Station undetected, these whackos claimed. Did I want to comment? Next, a conspiracy-minded political commentator whom I'd never heard of claimed that we spoke. He said I agreed with his take that this was all a stunt designed to propagate liberal lies and come after people's guns. Did I want to comment?

This was an abridged list of the bullshit I dealt with in the week that followed. I didn't comment when asked, but here's what I would have said if I did: Sam and Xander had nothing to do with each other. Sam got lucky by spotting the bomb, then unleashed on Xander in self-defense.

I tried to stay off Twitter. But I was powerless. I read the hate spewed about me, Sam, Xander. In a way, it distracted from the larger unfathomable loss of Sam. Social media, my new drug of choice. This until my therapist made me delete the apps from my phone, like Gelb had.

Somewhere in the haze of my doom-scrolling, I came across the news that answered some of the remaining questions about Xander's intent that morning.

New Evidence in Penn Station Bombing Case Leads to More Arrests, the headline read. Underneath were mug shots of three terrifying-looking men, alongside the subtitle: *Police trace bombing materials back to far-right group leaders, complicating the motive of suspect Xander Shine.*

I needed to wipe my eyes to make sure I'd read right. The article explained how the police received evidence that Xander had never intended to detonate the bomb inside Penn Station. He merely sought to take his own life in a shocking display that simultaneously thwarted the plans of some paramilitary, neo-fascist group that Xander's cousin Lance had joined. The group had planned to travel to Washington, D.C. in anticipation of political conflict surrounding the upcoming elections. Xander's cousin, Lance, intended to use the suicide vest at one point. Or not. When push came to shove, a person would be hard-pressed to follow through with something like that. Either way, Xander had only planned to create a small fire inside the station before turning the gun on himself. By intervening, Sam had done Xander the most sick and twisted favor imaginable: He granted Xander his wish to depart the world.

"We were grateful to receive some new evidence that spells out the facts in a very clear manner," Agent Ramirez said in the article. "In my nine years on the force, this is one of the stranger cases I've worked on. But we can now be certain that these arrests may in fact prevent politically motivated violence in the future, which is what we in law enforcement set out to do every day."

I scanned the mug shots of Lance and his accomplices, Mike Detrick and Ian Hart. Scruffy beards and tattoos covering their beefy necks. You could practically smell the cigarettes and whiskey on them. Something about Lance's eyes struck me as wistful, sad even. He had boyish plump cheeks under his wide awe-struck eyes, giving the impression of being in over his head. A brainwashed pawn to a larger plot. The suicide vest that belonged to him some depraved attempt to prove himself.

AUDREY

I tried to make my mind fit around the facts: How could Xander, a high-school student, have deceived these terrifying, military-trained men? How could he have pulled off something so complicated and dangerous, so batshit crazy? The only way I could make sense of it was to draw the connection to Sam. Look at Xander with his morbid intent, Lance with his forlornness. Look how far all these broken young men were willing to go to carry out their suicides. It wasn't like Sam and Xander's struggles were that much worse than anyone else's. They felt similar forms of disillusionment, but also had it far better than many. So why did they act?

I settled on some explosive combination of genetics, brain wiring, and home life. In Sam's case, the drugs acted as the spark to the tinderbox set down by our breakup. Much later, I read how there were many more suicides than homicides in the United States every year, despite the wide disparity in media attention. *Silent killer* was a recurring phrase used to describe the epidemic of self-loathing people experienced. But what about those of us left in their wake? Those of us left behind to grieve and attempt to rationalize what could never quite be understood. The people who killed themselves were off the hook, in many ways, saddling others with a weight they could no longer bear.

I never told my mom or brother about my rash decision to take that bus ride out to Bayside. I'd never tell anyone, ever. But I knew Holly must have been going through the same pain as me, if not far worse. And her, I *could* tell. She'd understand. I saw in her, so plainly, the victimhood she experienced through no fault of her own. All these repressed, sad little boys.

An ache resided in the most sacred layer of my core, screaming out to me to find her. Not that I believed I could. Or that I'd ever work up the courage to try.

42

HOLLY

I sat at the kitchen table, an array of pink and white and green flash cards spread out in front of me. There was a test the next day. Even as my entire world exploded, there were still tests, after-school clubs, assemblies, school plays. I stared at the card that said *Bromine*, tried to remember what I'd written on the other side. A minute of brain static came, the words locked behind a gate I couldn't open. I surrendered. Flipped the card over to read the number and type. *35, Halogen.*

From the other room, my dad let out a guttural noise in response to the show on TV. He had the day off from work. I took a disinterested bite of toast, applied more butter to the next one.

To concentrate, I'd left my phone on the counter, giving off its own gravitational pull on my attention span. Several days had passed without word on Xander's condition. I tried to maintain my distance, at least during the daytime, when I had obligations like school to keep me busy. My therapist told me to stay off social media, an instruction I largely followed. Lying in bed at night, though, I'd picture the possibility of speaking with him again. *What the hell were you thinking, dude?* I'd hear entire conversations, even arguments, between us in my head. But the more I let my imagination wander, the worse the pain seemed to get, like a bruise I knew I shouldn't touch. But couldn't help myself from poking at.

My dad came back to the kitchen to refill his cup of Coke Zero. I was over-alert to every sound—the ice clanking inside the freezer, the fizz of the soda.

"Have you seen my keys?" my dad asked, somewhat absently.

"I think they're on the hook by the door?"

"No. Not those. I need to stop by the office tomorrow and I can't find that little plastic thing that gets me in."

He rummaged through the drawers underneath the kitchen counter.

"Fob," I said. "That's what you mean."

"Sure. Have you seen it?"

I shrugged. He stopped pacing and looked at me for a hard second, then moved to open a window on the far side of the table.

"It's warm in here, isn't it?"

"I don't know. I'm fine."

"How's the studying coming along?"

I shrugged again, pulled my hands into the sleeves of my sweatshirt.

"What's on your mind?" he asked.

Did he really want to know? Or did he simply think this was what a good, interested father should do? It's not like I was going to spill my guts out to him, right then and there: On my mind was that my best friend was probably dead. People were writing a million hurtful things about him on social media. And ever since that Sam Reid guy died, the volume rose to eleven. New facts and quotes seemed to trickle out every minute—likely growing in the hour since I'd been without my phone. And I was just supposed to sit there, pretending like everything was normal.

"It's just hard to concentrate right now," I said.

"Want me to see if I can get you an extension?"

"No," I said. The thought of inviting more attention repulsed me. "It's fine, I just have another half hour to do. I'll be okay."

He nodded, stood, told me he'd leave me to it. I knew he was taking extra care to protect me, keep me safe inside my cocoon. Still, I couldn't quite accept his protection. At least not yet.

Suddenly, the flashcards didn't seem so impossible anymore. I managed to make one of two of the elements stick, followed by several more, even if I knew this information would leave my brain as soon as I handed in the test. I felt like I'd finally settled into a groove, in fact, when I heard a knock ring out from the front door.

I thought little of it. There were lots of knocks on our door happening that week. Nosy reporters hung around as the story took on greater and greater significance. We discovered how to ignore them, shoo them away. My mom was still coming and going from the hotel to the house, bearing groceries or coffee and donuts. Joan and Remy would swing by to check in on us at least once a day.

So when I heard my dad scoff in response to the knock, get up from the couch to open the door, I was more annoyed than anything. *Who now?* I thought over the interruption to the little pocket of concentration I'd found. I eavesdropped with only the mildest interest.

But then I heard her name come out of my dad's mouth.

"Lisa. Lisa, right?"

A thunderclap through my chest. I dropped the mechanical pencil in my hand, pushed back from my chair, rushed to the foyer. There, my eyes met Lisa's. I saw it in her sallow cheeks. Her gleaming red eyes that had experienced three days of pure hell.

"He has some peace now," Lisa said, her voice a crackling

whisper. She walked over to me with her arms outstretched. Tears exploded from my eyes. A thick, coiled rocking in my chest. I fell into her arms.

I pulled back to see her face, so twisted and beaten down I could barely stand to look. Standing in the foyer, just the three of us, a strange question entered my head: Had she and my dad ever met? We'd only hung out at Xander's house, me and Xander. But they must have known of each other in the distant gossipy way that parents of kids in the same grade all did: the basic details of where one another lived and worked, peppered with the occasional rumor, like when Xander's dad crashed his car into the divider on Northern Boulevard after a night out drinking.

The look on his face was one I'd never seen before, a pity so deep it bordered on disgust. He seemed to grasp the gravity of what losing a child meant. I derived a certain comfort from that unspoken recognition.

"I came straight here from the hospital," Lisa said. "You were the first person I wanted to tell in person. He loved you so much, Holly."

I moved my hand to cover my mouth. It felt odd, at first, like being forced to the center of a stage knowing none of the lines. But then I understood. She knew how much it would mean to me to be one of the first to know. Me and my fragile teenage sensibilities. What kinds of things had Xander told her about me? To that point, I'd been so fixated on how he influenced me, I never considered how I may have influenced him. But Lisa must've seen how I lifted him, kept him out of trouble, as much as possible.

"I'm so, so sorry," my dad said as I pulled back from Lisa's embrace. He put his arm around me. I couldn't believe how far we'd come. He didn't know of Xander's existence less than a week ago. Now he was the one to console me over his loss.

Lisa explained how Xander had lost so much cognitive and physical function, she had no choice but to pull the plug.

By ending his suffering, she could start on the hard work of healing her own.

"I'm here for you," she said. "We have each other now."

She looked at my dad, nodding.

"You're going to be so strong, I know it."

My dad offered her water, tea, the chance to sit down at the kitchen table and talk more. But she had other stops to make, people to inform, logistics to sort out. She looked out the window towards her car, parked at a haphazard slant in the driveway.

"Paige is waiting for me in the car," she said. Through the window, I thought I could make out another figure sitting in the passenger seat: Russell, Xander's dad. Despite all he'd put them through, it made some sense that they came together as a family, now, if only in self-defense with the whole world lined up against them. "We're holding a small funeral tomorrow. No pressure at all to come, but I wanted you to know."

She took me by the hand. She looked as if she wanted to say something more, but couldn't find the words. For the first time, I noticed her clothing. She wore a dark green corduroy collared shirt over a simple white T-shirt—ever the part of the professor at a big urban university. This stood out in my recollection. She looked cool even when she wasn't trying, even if these clothes were the last thing on her mind getting dressed that morning.

43

AUDREY

Sam's funeral took place on a Monday. Joined by my dad, and encouraged by my therapist, who said the closure might do me some good, I agreed to attend the burial portion of the ceremony. Thirty or forty of us gathered at the cemetery on Long Island, where the wind cut through the hoarse, Hebrew words of the rabbi. He honored Sam and his love for his family, friends, and music. He didn't utter a word about the Penn Station incident the previous week, and this felt right. Sam's suicide all but negated any heroics he may have displayed. A high-wire act that culminated in too much pressure, too quickly, where Sam lost his footing.

From the outside of the semi-circle around his grave, with Gelb and Amy and my dad by my side, I noticed the expressions on people's faces—ranging from shock to disbelief to mild disinterest. I wondered how Sam might feel to see his closest friends and family gathered here to mourn and memorialize him. He may have relished the spotlight in his flair for the dramatic. But the more I thought about it, the more I saw how disappointed he would have been. The ceremony was so short and spare, so frequently disturbed by the wind, that it never seemed quite real. The only ones displaying much emotion were Sam's mom and aunts, making quite a big show of it. The intensity of their sobs and wails seemed to cheapen everyone else's emotions by comparison.

Guardedly, I tried to read between the lines of Sam's dad's stoicism. He laid an arm over his wife's shoulder, occasionally shook his head back and forth. I knew Sam feared his dad, but I didn't learn the extent of their fighting until Sam's mom told me after our breakup—the brick that Sam put through the window of his car, the ensuing months of silence between them. Of all the secrets Sam kept from me, this one hurt most sometimes, given how open we were with each other about our families. But I could understand his withholding. Sam carried deep shame over his dad. Len never gave up on trying to shape Sam, when what his son really needed was the opposite—recognition that they were different people. They may never have agreed on Sam's career direction.

"It's tradition in the Jewish religion for the mourners to take part in the burial process," the rabbi said in his practiced avuncular tone. He gestured to the shovel standing upright in a pile of dark brown soil. "So we first invite the next of kin to pour soil over the casket, to signify the shared nature of the task and our binding together on earth."

Sam's dad stepped forward, using the back of the shovel to scoop a small portion of dirt and drop it down. A harsh crackling rang out over the wood. I looked at my dad. "The back of the shovel is very old-world," he whispered. "It's supposed to signify reluctance."

Sam's mom stepped up next, followed by his cousins and uncles. They approached the grave and heaved rocky dirt down on the casket, clattering so loudly I feared the wood might break. The rabbi continued to gesture and invite others to join in this surreal, haunting ritual that I'd never do myself. I could hardly watch from a distance. Sam's mom covered her mouth to hide the wails that came out of her. When I approached her after the ceremony concluded, I hugged her out of our shared cultural fluency, if not forgiveness for what she said to me the week before. "Thank you for coming," she whispered in my ear. I said nothing in return, but she didn't notice or mind, her eyes boiling red as we pulled away. Meanwhile, Sam's dad walked right past us.

Once we reached our car, Amy informed me that Gelb would soon enroll in a rehab program in Pennsylvania. Amy delivered him an ultimatum: no sobriety, no wedding.

"If I spend another eight years like I have the last eight," Gelb said, his eyes huge and clear, shoulders stooped, "I'm simply not going to make it out alive."

Gelb's legendary appetites had finally caught up with him to bear out the worst fate imaginable—the death of a close friend. Maybe it shouldn't have taken something so severe, but the thought of Gelb entering a rehab facility for 30 days comforted me, if only because it might ease his guilt. He looked so torn up and lost, as Amy filled in the remaining details—arrangements to drop him off the following week, visitations every other weekend—I wanted to reach out my arms to hug him. He merely listened and nodded along, though, uncharacteristically quiet.

"Seems like we'll have lots of ladies' nights coming up," Amy said behind a tight smile, trying to lighten the mood. "Please, come over any time."

I would end up spending a fair amount of the following month at Amy and Gelb's apartment, partially to provide each other with the company we desperately needed. But also, as a more symbolic way to paper over the tracks Sam left behind. Maybe my bitterness wouldn't allow his memory to tarnish what was rightfully mine, including our apartment I kept for the two months it took to find a subletter. A period where I slept at Taylor's or my parents' most nights, unable to suffer the emptiness of our bed alone. But each time I walked into the lobby of Gelb and Amy's building—for game nights with friends, a Saturday morning bagel—another piece of our breakup seemed to wash away. Not that it didn't hurt still. There in plain sight were the potted plants, the Renaissance artwork, the gilded furnishings that surrounded our last, spiteful few words.

But this I want to emphasize more than anything: Things have gotten really good for me over the past year. I don't have any explanation other than to say I feel like can breathe again. Living alone, I've started studying for my secondary degree in education administration—a process I'm not sure I would have had the space or confidence to undertake with Sam. I've spent hours with my therapist unpacking how liberated I feel from the worry of nipping and tucking away at some faraway future. Some life Sam and I never could have attained together.

It's still hard for me to believe I ever bought into our fundamental premise: When one little job offer came through for him, we'd be well on our way to the life we always imagined together. Apartment, engagement, marriage, kids. Under the influence of hope, I recognize, it's easy to fall into a pattern of denial. I should have confronted him much sooner about the late nights he came in from work, starry-eyed and chatty, fueled by his happy mix of benzos and alcohol. I should have pushed him harder, sooner, into therapy. By the time he seemed ready—backed into a corner that week, lip service as much as anything—it was too late to make a difference.

Sometimes, passing someone on the street, I'll mistake them for Sam. Full pink lips, wispy red-and-brown beard. I almost like seeing how wild I can let the delusion run, to where I can even hear his voice, pleading with me. *We'll be so good*, he says. *We'll celebrate by booking a weekend trip to Chicago. Then we'll start looking for new apartments together.*

And yet there was always time to turn back. With our whole existence orbited around his self-pity, any challenges I faced were little more than cute: students acting out in class, a mountain of secondary education applications. Even when I knew better, I learned how to hide or suppress my problems. They couldn't hold a candle to the monumental sadness he felt when he received another rejection, or faced his father's wrath. A key reason for therapy, I thought, but what I never could have accounted for was his turn towards violence. The rage he unleashed with his golf-club heroics and in the aftermath. His turn towards self-harm.

Sam consumed the entirety of my attention, and then some, for years. With him out of the picture, I now have the space I need to concentrate on my career, my students and even my brother, still battling his own demons. We hang out every Sunday night at my apartment, where we watch reality TV, laugh at dumb internet memes, and share what's going on in our lives. I've told Taylor about the excitement I feel over the prospect of seeing other guys. A little thrill rises in my chest each time, waiting for someone new to text me back.

The other night, Gelb and Amy joined us for pizza and a movie. I couldn't help but get sentimental from the banter Gelb and my brother exchanged, feeling the conspicuousness of Sam's absence more than I'd like to admit. But it was nice to see the beginnings of something different and new forming. Some strange, unspoken comfort in observing each other's distinct relationship to the trauma we all faced together. For Amy, this meant looking ahead, indulging me in every detail of their wedding coming up that summer. I enjoyed seeing her so energized. Gelb, on the other hand, was more reflective. He still seemed hung up on trying to rationalize it all. A goal he tried, at one point, to drag me into by cornering me in the kitchen.

"I thought you might like to know I'm beating myself up less and less over what happened that day," he said, just the two of us alone in the kitchen, refilling our water glasses.

"That's good to hear," I said, breathing through the discomfort. His green eyes shone bright and clear. He'd put on some weight, and didn't limit his intake that night, but I thought that food was a better, easier habit for him to confront next. His habit of springing uncomfortable topics on you clearly wasn't going anywhere anytime soon.

"I regret the drugs and alcohol obviously, thinking that would be any of type of solution," Gelb went on, piling M&Ms into his hands. "But the deeper shit is the fact that we couldn't speak to each other like adults, you know? Sometimes I think if we just sat down and talked and allowed ourselves to feel uncomfortable with the sadness, maybe none of this would have happened."

I nodded as if I agreed. "Yeah. Maybe."

"What Sam did was the easy way out," he said. I looked down, not knowing what to say. "Sorry, I don't mean to get into a whole thing. I just think that Sam didn't want to put in the work. I'll leave it at that."

He left the kitchen to join the others in the living room area, and no one spoke about Sam or anything so serious for the rest of the night. But the more I thought about what Gelb said afterward, the more I wished I would have pushed back. It sounded like a convenient way for him to punch down at Sam. To show me he'd *put in the work* that Sam never could have. But Gelb missed the muddier and more basic truth of the matter: In the 48 hours before he left his entire circle of family and friends behind, Sam committed an act of real heroism. He sought to do good in that moment. He simply had no internal foundation to fall back on in the wake of such a sudden high. He lacked the coping skills to handle the ramifications of his own actions, the heroism and the lying and the drugs. It's for this reason that I can never view Sam or Xander as hero or villain alone. Look at that yellow lighter Xander carried. He brought it to create a small fire and stop another, bigger conflict from happening the following week. That doesn't redeem his actions. It's only what makes him more like Sam than not. They were both human, both capable of applying the worst of themselves to their otherwise noble deeds.

This is what the media and everyone else get wrong all the time: Suicide isn't wrong because it's the easy way out of your problems. It's wrong because it's an act of violence. Not only against yourself but against everyone you know, leaving them the most damaged of all.

———

After two weeks of staying at Taylor's, I decided I needed to return to our apartment. Enough time had passed. Enough idling.

My mom joined me. When we opened the door, the smell was what got me first. Traces of his oaky scent still lingering. Tears fell from my eyes. Every corner bore another reminder —the books Sam collected on the shelves beneath our TV, the photos of us together, the concert posters of the bands he loved. A Knicks beer koozie left out on the ottoman. His guitar remained in its stand in a corner beside the couch, the deep blue of the body glowing, alive. A flock of riffs played in my head, the soundtrack to our better days and nights. Some days, I'd come out of the bedroom to see Sam hunched over his computer, big headphones wrapped over his head, a web of gear spread out on the desk. Sam's uncle Ray had passed the guitar down to him years earlier, and I remembered how hard the loss of his uncle hit Sam at the time. Ray was a successful working musician, a studio session guitarist with a few writing credits to his name. He mentored Sam through musical aspirations of his own, encouraging his constant practice and recording. When Ray passed, though, Sam's hopes of succeeding as a musician seemed to die with him.

I took the guitar in my hands, always heavier than expected, and wiped away some dust that had collected along the neck. From behind the couch, I fished out its soft black travel case, clumped and covered in even more dust. I strummed the strings once, producing a broken out-of-key sound. A sound that seemed to tell the whole story, reverberating in my head for minutes afterward.

I placed the guitar back in its case, which gave me the strength I needed to pack other items, too. Soon I settled into a weekend-morning-like tidying rhythm, treating it almost like a game I knew I could win. I packed up his every pair of underwear, sock, work folder, guitar pick, hat. I feared any items left out would take on a new life of their own, like ancient tombs left open, haunting me and everyone forever.

"Oh, no," I heard my mom cry out, accompanied by a popping in my ears. I came out of the bedroom to see her standing over the open duffel bag full of his ski boots, helmet, jacket. Her face was puffy and red, the sight of her crying so shocking and rare that it caused my breath to catch. "His ski clothes."

I walked over and embraced her, letting her cry into my shoulder for a change. Was this the first time she cried after we learned of Sam's death? I couldn't quite remember, or maybe I didn't want to. She was always so willing to sacrifice her emotions for ours that I couldn't help but find it endearing, almost. A reminder of our ski trips had finally drawn out the submerged grief in her. The thing she cared about the most in this world.

"Did you say Sam's mom was coming by?" my mom said through some dying sniffles. She pulled back from me, grabbed and unfurled a garbage bag. Just as suddenly as she burst into tears, she swung back to the job we came here to finish. She couldn't allow herself to dwell too long in the realm of *feelings*. Not when there was so much still to do.

"We've been texting," I said. "She said she might stop by, but I don't think she can bring herself to do it yet."

She nodded, turned her attention back to the piles of clothes and other ephemera. She must have been as happy as

I was to have a task laid out before us, each bit serving as a perverse sign of progress. We folded more shirts and pants, stacked everything up inside of garbage bags. We didn't quite finish the job, but took pride in the small step we made toward putting Sam's memory behind me.

More partially productive days like this passed in a haze of grief, confusion, guilt. I still couldn't sleep much. I stayed at Taylor's apartment each night but forced myself to visit the apartment at least once a day, to prove that I wouldn't hide from the challenge. In the meantime, some of Sam's family members reached out to express condolences and comforting memories of him. The conversations helped more than I would have expected. They honored Sam for his sarcasm and quirks. I'd take any moment of lightheartedness over the near-total amount of time I spent grappling with his darker side. The one I had not fully understood.

Somewhere within that foggy span of days, I received a call from Beth, Sam's mom. She hoped to meet in person.

"I want to say sorry for my rash response that day on the phone," she said. "I'm hoping we can clear the air." I thought back to the hideous moment when she called me a bitch—suggesting, in fact, that Sam's dad Len had been the one to first invoke the word. Beth and her husband, always such perfect stereotypes. They always needed to find someone else to blame, didn't they? Even if that meant pouring acid into the wounds of the only other person who cared. They couldn't imagine a world in which an apology wouldn't be good enough. They apologized only so that they could move forward and pretend it all never happened. But an apology couldn't erase the pain they caused me. The years of pain they caused Sam.

"It's fine," I told her over the phone anyway, knowing I'd never get through to her. "Heat of the moment and all that."

A few days later, we met at the apartment, where she came to collect the bags of clothes and boxes. Her face looked thin, eyes pink and rheumy, concealed by thick layers of makeup. I thought I could smell traces of cigarette smoke behind her perfume. I rarely saw her without a full face of makeup or blown-out hair, bleached-blonde and swept into a neat row of bangs. She sat across from me at the kitchen table, the place where Sam and I had shared so many meals, laughs, frustrations. Even with almost all trace of him gone, his memory still seemed to lurk in the foreign quietness of the room.

"The most important thing for you to know is that it's not your fault," she said, her voice shot through with cracks of devastation. "I know Sam always loved you, Audrey. And I know you tried to help him when no one else could."

Tears battered my eyes, impossible to avoid now. Beth reached across the table, her hand trembling as she took mine. In that moment, I recognized her strength, oddly enough. I clung to the bravery it must have taken to come see me face-to-face. To try, in the only way she knew how, to mend the wounds between us.

"There was nothing any of us could have done," she said.

"Maybe," I said, reaching for the box of tissues to dry my eyes.

"Sam struggled more than any of us really knew, and he made choices that were beyond our control."

"Len," I said, the mention of her husband's name piercing through the air. Her hand retracted from mine. "Why did he always have to put so much pressure on Sam to be something he wasn't? Why couldn't he just leave him alone? Why isn't he here right now?"

My ears smoldered from the inside out. Lava spewed from my brain. She grimaced, clicked her long nails.

"I may not always agree with Len's methods," she said. "But he was trying to help Sam, help *you*. We only wanted a better life and future for you guys and your potential family. There was nothing wrong with trying to persuade Sam to earn a degree. But I recognize he took it too far—and that's the part we regret."

I wouldn't suppress the truth, now that we'd come this far. "But it wasn't like Sam was ever unemployed, or all that needy. Sure, you guys helped with some payments here and there. My parents do the same—and they don't hold it over me. I just think, that's the part that *was* in your control."

"I hear you, Audrey, okay?" she snapped. "We weren't good parents. You don't need to belabor the point."

"That's not," I said, but caught myself. Because, what was there to say anymore? I recognized this quality of hers, one Sam and I had talked about often: her self-victimization. It wasn't just Sam's troubles that ran deep, like she had suggested. It was hers and her husband's. The troubles that began with their own parents and grandparents stretched back many generations.

We stuck to softer, more practical matters from then on. The subletting of the apartment, for instance, which my dad was managing. We even shared some mutual disbelief over all the crazy things people were saying and writing on social media, scoffing over how quickly it had snowballed.

After a while, we returned to the primary task at hand. We hefted black garbage bags full of Sam's belongings down to the lobby, packed up her car. Our steely, work-like approach felt like a mending of fences, in its own way, a necessary step to healing. A type of closure and foundation at once: the logistical sorting out of all of Sam's worldly belongings returned to his family of origin.

That foundation served me in a sense, too. Later that day, I met with my therapist who encouraged me to form a daily exercise plan. I'd wake up with the sunrise every day to work out: jogs through the early-morning Manhattan streets, even in the bitter cold. I'd dodge young mothers pushing babies in strollers, deliverymen wheeling hand trucks. The simple act of breaking a sweat, every day, could be so powerful. The tiniest hit of adrenaline first thing in the morning. Not that there still wouldn't be moments, doubts, sleepless nights. But I meant what I said about not succumbing to the same despair that took hold of Sam.

I've never once failed to drag myself out of bed in the morning to work out. I've found the strength to run, take a yoga class, a short online arms-strengthening class. I've seen firsthand the dangers of relenting to the tricks your mind plays on you when you lose control. I watched Sam enter that steep and rocky and roped-off terrain, and I've determined I'll never trespass there.

44

HOLLY

They left empty Snickers wrappers in my locker. Ash trays emptied on the doorstep of my dad's house. Notes online calling me a cunt and whore and fat bitch. *I wanna stab you to death and play around with your blood.* All because I ever had the nerve to feel romantic love for someone as outcast as Xander.

Could I blame them? Maybe only partly. How would you react to a classmate threatening your life? The grief Xander's mom Lisa must have received—the hate mail and cold shoulders from full-grown adults who were supposed to know better—felt like a worse violation, grosser and eviler for its forethought.

Everyone knew Conner was behind the tweets. But as always, the school couldn't do much. Not without opening an official police investigation, subpoenas, affidavits. By the time anyone could begin prying, the Twitter eggs had gone dark. Conner and his crew knew how to test the limits. They didn't mind being called into the principal's office every few weeks to answer questions. Deny, deny, deny.

A few months later, Hal discovered that Teddy—his closest friend—had set up his own Twitter egg to join the festivities.

One post implicated Hal himself, suggesting that he'd aided Xander in his plan to escape the field trip that morning. Hal broke ties with Teddy in the end, but that didn't mean Teddy lost friends overall. He'd earned a different set of friends with his posts: Conner and Drew. Xander turned out to unite kids who never would've spoken otherwise. But Xander couldn't defend himself against their attacks anymore, so the blame trickled down to the next best thing. Me.

I couldn't bring myself to attend the funeral. I didn't trust my emotions not to come pouring out in some foolish, humiliating way. Instead I stayed home and slipped into the routine that would become all too common for me over the next few months: lying in bed or on the couch, eating a bowl of Cinnamon Toast Crunch, watching shows I'd missed from previous decades. *Lost, E.R., Heroes.* My pain required the full escapism of other times, places, dimensions, worlds.

Outside, the planet continued its brutal, unforgiving turn. I'd finish out the school year in Bayside, but couldn't stomach the thought of going to college anymore. Over the months, I received acceptance letters to many of the small liberal arts schools I'd visited in upstate New York, Vermont, and Massachusetts. But I had no interest in adjusting to a new place, choosing a major, making new friends. Not when the one I'd grown closest to had turned his back on me in the extreme way he did. Predictably, this kicked off a series of discussions-slash-arguments with my parents that resulted in me taking a gap year in San Francisco.

At school, at first, most kids kept their distance. I walked the halls between classes with Remy by my side like my own personal bodyguard. A role she welcomed. But I still couldn't bear to read the news from that day. I knew developments were ongoing, the trial set to begin early the following year.

But everything was so raw still. Other kids and community members would give these interviews to reporters about Xander, his cousin Lance, and Lance's friends. The story captured the public's imagination in a way that created stark divisions between families and teachers and politicians over the complicated questions Xander's actions raised: How did no one think to monitor Xander's and Lance's activities? Why didn't the cops raid Lance's home sooner? And even if Xander didn't share the same politics as his cousin, was the threat of violence *ever* ethical? Everyone seemed to think something different.

My mom has pointed out how nothing in the story fits our society's traditional definitions of hero, villain, or victim. When the cops found Xander's journal entries on my computer, they saw, plain as day, his plans to undercut Lance while taking his own life. The lighter he had on him was only meant to cause a small fire. The gun he meant to turn on himself.

Lance and his friends were planning to travel to the protests the following week, but they didn't have any concrete plans, at least not yet. Xander turned out to be right about that part. They were merely storing the weapons to protect themselves in the event a Second Civil War broke out, an event they saw as all but inevitable. But now that those weapons carried out some actual purpose, amounting to little more than a morbid prank on Xander's part, it meant Lance and his friends would be serving prison time.

"People are too simple-minded to understand how Xander could have done what he did," my mom told me one day over the phone. "No one really appreciates the nuances of mental health. Look at Sam Reid. The guy went from hero to suicide in 36 hours."

I'm not sure if I agree with her or not. What I keep getting hung up on is how Xander could have been dumb enough to take up my suggestion. For all his smarts, he seemed to succumb to the most impassioned, most irrational instinct inside of him. Too blinded by his pain to think or care about the potential for backfire. Since he was still a minor, Xander's journals remained sealed during the trial. But I knew deep down I did push him, to some extent. Could I have done more to stop him? It destroys me to think I could have.

My dad, for his part, has kept his mouth shut. In the months that followed, he fielded all the inquiries from reporters, some of whom were brazen enough to approach our doorstep again. He's been more than happy to be the one to tell them to *fuck off*.

Over time, the story has faded from the news, beyond the small pockets of internet commenters and amateur true-crime sleuths. Everyone else has moved on to the next political conflict or natural disaster or viral sensation. Lying awake in the middle of the night, though, I'll sometimes picture myself sitting down with a reporter for an interview. Maybe it's because I never got the chance to have that conversation with Xander that would have cleared everything up, but I'm not sure I'll ever say I *blame* Xander. I blame the cops for not doing anything sooner, and I blame the media for invading our privacy. But not Xander. His heart seemed to be in the right place. He was genuinely hurting inside, the victim of emotional and physical abuse from his dad. Yet he was so fixated on being both epic and noble in his pain, the best solution he came up with was to strap on a bomb, cause a frenzy, and let everyone else suffer the consequences. This, I've learned, is how the male species thinks: *I need to exorcise this anger from my body, no matter the consequences. Everyone else can deal with it.*

Just because I understand, though, doesn't mean I'm not haunted. Memories of that week still overwhelm my obsessive thoughts, still show up in my super-intense dreams. The only thing that seems to stop me from obsessing over all the *what ifs* is my art. Not that I dove back in right away. It took about six months before I felt ready. Six months of feeling sorry for myself, eating cereal in between periods at school, before I broke out the old kit.

The *body project*, I sometimes called it: an undertaking far bigger in scale than the original sketch I offered to show Xander that morning before we boarded the train. There were so many ways a body could trap you inside of your own skin, betray you when you needed it most. Crippling migraines. Medieval amputation of limbs. Excruciating menstrual cramps. Fevers that paralyze your whole lower body.

I began by applying the techniques most familiar to me from my art classes—a series of charcoal pencil sketches followed by a faithful acrylic mix. I played with the light from the first sketch—a version far too bright, another too splotchy and coarse—experimenting with the shadows, considering new sources of light, new angles to draw from. A little later, I separated the individual sketches into panels. The space in between the panels there to signify my disembodiment. My body being pulled in all directions at once.

Pretty quickly, my dad noticed the smell of fumes drifting down the hall, the unhealthier lengths of time I was spending inside my room. There were already plans for me to move out to San Francisco with my mom, so there wasn't much he could say. But then, one day, he did me a favor I never thought possible.

"I'm going to clear my hockey equipment from the garage," he told me, standing in the doorway of my bedroom as I texted with my friends. "I figure you can use the space and you know, there's better ventilation in there. All these chemicals can't be good for your lungs."

"It's fine. You don't have to."

"No," he said. The unspoken sacrifices of parenthood had unraveled in him. An unraveling I struggled to stomach. "I want to."

I nodded, thanked him, fought back tears. There were subtler shifts in my dad's behavior, his development from the person who was married to my mom. He treaded lightly with me in my remaining days in the house, didn't pick fights like he used to. His decision to start anger therapy, of his own accord, came as a surprise, even if I only learned about it from my mom. And while I wouldn't say he deserves the credit for my artistic exploration, the space would, if nothing else, accelerate the creative process.

As soon as I told Remy about the new garage space, we began taking weekly trips to the art store, buying seed oils and watercolors and impasto mixtures that would dry in a rough, broken texture on the canvas. After the events of the fall, Remy was the only one of our friends who continued to act like herself around me. She didn't treat me like a victim who couldn't bear to hear the truth of things. We even joked about Xander sometimes, wondering what he might think of the sketches we drew—the absurd, pop-art juxtapositions of celebrities and household Clorox spray bottles. We guessed he'd be nothing but proud of our absurdity.

This wasn't quite the case the few times we hung out with the larger group. Teddy and Piper were always too careful not to say anything offensive, not to smoke or drink, either, and I couldn't stand staying for more than an hour or two. Probably, they spoke about Remy and me behind our backs, jealous of our exclusivity. But that's not the type of thing I worry much about anymore.

The biggest adjustment, these days, is the tender new dynamic between me and my mom in San Francisco. We'd been apart for two of my teenage years, a period my therapist would call *formative*. A bigger hurdle to clear than I would have guessed. Her singing voice that used to bring me so much joy as a girl has taken on a thin, spooky quality. I'll wake sometimes to hear her humming from the other room. Her voice seems to pry open old bruises under my skin. I'm too afraid of offending her to tell her to stop. Either that or I simply can't find the strength. Because the other part I'm adjusting to is the gentle but consistent pressure she's putting on me to make something of my art. "Look," she said the other day, pointing to the laptop screen in front of her. "There are application deadlines for several art schools in the area coming up. Want me to help you with one?"

My lungs pushed out a groan. It had only been three months since I moved to San Francisco. "How many times do I have to tell you? When I'm ready."

She threw her hands up and smiled neutrally, and I gained some relative appreciation for my dad then, who never commented on my art. But in these moments, I can't help but think my mom is using me to vicariously live out her own, hindered acting career.

"Hey, can I tell you something?" my mom said, fixing me with a mischievous smile that made me want to smile back, even though I didn't.

"What?"

"I'm proud of you."

"Please."

"Nope," she said sarcastically. "You're going to figure it out. You can take as much time as you need. But I have so much belief in you, it's scary."

We ended up talking for a long time—not just that day, but over the months. We've talked about family history that I never knew, my great grandparents who immigrated from Scotland through Ellis Island and opened a butchery on the Lower East Side of Manhattan. She's told me about the theater group here that she's joined on a part-time basis, performing once every other week on Saturdays, and another actor, Andy, who stays over some nights. I enjoy seeing them get all hopped up in anticipation of an upcoming performance. To see them sing their hearts out to some old Sondheim score for an aging, 150-seat crowd.

We've even spoken a little about the other couple involved in the Penn Station incident that day. I've seen pictures of Sam and Audrey online. I read the small tidbits of their personal lives the media reported on, treating them as roughly as they did ours. But it made me feel oddly better, less alone in a sense, knowing that my relationship with Xander wasn't the only dysfunctional one to come out of the situation. The unthinkably sudden nature of Sam's rise and fall consumed much of the attention. I was largely shielded from the public's awareness. The handful of Twitter trolls from our school came and went with little more than a whimper. But the parallels between Sam and Xander didn't escape me. Sam with the world at his feet, meeting the same doomed fate as Xander. Audrey stood behind him, of course she did, left alone to endure the blowback. Speculation roared that she drove him to commit suicide. Though I didn't know what to think. Only that I felt pity for her. In some sense, I looked up to her for facing it all.

"Behind closed doors, everyone has their own shit," my mom said the other day. "Only a small fraction of it makes it out there. And when it does, people love to gawk and turn their noses up. Inside, though, we're all the same."

Every day I can see how much more settled she feels in San Francisco. Me, on the other hand, I'm a work in progress. I still haven't even put all my clothes away yet. The bed in my mom's spare room is so different from my bed in New York, whose lumps seemed to fit the crevices of my body perfectly. The bed here is stiff, strange. I can't imagine ever getting used to it. Even though I know, day by day, I am.

On weekends, we take our bikes out through the parks together. We'll go for picnics with the new friends she's made. We've even created our own rating system for all the cold brew coffee in town.

"I do miss Broadway," she likes to say, far too often, any time we talk about New York.

In time, I've surrendered the petty grudge I held against her for moving here to advance her career. We've talked about so many things that have made life feel normal again, and the one thing we haven't talked about is the one that will never be normal. She knows I'm exploring it in my art. She knows how much, or little, I speak about it with the therapist I see. And she knows enough to give me space.

So up late at night, painting, I've found the one place I can escape to without the need for words. I can never seem to find the right ones anyway. I know at some point my mom and I will have a long, emotional conversation about everything. But right now, I'm content with the shape of our quiet little life in San Francisco. I'm content to muddy my hands with the supplies—the charcoal, the acrylic, the oils. The burst of panels is always there to tinker with, to work and polish until I can get it right.

45

AUDREY

I pace the hotel room, thinking of someone to call. But there's no one I feel like I can trust. Not with this.

She's the only person who still drifts into the danger zone of my obsessive worry. Holly. I lie awake some nights wondering what I might say to her. I've written several versions of a letter explaining why I felt the need to show up in Bayside at the most panicked times of either of our lives. But I know admitting that wouldn't do her any good; it would only serve me. Yet there's nothing illegal about wanting to see for myself that she's doing okay. Is there?

Bright afternoon sun filters in through the window. It's September. Almost a year has passed since the incident. I've moved on. I've convinced myself that I've moved on, anyway, and spend every night trying to figure out if there's a difference.

I fiddle with the thermostat on the wall. In the hour since I checked in, I've been unable to get the temperature right. The A/C clicks on and pushes frigid air through the vents. Better than the sweatbox of the last ten minutes, I think. I sit on the mattress, pick up the phone to call the front desk to see if they can send a repair person. But when I look at the phone on the nightstand, the printout sitting there stares back at me. A simple black-and-white design featuring Holly and three other young artists at the community college. I place the phone back down into the slot. No sense giving up now.

The exhibition starts in an hour, according to the poster. It's embarrassing to admit how I found out about it. Once the media attention died down, I felt compelled to keep tabs on her, so I set up a Google search alert for her name. A maternal part of me feared she might slip into complete despair, off the edge of the earth, if I didn't keep watch. Probably, she did, at least for a while. But I couldn't bear the thought of passing up the chance to see her, speak to her, share our distinct relation to the events of that week. We were bound, in a sense, for life.

Cold air spikes through the room again. Goosebumps rise on my skin. I rush to the thermostat to shut off the A/C. On my phone, I see my mom and Taylor have checked in on me on our group chat. They know why I'm here. They don't understand. Not in any real way.

When I told my mom and Taylor about my plans to travel to San Francisco, they offered to join me for support. They had a habit of forcing their way into family travel plans, but I turned them down. "If things go bad or wrong," I told them, "I don't need you reminding me this was why I never should have come to begin with."

A few minutes of relative comfort pass, the room suspended in a purgatory-like state between warm and cold. After replying to Taylor and my mom, and skimming idly on my phone, the hotel room returns to its former stuffiness. I can't stand it for a minute longer. I need to go outside, to walk and take in fresh air.

It's mid-afternoon in San Francisco, this normal and clean city I have no business being in. I grab a coffee at one of the local coffee shops. Outside, I notice how the one meteorological phenomenon I know about San Francisco, the fog, has taken the day off. With the sun strong on my neck, I meander past the rows of department stores, green spaces, grocers, theaters, beer halls, cafes. I try to ignore the thrum of my restless heart. I take out my phone to see that my walk has taken me 12 minutes closer to the gallery space. I plug in the address and walk the remaining ten minutes to the gallery, a square brick building overlooking San Francisco Bay. The revolving doors loom like a dragon guarding a princess in a fairy tale. There's still time to turn back, I remember. Head straight to the airport and board the next flight back to New York. Leave all my clothes behind in the hotel room. A fair trade for never having to remember I thought this was a good idea.

A few more minutes pass of pacing, thinking, sweating. There's a ball of something hard and wicked in my chest. But then a cheesy phrase enters my mind, the catchphrase of one of my workout instructors, of all things: *You didn't come this far, just to come this far.*

I'm reminded of the work I've done over the past year: the early morning wakeups to run, enduring the freezing cold over the warmth of my bed. *I didn't come this far just to come this far.* Some good can come out of this still, I think, some letting go or contentment, if not closure.

A warm burst of air flows out from my lungs. I begin ambling over to the entrance. Forces outside of my control propel my arms and legs through the revolving doors. A middle-aged woman with bright green, inviting eyes sits behind a white plastic table. She says hello.

"I'm here to see the student exhibition," I tell her.

"Oh, lovely. Please, just sign in on the sheet for me. Here you go."

She doesn't pick up on my frayed nerves, of course she doesn't. I'm not the tiniest bit odd or suspicious to her. She hands me the clipboard, only fifteen or twenty names on the list, and I write my first name, *Audrey*. That's when I freeze with doubt. Should I use a fake name? What if Holly looks over the guest list and I've decided not to speak with her? I write some muddy script for my last name and set the clipboard down on the table, dart past the woman towards the elevator bank.

"Do you know the way?" she calls after me.

"Oh, yes. I mean, second floor, right?"

She smiles. "Third floor, make a right, and it'll be the second door on your left."

I turn around. "Got it, sorry." I point to the paper coffee cup in my hand. "Too much caffeine already today, you know—"

She smiles and nods, and I pretend not to jump out of my skin. I take some deep breaths on the elevator ride, try to remain calm and focused. I'm here for support, to show genuine interest in her. What's so wrong with that? Nothing, maybe, except for the demon in my chest that won't stop thrashing.

When the elevator door slides open, a low hum of activity becomes audible as the doors to the gallery spread open. Little separates me from the glass enclosure framing the room. The sound of major-key music, beckoning from down the hall, reminds me of Sam. He loved to explain the difference between major and minor keys, no matter how long it took me to understand. These random reminders of him always hit me with sadness and gratitude in equal measure. Sudden memories of the stupid, intense love we shared.

I walk towards the door and look through the glass, my reflection superimposed over the spread of the gallery: clumps of people talking or circling a large sculpture, canvases hung up on the surrounding walls or propped up on easels. It's a beautiful, open setting. Whitecaps reflect on the bay in the distance.

Then, from the back of the room, I see Holly. She's standing in the far-left corner wearing a black hoodie and jeans, her hair highlighted red. The artwork pulls at me on some unconscious level. Disembodied, I walk into the room and up to her exhibit, praying she won't recognize me. I stare at the galactic burst of panels she's constructed, each depicting what looks like abstracted limbs and body parts, severed or broken or bleeding. The space in between the panels is striking for what it leaves out. You see only the tops of heads, sparkling with beads of sweat, torsos bruised with wild streaks of purple and red. The sketches are otherwise grayscale, foregrounding the spare eruptions of color.

And it's while I'm taking in all of this—the broken textured quality of the paint, the arresting pops of flashbulb light—that I feel tears filling my eyes. My throat emits this laugh-cry, this beastly type of sound, because I can finally see what those spaces represent, all that juxtaposition of light and dark. It's Holly reclaiming her story. She's recognizing the parts of herself she'll never quite reclaim, but relegating us onlookers to the background—hiding from us what we don't have the right to see. She's felt the same pain as Xander and Sam and me, but she's done something else with it. She's done the thing almost no one does. She's converted her pain to love.

I can see how much time she's spent perfecting the shadows, the spacing, and the color scheme. It's so moving that I'm satisfied completely. I can go back to my hotel room and sleep the rest of the day knowing Holly has found a way to capture her lived experience, to work through it and overcome it. But the awe I feel stops me in my tracks: I stare and stare, and I don't stop staring until I feel someone tap my shoulder and say, "Ma'am, are you okay?"

It's not Holly but Holly's mom, Sandy. Up close, I see her scholarly face. Her deeply kind eyes.

"I'm okay," I say, noticing just how wet my eyes are, how strained and swollen my face must look.

"Wait," says another, smaller voice. I turn to see her, Holly. "Audrey? You're Audrey, right?"

I nod and cover my mouth, the tears falling down my face rapidly now. She smiles. She seems happy to see me, and in that instant, the ball that has been hardening inside my chest since I left New York seems to crack.

"Yes. I'm Audrey." We look into each other's faces, blinking and looking down at our feet like a pair of shy toddlers meeting for the first time.

The ball in my chest melts and floats away, and we start talking.

ACKNOWLEDGMENTS

A big beautiful team of people has been there to provide me with stunning editorial advice, inspiration, and emotional support through the years-long making of this book.

Thank you, first and foremost, to Susan Scarf Merrell. You saw this book's potential at a time when few others did. Your invaluable mentorship and wisdom have been the steady rock for me at the center of turning this batshit dream into a reality.

Thank you to everyone at the BookEnds writing program at Stony Brook Southampton, but especially my loyal pod mates Sandra Leong and Greg Phelan. You both helped shape some of the book's vital embryonic material—and I'm forever grateful for the intellectually stimulating and playful dynamic we formed together. Vanessa Cuti and Caitlin Murphy, I'm thankful for the insights you each shared, helping to refine the book's opening structure. Thanks also to Maggie Hill and Sue Mel for your willingness to chat through the (many) pitfalls of publishing.

Big shout-out to Diane Glazman. A conversation with you in 2020 gave me the spark and confidence I needed to expand the structure of the book from one narrator to four. I'll always be grateful for that crucial moment in the evolution of this project.

Thank you to Robert Schirmer and Rachel Weaver for always offering smart, sensitive editorial feedback. Thank you to Prof. Brian Nussbaum at the University of Albany for getting on the phone to talk through the logistics of a fictionalized domestic terrorism incident.

Thank you to the professionals who have listened to me sulk, whine, and ultimately assemble the strength needed to put my work out there. Talia, Sara, Tina, Lindsay, and Kelly: I don't quite know who I'd be without our sessions together. I do know it would be a pale husk of the person I am today—and I'm so thankful to have found people and resources to help me through times of crisis, not to mention the everyday slog of being human.

Thank you to my parents Lorri and Danny Klonsky, as well as my sister Sloane Klonsky, for always standing by me and delivering me tremendous strength in times of need. You don't know how much it has meant.

Finally, thank you to my wife, Sydney Friedman, for, well, everything. Thank you for being my alpha, beta, and gamma reader. Thank you for loving and putting up with me. You are my eternal light and joy. I'll never be able to thank you enough.

ABOUT THE AUTHOR

Evan Klonsky is a New York-based writer who currently works for the nonprofit group Physicians for Human Rights. His work has appeared in national publications including *Newsday, Inc., Relix, The Esthetic Apostle,* and PopMatters. From 2018-19, he was a fellow in the BookEnds program at Stony Brook Southampton. This is his first novel.

http://www.evanklonsky.com

 instagram.com/EvanJKlonsky
 linkedin.com/in/evan-klonsky-38450822

www.ingramcontent.com/pod-product-compliance
Lightning Source LLC
LaVergne TN
LVHW091715070526
838199LV00050B/2411